# Broken Down Summer

By John M. Dargo

# Broken Down Summer

Editor: Editions Editing

ISBN-13: 978-0-615-39526-5

To contact the author, visit www.johnmdargo.com

Milton Press Publishing
Shelbyville, KY 40066

My many thanks to Sandy, Bill, and Virginia for their encouragement and expertise.

Also, special thanks to Detective William Sumpter (LAPD ret.), for his advice on the methods and inner workings of the Los Angeles Police Department.

iv

# Tuesday, August, 23<sup>rd</sup>

The man's voice came across cold and had a slight accent.

"So if you want to see your wife and daughter alive again you'll listen closely."

It was the tattooed guy with the gun doing the talking. At least that was the best David Watts could tell from what he had observed before having been so abruptly blindfolded.

"I will call you on your cell phone at exactly six o'clock tonight. Understand?"

David's arms hurt from being yanked out of bed by his elbows. His wrists had been tied behind his back before he was grabbed up; his shoulders, seemingly, almost pulled from their sockets. He was having trouble breathing too; the duct tape over his mouth partially covered his nostrils. But he managed to nod his head to the question.

"Good. At six o'clock when I call I will tell you where to deliver the money. You will have the money in cash, one hundred dollar bills, all $120,000 of it. Understand?"

"My God," thought David. "Did he say $120,000?"

David shook his head.

A blow struck him on the cheek and he fell to the side. A muffled scream emanated from his wife, Marianna.

"It is simple enough you fucking moron. You get the money and I call and tell you where to take it, or your wife and the kid die. Now, do you think you got it this time?"

David's head swam as the intruders lifted him back to his knees. He still didn't "get it", however this time he nodded as if he did.

"All right. That wasn't so hard, was it? Now I think we have an understanding."

Then the voice turned away, "Empuja este pendejo abajo la cama."

David felt strong hands on him once again and his arms were suddenly freed, the duct tape around his wrists having apparently been cut. He started to reach for his blindfold, but before David could raise his hands someone grabbed him underneath the arms again and forcefully guided him beneath the box springs of their bed.

"Don't even think about crawling out from under there until we are gone, got it?" came the same man's voice, this time from nearby. "And don't call the police. If there's police, then they die."

David lay still. He could hear the men leave the room for the hallway. A few murmured words were followed by many footfalls and the sounds of some struggling. David thought he could also make out Marianna and Julia's muted cries. Then came the sound of the front door closing, followed by silence.

He was alone.

The day was going to be a scorcher. Detective Brenford Stokes could feel the sweat accumulating around his neck. The temperature had already reached well into the nineties, even though the detective's watch told him it wasn't even 9:00AM yet.

In the Boyle Heights area traffic on Cesar Chavez Avenue in front of him barely moved. Just to the east a road crew had one of the lanes blocked off, disrupting what was normally an already poor morning rush hour. Pedestrians along the sidewalks kept to a leisurely pace in the heat, mainly Hispanic youths, mostly with their baggy shorts well below the knees, some with their baseball caps offset at an absurd angle. There were some elderly passers-by also, but most people of working age had by this time disappeared to their various places of employment.

These comings and goings on the main thoroughfare, however, were not of all that great an interest to the detective. Most of the hustle and bustle surrounded the Cesar Chavez corridor, almost a block north from where the detective sat in his specially unmarked Chevy Malibu. What did interest the detective, however, was the activity, or lack thereof, at a two-story duplex just south of Cesar Chavez.

Stokes's interest in the duplex stemmed from the location's alleged illicit involvement regarding underage girls.

Acting on a tip, the department had set up a round the clock surveillance on the property. The tipster had suggested that the duplex was being utilized as a waypoint for an underage prostitution ring. The vice squad was now in their third day of monitoring the traffic in and out of the building. So far they had seen nothing out of the ordinary, but only three days in, that wasn't really a surprise.

Detective Stokes worked the shift alone this morning, just like he had for the last couple of days. The night shift was set up in pairs, but the day shifts were loners. The reasoning for the light day duty stemmed from the belief that most illegal activity would probably occur after dark when it would be easier to conceal the smuggling of human chattel onto and off of the premises. Besides, a pair of individuals was easier to spot, and being one-half mixed African American and Hispanic himself, Stokes didn't need some pale guy sitting next to him blowing his cover.

Stokes sipped his coffee as he waited. The drink had cooled off, despite the specially insulated container he had recently purchased. That irked him. He liked his coffee hot, even on warm mornings such as today. What's more, a fly kept landing on the lid of the mug, and Stokes had to continually shoo it away. Another couple of flies buzzed around inside the front windshield. The detective began to wonder where they were all coming from, when he caught sight of an overfilled trash can on the sidewalk just behind his vehicle. He hadn't noticed any smell before, but the odor was now brought to his attention. As the day warmed the stench from the container had insidiously begun to permeate the interior of his car.

"Wonderful," he thought. "At least I'll smell like I'm undercover."

Stokes briefly considered rolling up the Chevy's windows, but given the rising heat, he opted against it.

In the early morning light and with a flashlight pointed in his face it had been hard to see much. David had been asleep, with his wife, when Marianna's scream had awoken him. He simply had not had time to react before the barrel of a gun had been placed against his head and three or four men stood over him. Then they had blindfolded him.

But before the duct tape had covered his eyes, David had been able to make out a few marginal details of the kidnappers. The first thing he had noticed was that the men appeared to be Mexican, or at least of dark complexion. The second thing was that the attackers had been heavily tattooed. Aside from that limited descriptive observation however, he was completely in the dark as to what had just happened.

David waited until he was sure the intruders were gone before he removed the blindfold and duct tape from his mouth. He crawled from underneath the bed and stood. Between the anxiety of the moment and the lack of oxygen from the duct tape, he felt light headed. He tried to catch his breath. His left arm hurt and he wondered if maybe he was going to have a heart attack. But his breath quickly returned and he decided the pain in his arm was simply a result of his rough treatment at the hands of the kidnappers. At least he hoped. He couldn't afford to be hospitalized; a heart attack now and his whole family might die.

David looked around the room. The bedroom showed little sign of a struggle. Other than the bedspread and sheets having been thrown to the floor everything else seemed in order. In the hallway a picture had fallen from its hanger and the glass had dislodged from the frame. David checked the living room and kitchen; they were tidy as always. It almost seemed as if nothing had occurred.

Except now, of course, his wife and daughter were gone.

Then David saw the front door. The knob sat askew and part of the inner frame appeared damaged. He went to the door and grasped the handle and tried turning the knob. It opened, but the mechanism bobbled loosely in his grasp and was obviously broken.

With the door ajar David peered outside. Surely the intruders were gone by now, he thought. He didn't see any car out front, only his gray compact in the driveway. He stuck his head out further and looked up and down the street. There was nothing unusual. He backed into the foyer and tried closing the door. The mechanism latched, but just barely. He tried the lock next, but nothing happened. They had completely disabled that. David wasn't sure how they had broken through the door, but from the look of the framework it appeared as if they might have used a crow bar or some similar object.

So he couldn't lock the door. It hardly mattered, David had more important worries. At least it would latch closed.

On his way back to the bedroom he stopped and used the bathroom. He also took two aspirins. He had heard that you could actually ward off a heart attack with common aspirin.

After that, he didn't know what to do next. He didn't have $120,000. He had no way of cashing in anything for even close to that amount, either. Hell, they didn't even own their own home.

David Watts had never been in trouble, not since he was a kid, and he really didn't know if he could handle a situation like this without any help. He was fifty-three years old and terribly out of shape. At five foot nine and two hundred and forty pounds he was also a good deal overweight. His occupation as a part time high school biology teacher had not prepared him for a situation such as this. He really knew nothing about the law or the criminal justice system. He especially didn't know anything about kidnapping or how to go about raising a ransom to get one's family back.

So how was he supposed to come up with $120,000 before six o'clock?

The fact was, that without equity in a mortgage or any substantial savings, he probably couldn't raise $120,000 even if he were given a whole year to do it. He had no idea where to start or even what to do next.

"This is absolutely crazy," he mumbled out loud to himself.

And why $120,000? Why not $100,000? That seemed like a more reasonable sum. And why their family? Why not a more well to do family from Beverly Hills or Malibu? Why one from Silver Lake? It just didn't make any sense.

David walked to the third bedroom in their home. He and his wife used this room as a small office; it was where they kept their computer. There was also a printer, a desk and a file cabinet. David went to the desk. He opened the top right hand drawer and pulled out the family checkbook and looked at the register. They had just over seven thousand dollars. There was also a savings account, which had been left idle for quite some time. He wasn't exactly sure where he'd last seen the ledger for that, but they kept it somewhere in the desk. Last time he had checked, however, the balance had been around fifteen hundred dollars. Even with interest it would still be well below two grand.

David opened the upper left hand drawer where his wife's account book should have been. Marianna had a separate, smaller checking account, in her name, though both spouses were noted as cosigners on either of their two accounts.

The checkbook wasn't there.

David went into the kitchen and found Marianna's purse, it sat right where his wife usually kept it on the counter ledge. He opened the purse and, after a moment of searching, found the checkbook in a side pocket. He opened it and looked at the total. The register read $247.15. That would not help.

So all together the three accounts might add up to about nine thousand dollars. That left him roughly $110,000 short of the amount he would need to free his family.

On the east coast it was approaching eleven o'clock and Harold Reed was sitting at his office desk in a large insurance company when the phone rang. Mr. Reed was with another of the company's Vice Presidents at the time. He was a little annoyed at the disturbance; he had told Sherry, the receptionist, to hold all his calls. Not that his meeting with his fellow VP was all that important, they were actually only discussing lunch plans, but Sherry didn't know that, and the point was, when he said he didn't want to be disturbed, it meant he didn't want to be disturbed.

"Just a second Frank," Reed said to the visiting VP seated in front of his desk. "I have to see who this is." The executive leaned his leather chair forward and reached across his desk for the phone.

"Sherry, I'm still with Carson. I thought I said I wanted you to hold all my calls."

There was a pause as Reed listened to the woman's explanation for the interruption. After a moment his brow furrowed. He was hearing something he didn't like.

"All right, all right. I got it. Thanks, I'll take it," he said and pushed the button down disconnecting himself from the receptionist.

Harold Reed shook his head and addressed his co-worker, "Sorry Frank, I have to take this call. It's my ex-brother-in-law. Wish the guy would quit calling me. Thinks we're still friends or something."

Frank nodded, "It's OK. I need to get going anyway."

"Hell, it's been seven years since the divorce. Can you believe that? Knowing how this guy operates, he'll probably be wanting to borrow money or something."

The other VP rose to leave. "Yeah, nothing worse than an ex-bother-in-law." Then the man added, "That is except an ex-wife."

Both of the men laughed.

"Yeah, really. Hey, I'll see you at one o'clock, we'll do the sushi place then." Harold held his palm up in a gesture of goodbye as the other man turned for the door.

Now to David Watts, he thought. Reed would try to make it short – the guy was such a nuisance. He pushed the button for the line where his ex-brother-in-law waited.


"Only three more hours," Detective Stokes told himself. Three more hours and the next shift would be coming to take over at noon. He wanted a shower and then a nap, badly. As a matter of fact he had become a little concerned he might actually doze off right there in the car. He tried to down a little more of the coffee, but it was tepid by now and really wasn't worth drinking. He looked at his watch again - 9:02AM. Sweat ran down his cheek from where his closely cropped hair met with his temple.

It was getting hot now. Frustrated, Stokes fumbled under the seat front beneath him. He felt to the driver's door side and then toward the middle of the car, before he finally found what he was looking for. He pulled the item from below the seat and flipped the switch on the side of the small casing. On top of the case a three-inch red rotor blade began to spin. The rotor put out a wisp of air for a moment and then the blade slowed. The battery was dead. Stokes had known that to be the case before he had even tried it. The little fan took a single AAA battery, but all Stokes had were the AA size for his flashlight and some surveillance equipment. He tossed the fan gadget back under the seat. He'd probably go through the whole process again tomorrow.

Looking up, the detective noticed that while playing with the miniature fan, he had failed to keep an eye on the changes in the landscape of the duplex he was supposedly observing. An individual had now appeared, seated against the wall of the two-story dwelling. The man sat in one of those metal folding type chairs, right at the entrance to the alley-like driveway. He didn't seem to have noticed Stokes, at least not yet, though the man appeared to be keeping a wary eye on the narrow street and the surrounding buildings. The man wore long blue jean shorts and a white wife beater tee. Due to the distance from where his vehicle sat, it was hard to tell for sure, but it appeared the man had several tattoos around his neck and another larger one on his right bicep.

Detective Stokes took a look up and down the street himself. It didn't hurt to be too careful, and the new man's presence indicated to Stokes he needed to keep his guard up. The situation could be totally innocent, but most likely the tattooed individual would be a lookout for one of the local gangs. There was probably a regular routine of drug trafficking on the somewhat enclosed side street. You could pick almost any area street at random and there stood a good likelihood of that being true. Of course, there was always the off chance that the tattooed guy could be involved with the criminal activity that vice was actually there to monitor, but Detective Stokes doubted it; so far it looked like the department had found another waste for its time.

Just as Stokes considered this, a black sedan turned off of Cesar Chavez in his direction. The detective perked up a bit when it appeared as if the car would turn into the target driveway, but instead it pulled into the driveway of the next duplex, the property just closer to the location where the detective watched from the opposite curb. Stokes was about to relax back into the front seat of the Malibu, when the front passenger door of the dark sedan opened and a young girl stepped out. An adult male followed the girl from the car. The man lifted the child in his arms and carried her into the lower entrance of the duplex. Immediately after the girl had been ushered inside, the rear door of the sedan opened and an adult woman exited the vehicle in much the same manner as the child had; again accompanied by another adult male. This time the man was really large however, and he held the woman's arms by her side as they made their way into the residence. All of the individuals appeared to be darker skinned, Latinos.

"Wow," thought the detective. "Looks like we've got a winner."

After the two female passengers had been escorted inside, a third man stepped from the rear seat of the car. This man was slightly lighter skinned, tall and slender, though of somewhat muscular build. He had long hair and wore a sleeveless Lakers jersey; his arms were heavily tattooed. After exiting the rear seat, the individual opened the front passenger door and climbed in. The dark sedan backed out of the driveway before the driver turned the vehicle in the direction from which it had approached and sped away with the tattooed man beside him.

This turn of events was quite a surprise. Stokes hadn't been told the residence next door might also be involved. Maybe headquarters had been mistaken about the tip and placed the surveillance on the wrong property. It didn't matter. Something was going down at the closer duplex and it wasn't good. The woman and child seemed pretty obviously under duress and it appeared they had been taken inside the home against their will.

Stokes was sorry to see that two of the four possible perps had left. Hopefully they would return before he and his fellow officers made any move on the place.

Detective Stokes called his observations in to headquarters and asked for a full perimeter stake out.


David Watts hung up the phone. The only person he knew who could possibly help him raise something in the neighborhood of $100,000 was his ex-wife's brother, Harold Reed. The man was a VP of a Fortune 500 insurance company and worth several million dollars. The problem lay with the fact the guy was an asshole, and, in David's opinion, an asshole of the first magnitude at that. Reed made no pretense of his dislike for David. And it didn't help either, that David had absolutely no relationship with his ex-wife Susan, Harold's sister. Reed was not going to do him any favors based on her good will. David hadn't seen Susan in five years and hadn't even spoken with her in four, ever since she had asked him to please not contact her again. They didn't have any children and there was no reason for them to communicate anyway, so David had obliged his ex-wife.

What surprised David however, was that, though his bother-in-law had been his normal obnoxious self, and pissed off that David had even asked such a request, Reed had actually said he would consider helping him out. Reed was looking at getting the money together and would possibly have it available tomorrow "if needed." That was a stunner. David had almost not even called the guy.

A moment earlier, raising $120,000 had seemed like a ludicrous proposition. But now it looked as if David might actually be able to make the ransom demand. Marianna and Julia could be back so fast it would be like they had hardly been gone at all. He just had to hope that the kidnappers would be willing to wait until tomorrow for him to deliver the cash. He also needed to make sure the six o'clock phone call from the kidnappers went off without a hitch.

David found his cell phone and checked the battery, it was about halfway charged. He turned the phone off and plugged the device into the wall. He wanted to make sure there was plenty of juice; he didn't need the thing cutting out on him in the middle of the call.

David's attention now turned to another matter; whether, or not, he should call the police. His first instinct had been to include the authorities; he was way over his head in trying to deal with a kidnapping. But their assailants had instructed him that his family's lives depended on his not contacting the police. He wasn't sure what to do. He had already secured the money, with little outside help. Maybe he could see the ordeal through without having to bring anyone else in, at least until his wife and child had been safely returned.

But even after he had gotten Marianna and Julia back, there would still be one big problem to solve. That would be the problem of the borrowed money. How was he ever going to pay Harold Reed the $120,000 back? The thought made him want to vomit. He would forever be in that asshole's debt and Reed would never let him forget it.

David actually felt nauseas. And he had the whole day to wait and worry about what was going to happen. He just hoped Harold Reed wasn't pulling some sick joke on him. David had explained it was a matter of life and death. Reed had wanted details, but David had managed to keep the man in the dark. Now it became a waiting game; till six o'clock anyway.

David decided he needed to shower, something from his normal routine. Besides, that way if he vomited he wouldn't have to clean it up.


The shirt was now stuck to his back. Detective Stokes hoped, however, that he wouldn't have to be waiting there in the heat much longer. Stokes had received approval for two additional units to keep the duplex property under surveillance. One to observe the street front and the other for out back, just in case the suspects got wind they were being watched and tried to exit out the rear. Stokes would be leaving when the other undercover officers arrived. In order for the officers to legally enter the premises the detective needed to get back to headquarters and fill out a warrant. That would take a couple of hours, and then he'd need to track down a judge to get the warrant approved. Later, if things went as planned, Stokes would be back on location for the bust.

"So much for my nap," he thought, and forced some of the cold coffee down his throat.

The tattooed man in the chair next door, at the original target residence, stood up and looked around. Once again, it didn't appear that the man had noticed the detective as he sat across the way. Then the man turned and entered the side door of the first duplex.

Stokes decided this provided an opportune time to remove himself to a less visible location. He started the car and pulled out on to the nearly empty side street. When he got to Cesar Chavez the traffic was still heavy, but not quite as bad as it was before. He made a right and proceeded into the traffic past the construction zone squeeze. A taco wagon didn't want to let him merge over at first, but Stokes pulled his badge from his front pocket and pointed it at the driver. The dark skinned man apparently didn't want any trouble and backed off, letting Stokes have the right of way.

"Probably an illegal," thought Stokes. "That always scares the shit out of 'em."

At the next intersection Stokes made a right, and then he did the same again at the next intersection. He pulled to the curb when he reached the crossroads for the side street where the duplexes lay. Then he radioed in for the back up cars to meet him at the new location.


The shower was just what he needed. The nauseas seemed to pass as he stood under the running water for a while. Things were actually working out OK so far, he kept telling himself. But the stakes were so high, and David was afraid that, somehow, he was going to bungle it.

He went over the list again. First, he would have to retrieve the money; Reed was going to call him in the morning with the information as to which bank he had wired the funds to. Second, he needed to be ready to get the call from the kidnappers; along with receiving the drop instructions, he'd have to explain that the cash would only be available the following day. Third, he'd have to go get the cash and take it to the location the kidnappers had selected. David just hoped the drop spot would be a public place somewhere, and not a location where the kidnappers could just take the money from him without handing his family over. So that begged a possible fourth item on the list, if they didn't release Marianna and Julia at the cash drop; then when would he get them back? This thought made the pain in his chest return again.

David turned off the shower and ambled into the bedroom. Though some of the cooler air from the previous evening remained inside, the heat from the mid August day had already begun filtering into the home. He moved to the window and opened the lower portion of the shade and turned on the compact air conditioner unit. David let the fan blow on his back a moment before he turned and sat on the bed. The sheets were still on the ground, but he didn't care. David lay back and closed his eyes. He pictured Marianna, her beautiful brown eyes, her tan complexion, her dark hair, and her full bosomy figure.

They had been married almost two years. Marianna had been thirty-seven when they first met. She had been working in the school cafeteria where he was a teacher at the time. When David first saw her behind the lunch counter she had stood out from the other women in their drab kitchen outfits. Her eyes had twinkled, and her full figure had been unmistakable, even with the one-size-fits-all aprons.

He had asked her out.

First it was only lunch, but soon it had been dinner, and then, inevitably, they had become romantically involved. Within a year they knew they had found something special. Marianna was very simple and uncomplicated, and David loved that about her.

The only surprise she had ever pulled on him had actually ended up becoming one of the biggest joys of his life. Not long after they had set a date, maybe a month or so before they were actually to be married, Marianna admitted to David that she had not been completely truthful. Originally she had told him she had no immediate family, she was an only child and her mother and father had been killed in an automobile accident. But what she had failed to tell him, at first, was that two and a half years earlier she had given birth to a baby girl. Marianna had been ashamed because the child had been born out of wedlock. Though she didn't attend to church as she should, Marianna had been raised a good Catholic girl, and good girls didn't do such things, no matter their age or their circumstances. She had asked David for his forgiveness and understanding, which he, of course, had offered.

That was how David had found out about Julia. The little girl had been living in Saltillo, Mexico, with Marianna's aunt, while Marianna tried to make a living for the both of them by working in the states. It was tough being so far from her daughter, but the woman had done the best she could to provide for her small family.

So it was that Marianna had approached David asking for forgiveness for her secret, and also whether he would welcome her daughter into their new home. She wanted him to accept Julia as his very own. David, of course, had said yes. That was all two years ago.

David glanced at the digital clock on the nightstand. The blue lights read 9:37AM. Eight and a-half hours yet till the call. "My God, I'm going to lose my mind before then," he thought.


It was around eleven o'clock when Detective Stokes arrived back at the Hollenbeck Divisional Headquarters on First Street. He had waited almost an hour for the two back-up cruisers to arrive on location. Then he had driven less than a mile down Soto to the headquarters building.

The air-conditioning in the station house made the dampness of his clothes all the more noticeable. His shirt plastered to his back felt like a wet sponge. At first the cool air had been a welcome relief, but now the cold perspiration made him feel clammy.

The detective turned on his computer and clicked on the desktop icon for filling out a search warrant. It took a moment, but then the screen popped up. It would take about fifteen minutes to fill the form out and then print the document. Then he'd go to the courthouse and find a judge.

Harold Reed couldn't believe what an idiot his ex-brother-in-law was. The man actually expected Harold to give him $120,000; just like that. Watts had said it was a "matter of life and death", but then wouldn't tell him what the hell was actually going on, or who's "death", or who's "life" had supposedly been placed in jeopardy.

And he needed the money by tomorrow.

That was a laugh; the jerk probably didn't even know it was nearly impossible to come up with that kind of money, in cash, that quickly. The funny thing was though; Harold actually had the resources to be able to pull such a financial move off. Not many people did. Harold had told David he'd get the money together so that it would be available for Watts to withdraw the next morning from an LA bank. That was the truth, well sort of. The money would be available, but Harold wasn't going to trust David with it. Harold had already decided that there was no way he would simply give the twerp $120,000. If given the option, Harold would have told the guy right away to go to hell and not even have bothered with the money. The problem was, that asshole of a brother-in-law of his had something on Harold Reed. And the guy was just waiting to use it.

The "something", was that David had caught Harold in a delicate situation with a woman, a woman who wasn't his wife.

While David and Susan were still together Harold had tried to act the part of the friendly brother. After all, you couldn't choose whom your sister married, and in order to please Susan, Harold had played along. He had even gone so far as getting David a membership into the exclusive club that Harold belonged to. That had been when David and Susan lived in New York. Harold hadn't expected Watts to actually use the membership, however. All the accoutrements of the club required that one be rather well off just to associate there. Drinks were expensive and just parking in the garage for a day would probably mean a whole day's salary for a teacher. But then Susan had made up for David's lack of income. She worked in the advertising business and pulled in six figures. That job had come after their marriage, of course. Harold was sure Susan would never have married the loser in the first place if she had been bringing in that kind of salary beforehand. But she hadn't been, and so they did, and so David had caught him.

Harold leased one of the private apartments above the club. He was having one of his not infrequent afternoon interludes, when David, who had caught wind of the leased flat, had seen Harold's car in the garage and, not seeing him in the club, had tracked him down to the apartment. Harold had been stupid and just opened the door. He was used to being in charge, in control; he felt safe where he was the boss. The danger of being caught had never occurred to him. David put on a show as to ignorance of what was going on, and had actually had the balls to not mention the incident to Harold's wife. But Harold knew it would only be a matter of time before the man came to him to call in the marker. After all, that's what Harold Reed would do.

And now the jackass wanted $120,000.

But Harold wasn't going to make it that easy for his ex-brother-in-law. As promised, Harold would have the

funds available in LA the next day; they just would not be
available to David Watts was all. Harold had already
booked a flight into LAX. The flight was scheduled to
arrive first thing in the morning. Then he'd get to the
bottom of all this. If the little twerp wanted to take his
money then Harold was going to make David explain
what exactly it was he needed it for. Harold would be the
only one who could withdraw the funds from the bank.
And then he'd follow the cash and make sure David
didn't lose it. And then they'd be even. Well, sort of.

 

David opened his eyes. He felt cold. He turned his
head and saw that the window air conditioner was on. The
clock said 11:58AM. How long had he slept he
wondered? Then he remembered his wife and child were
gone, and that made him feel even colder. He looked at
the clock again. He'd slept for over two hours.

David rose and went to the window and turned off
the a/c unit. He tried to clear his head about what he
needed to be doing. He had secured the money, through
the help of his brother-in-law; at least that's what Harold
had told him. So that was taken care of. And now he had
to wait for the phone call. Then they'd tell him where to
take the money. He'd pick the money up from the bank
and take it to the drop location and exchange it for
Marianna and Julia.

Simple enough.

But what if the kidnappers didn't release his loved
ones? What if, God forbid, they were already dead? If that
were the case, then they'd probably just shoot David and
take the $120,000. The possibility of having to face the
tattooed man with the accented voice again suddenly

dawned on him. It was a scary thought. The guy had been pretty rough with him the first time. And that had been when David had something the man wanted. Once the money exchanged hands, maybe the guy just wouldn't need David alive anymore.

If David owned a gun he'd feel better, he thought. If he brought a gun at least he'd have a fighting chance. But David had never fired a weapon in his life. Did he even know anyone who owned a handgun? He didn't think so. His chest started to hurt again. But he didn't have time to think about that right now. Could he even buy a weapon? No. There was that waiting period law.

"Damn-it," he thought. "Only criminals get guns." He'd be defenseless.

If he couldn't get a gun maybe he could at least get someone to go along with him when he dropped off the money. But who?

Then an interesting thought came to him … he could hire a private detective.

He'd seen it on television, probably hundreds of times. When you couldn't get the police involved then you went to a private investigator, which was how it always worked. And the P.I.'s always carried a gun, too.

That was the answer. David didn't have the type of funds to pay off the ransom, but he certainly had enough money to retain a private investigator. All he needed now was a phone book. He only had six hours.

Detective Stokes entered courtroom number five and approached the deputy who was serving as the sergeant-at-arms. Another detective stood beside the deputy and spoke with a young woman who was apparently serving as the judge's administrative assistant. Next to the group of people sat a wooden desk. On their opposite side the judge was seated on the courtroom bench, attending to the paperwork in front of him. He was in his street clothes. Typically judges didn't put on their robes unless an official court proceeding was underway. Today was an administrative day in Courtroom Five.

A uniformed officer was headed in the opposite direction with what looked to be a warrant. Stokes nodded to the officer as he passed. Detective Stokes entered the bench area and greeted the deputy on duty.

"Is the judge accepting warrants now?" Stokes asked.

"Yeah, but he's about to go to lunch," replied the deputy. "If you drop it in the box he'll probably be able to get to it a little after he gets back. There's a couple ahead of you."

Stokes had figured that.

"Something like one-thirty you think?"

The uniformed officer looked at his watch. "Somewhere around there. He could even get to you sooner, maybe."

"OK, thanks."

The deputy smiled, "Sure."

Stokes approached the desk. Several wooden trays were uniformly arranged on top. Various types of paperwork lay in each of the different trays; Stokes found the one marked "Warrant Applications". He dropped the warrant form he had prepared in with the other forms, and checked to see how many applications were in the pile. Stokes estimated it looked like there were about seven applications already ahead of his. That could take the judge as much as half an hour to work through. That meant the detective might have to wait an hour and a half or more, but he'd try to be back before the justice returned from lunch; Stokes could just sit in the courtroom and wait till the judge called him back to chambers. Then he'd have to answer some questions, but in all likelihood he wouldn't have any trouble getting the document signed.

Stokes decided he would make use of the time and take a break. He'd head home and grab some lunch himself. That would also give him the opportunity to take a quick shower and get into a fresh change of clothes. He was hoping for a long day. The detective was eager to see the warrant put into action before night fell, and he had every intention of being on scene when that happened.

There was no heading of "Private Investigator" in the phone book. That only added to David's growing frustration. So he tried "Investigators". He leafed over and found what appeared to be listings of the services he was interested in. There were a lot. He had no idea how he should choose a particular company.

"Just pick one," he told himself.

David placed his finger on the page.

His first attempt got no answer. The second phone number he tried was disconnected. There were about sixty listings, so he wasn't worried about running out of agencies, one of them would surely be staffed. His third attempt rang several times before a message machine came on; he was about to hang up when a live voice picked up the line.

"Stafford Investigations."

The man's voice came across as a bit out of breathe.

Having been about to place the receiver down, David was somewhat caught by surprise. "Umm…Stafford Investigations?"

"Yeah. Stafford Investigations." The guy sounded a little annoyed with the redundant question. "This is Jim Stafford."

David tried to do better. "Oh, Hi. Umm … I'm hoping you might be able to help me. I'm looking for a private investigator. Is that what your company does?"

"Yeah. We're a private investigation firm. Private detective some people call it."

"OK good." He'd found the proper listings. "I'd like to talk to you about retaining your services. Possibly just for a day or two."

"That's fine."

David wasn't sure where to start.

"Do you work by the hour, or on a per job basis or something?"

"Usually by the hour, plus expenses. What type of job are we talking about? Surveillance of some sort?" the investigator asked.

No, it was a lot more complicated than surveillance, thought David. "No, actually I need some pretty big help. I've had something happen and I've been instructed not to get the police involved. Something like that."

"You mean like a kidnapping?"

Wow, the guy was on the ball. David hadn't meant to give it away so easily. But maybe that indicated this Stafford guy might be the man David needed.

"Something like that. Can we meet and talk? I need to get help right away."

"Yeah, of course. Where are you now?"

"I'm in Silver Lake," answered David.

"That's not far. I'm in the Windsor Square area, off Wilshire. You could be here in about half an hour. Can you come by my office?"

Of course he could. "Yes, I can. Listen, this is an emergency. I need to discuss this as soon as possible."

"Yeah, yeah, sure. That's what I thought. That's not a problem, I'm here at the office now and don't have a client scheduled."

"And will you accept a personal check, or a credit card?"

"Sure, a check is fine. Just come on over. We'll discuss the fee when you get here."

David was relieved.

"OK, thank you very much. I'll be there as soon as I can."

"No problem."

David verified the address and hung up the phone.

He had five and a half hours.


Jim Stafford let out a big sigh.

"Finally," he thought.

The private investigator hadn't had a paying customer in over a month. But this guy he had just spoken with seemed eager to drop some cash on him, and right away, today.

Jim looked around the room. He needed to clean up a little bit before the client came by. There were empty coke cans and a couple of old fast foods bags lying around. He didn't get much foot traffic, so usually it didn't matter.

Stafford Investigations was located on the second floor of a small commercial center. The center was older, but the rent was cheap enough and that was really all that mattered. The cheaper the better. The only reason an official company address even existed was the impression it made on clients. Otherwise he could just as easily have operated out of his apartment. A bedroom could hold all the equipment he really needed to run his business; at least since he had become the sole employee of the company.

Until two years ago he had had a receptionist. And then a couple of years before that there had been a couple of college kids working for him, too. But now it was just himself. The office held what still remained of the business. There was a desk, he had been particular about the desk, he had insisted it be one of those old metal kinds, like the police used to have. There were two file cabinets, a couple of chairs for clients to sit in, a couch along the wall and a table which held his computer, a fax, and a printer, as well as an old coffee pot. Jim didn't like the computer on his desk; it didn't fit with the image. His desk had the phone, a gooseneck lamp and a paper tray. Taped to one wall were a couple of aerial photos of Los Angeles. The other wall was taken up by a couple of large street maps bracketing the file cabinets. There was a bathroom in the back. The front was pretty much one big window covered by venetian blinds.

Jim picked up the trash and tossed it in the wastebasket in the corner. He sat down at the desk and pulled his appointment calendar out. He knew he didn't have any appointments today but he wanted to put the new client's name down there anyway. He also wanted to scribble a couple notes around on it to make it look like he had some other meetings scheduled. He picked up his pen, and then it him.

"Shit," he said aloud.

He hadn't gotten the clients name. That was stupid.

He looked at his watch. It was 12:40PM. That meant the guy would probably be there sometime around one o'clock. He hoped. Why didn't he get the guy's name and phone number? At least he had aggressively pursued the client to come into the office. He'd even told the guy not to worry about the fee until later. That usually worked. Jim was good at closing the deals when he had the opportunity. He just hadn't had that many opportunities lately. Ever since the economy had turned sour business had been down. People weren't spending on unnecessary luxury items. And, apparently, private investigators were a luxury item.

Jim placed the appointment calendar back in the drawer. He found a yellow note pad and pulled it out. Not very impressive, but it would have to do. He got up and walked back to the table where the computer rested. It was on, but it was in sleep mode. Jim hit a couple of keys and the screen lit up. It said "Stafford Investigations" in big bold letters. He turned the screen a little so that it would be visible from where the clients usually sat. Next he opened a file drawer from one of the cabinets and pulled out about four files. He went back and placed the files on his desk. There was already a wooden tray on the desk with a couple of files, but those were dead files, workups he'd done; ones he hadn't heard back from the clients on. He probably wouldn't.

Jim stepped back and looked at the arrangement. At least it didn't look like the desk of someone who hadn't had a job in a month.

David Watts crossed Western Avenue and started looking for the turn he wanted. The PI had told him the building was only half a block off Wilshire. A block later David saw the road sign and made a right off the main boulevard. On his left he immediately saw the storefront. There was a barbershop below and a yellow sign with black lettering above. The sign read "Stafford Investigations".

The businesses had no dedicated parking area, so David had to drive his automobile a little further down the street and pull a u-turn using an alleyway opening. Fortunately, owning a sub-compact, maneuvers like that were fairly easy. When he arrived in front of the building he found a couple of open parking spaces on the street.

He'd brought his checkbook, but nothing else. What else would he need? Probably nothing. He just wasn't thinking very straight. It was going to be a relief when he finally had an ally in this mess.

David exited the car and walked to the front entrance. Stafford had a separate entrance from the barbershop, on the investigator's door the glass had been blacked out. David opened the door and went in. Upon entering he was met with a steep flight of stair. As he began to climb he suddenly felt very warm. He hadn't stopped to think about it until he'd gotten onto the staircase, but the day had already turned really hot. It was probably going to be one of those 105-degree days.

When David reached the top landing he found the upper door propped open. Before he had even left the final stair a figure appeared in the doorway.

"Hello there!" said the man, smiling. "You must be the guy who called."

The man stuck out his hand. David took it.

"Yes. I told you I'd be right over," he answered.

"Great. Guess you found the place OK then. I'm Jim Stafford."

"David Watts." David had to look up to meet the man's eyes.

"Nice to meet you Mr. Watts." Stafford backed up and opened his arm toward a couple of chairs in front of an old desk. "Please come in. Have a seat."

David took a couple of steps over to the desk and sat in one of the facing seats. Jim Stafford sat down in his rolling chair behind the metal desk.

"Can I offer you something?" the man asked. "Actually all I have is water. Or I could make some coffee if you preferred."

"No. I'm fine. Thanks."

Actually he was a little thirsty, but David didn't want to bother with that right now. He needed to get right down to the business at hand.

"So what can I do for you Mr. Watts? Or should I call you David?"

"Uh … David is fine."

"OK, David, what is it you would you like me to do for you?"

David saw the computer screen on the table, and a couple of pictures of LA taken from overhead. Behind him he heard a window unit air conditioner.

"I need someone to come with me on an errand. I have to meet with some people. Well some bad people, and there's going to be a lot of cash involved."

A lot of cash involved. Stafford liked the sound of that.

"Yeah, that's right. On the phone you said something about not having the police involved. Is this something illegal or something?"

"No. No. I'm not involved in anything like that."

That didn't leave many other alternatives.

"Well, you're not talking about kidnapping are you?" That would be a first.

David looked at the man.

Jim Stafford was tall and stocky, but not particularly athletic in appearance. As a matter-of-fact the man had actually moved rather slowly to his desk, almost as if he had a limp. He looked about forty-five or fifty years of age. Stafford still had a full head of auburn hair, but it was too long, and in general the man gave the impression of being somewhat unkempt. He certainly wasn't the picture of confidence that one saw on TV.

But could he do the job? That was the question. Unfortunately, David really had no time find out. It was going to have to be this guy or go it alone.

The investigator still waited for an answer.

"Yes. It's my wife and daughter. They were taken this morning." David could hardly bear to listen to the words as they came out. But it was a relief to have the thoughts shared with another human being, instead of having them just pounding around in his head, over and over again.

Stafford couldn't believe it, himself. He had really only been kidding when he had suggested it might be a kidnapping. That had sounded impressive, like maybe he had dealt with kidnappings before. But the real thing, that was another matter, maybe one for the police.

"Taken?"

"Yes," answered David. "When I woke up this morning my wife was screaming, and there were three or four men in my house. Before I knew what was happening they had me pinned down and tied my hands and put tape over my eyes. Then they told me they were going to take my wife and my daughter, and I had to do exactly as told if I wanted to see my family again."

Wow, thought Stafford. "And not to call the police?" he added.

"Yeah, and not to call the police, or they'd kill them."

"Do you know if they were armed?"

"Yes, before they blindfolded me I saw that one of the men had a gun."

Shit, this really was bad. "You mean like a handgun, like a pistol."

"Yeah." As David retold the story he realized it sounded horrible. And Stafford's reaction was confirming the same.

"And you didn't know these guys."

David shook his head.

"You didn't recognize any of them?"

"No. I barely had time to see them, and it was still pretty dark. But from what I could tell they were Mexican. Or from Central America, you know, Hispanic."

To Stafford, this sounded really bad. It was the worst type of kidnapping; committed by strangers, possibly gang related, and a ransom. Maybe not something he would normally want to deal with.

"Did they say how much of a ransom they wanted?"

"$120,000," David replied. That too, sounded horrible coming out of his mouth.

"Wow. That's a lot of money. Do you have that kind of cash?" Maybe a commission basis would make it worth his while, thought Stafford.

"I don't. But my brother-in-law is helping me. He's wiring the money to a bank here in LA. It will be available tomorrow morning."

"And when do they want the money by?"

"I don't know yet, but I think tomorrow sometime. They're supposed to call me at six o'clock and tell me what to do with the money."

Stafford leaned back in his chair and thought a moment.

David didn't wait for a response; he got right to the point of what he needed the man to do for him.

"I want you to be there when they call me. Maybe you can help me arrange for a place to drop off the money that isn't too dangerous. I mean like a public place."

Stafford nodded his head, "Sure, I can do that."

"And then I want you to go with me when I bring them the money. For the exchange." David looked to the investigator; he hoped he would get the same affirmative answer again.

The guy was asking Stafford to get right in the middle of the thing.

"This sounds like a very serious situation. You realize that? I mean somebody could end up getting killed."

Of course it was, didn't the investigator understand? "That's why I need your help."

Stafford shook his head, "I'm just wondering if maybe we shouldn't get the police involved."

That would certainly be easier, but David feared what the kidnappers would do if they found out. "No. No police. They specifically said they'd kill them if I called the police."

Stafford had never worked a kidnapping case before. It was really over his head. He usually just followed cheating spouses around or sometimes tracked down runaway kids. This was completely different, it was much more dangerous. But it was also potentially lucrative. And Stafford needed the money. Usually the riskier the job, the higher the pay, and with this one there could even be a large ransom in the mix.

His prospective client sat across from him, a look of despair and pleading mixed on his face.

It would be a risky assignment.

"OK. I'll do it," Stafford finally answered.

David sat back and looked at the ceiling. Then he felt tears welling up with the relief. "Thank you."

Stafford saw the emotional state his client was in.

"It's OK, it's OK. I'm here to help." The investigator smiled at the poor sap. "Everything's going to work out."

"Thanks," David answered. "It's just a relief. Without going to the police I didn't know what to do."

"Well, you did the right thing by coming to me."

Stafford felt genuinely pleased to be able to help the client out. This also seemed the opportune time to get some needed help for himself.

"You said you were going to bring your checkbook?"

"Yes."

"Great. Basically, for two days work you'd normally be talking about $500 a day. But considering we're dealing with armed men, and the fact I'll be accompanying you to the drop off, that makes it more complicated." Stafford looked for a reaction, but the client's demeanor remained the same. It didn't matter; the guy was really in a pickle.

"So let's say $5,000."

Still no reaction. He went for the closer.

"Can you pay that today?"

David nodded his head and got out his checkbook.


After returning from lunch, Detective Stokes hadn't waited more than about ten minutes for the judge to call him into chambers. The judge asked him a few rudimentary questions and then signed the warrant. It was as simple as that. Now the detective needed to go get some firepower.

Stokes stepped from the courthouse and into the midday heat. Across the street, his unmarked cruiser sat in a reserved parking spot. He had traded the undercover Malibu for the standard plain white Crown Victoria that he usually drove when not on stakeout. He had also taken a quick shower during his lunch break and thrown on a change of clothes. The shower had refreshed him some, but he had immediately begun to sweat again when he had returned to his car. At home, he had left the cruiser in the driveway, in the full glare of the sun. And it had been horribly hot inside when he had climbed in.

It was days like this that made him wish he could park inside his garage. Like a lot of southern Californians', Stokes didn't use his garage much for the storage of automobiles. Given the temperate winter weather, a lot of Californians just left their cars outside all the time and used their garage as extra storage space, or maybe a workshop or something. Stokes didn't think many people used their extra space quite the same way he

did, however. Stokes' garage was basically a shelter for
sick or homeless animals. And, of course, it wasn't really
so much his garage, as his wife's. Debra was an animal
lover. It didn't matter what kind of animal either; big,
small, furry, feathered, scaled, slithering, jumping or
crawling; she loved them all. Debra's mother had been a
veterinarian and she had exposed her only child to all
kinds of creatures, even letting her care for some of the
wayward animals that sometimes made their way into
their home. When the older woman had passed, Debra
had adopted a couple of the longer-term projects she'd
grown attached to. And now that she was an adult, with a
part-time career, she still couldn't pull herself away from
the critters.

Stokes assumed some of the animal attachment came
as a substitute for what might have been a larger family
life. Unfortunately, try as they might, not long after he
and his wife were married the couple had found that they
were physically unable to have children. The doctors had
explained about the specific malformation of some part of
his wife's anatomy, but Stokes had never really fully
understood. All he knew was Debra would not be able to
bear him any children. Which was all the larger a shame
because he knew Debra would have been a wonderful
mother.

Stokes felt especially saddened, not so much for
himself, but for his wife. On top of losing her mother so
early, this had been really a crushing blow for Debra.
What's more, she had no siblings and her final relation,
her father, had been estranged from her for years. Except
for Stokes, Debra really had no other family.

And then they had found there would be no children
either.

Like many other childless couples, they had considered adoption. But the waiting periods were so long and then, even with the wait, the chances of ever actually getting a child were still remote. They had put off the decision to apply till another time, and, somehow, that time had just never come.

So their garage, hell, most of their home, had become a sort of unofficial animal hospital. In view of their lack of children, the fact was, the animals filled a void. And, if truth be told, Stokes also found himself more than just a little enamored with many of the pets.

Debra had a special permit for some of the more exotic animals she cared for. But there were others she kept in their possesion knowing full well they were in violation of animal control laws. Stokes had tried to reason with her, but when it came to their zoo, there was no middle ground. So he just looked the other way. Besides, it was nearly impossible for animal control to keep track of the myriad of creatures now living on their property anyway.

So with the menagerie in the garage, the cruiser had been left sitting exposed in the driveway for an hour. Even though he'd run the a/c at full blast on the way to the courthouse, Stokes had begun to perspire, again. As he left the cool of the court building he was still sweaty.

The detective unlocked the cruiser and climbed in. He had tried to find some shade to park in, but there just hadn't been any available. The steering wheel felt hot, so he held the wheel along the bottom of the rim while he started the engine. He turned the a/c on and turned the fan on high. Stokes placed his hands in front of the vents and felt the air; it was only just barely cool. It would take a minute or two with the engine running for it to kick in.

That was the best he could do. He backed out of the space and then pulled forward. Then he made a left out of the lot and headed for Soto. He was only a couple of blocks from headquarters.


Jim Stafford was almost gleeful. He held in his hand a check for $5,000. He hadn't seen that kind of money in a long while. His glee was slightly tempered, however, by the commitment for services that the fee had obligated him to. The particular circumstances of the job he had been contracted to do were a little rougher than he was normally used to. He was going to have to be on his toes on this one. But, as Stafford considered the transaction further, he realized he'd made the right decision; at least he had the check. Now he could pay the rent, both rents. And still have something left over. He looked at the clock on the wall; it read 1:45PM.

He had agreed to meet at the client's home at five o'clock, well before the ransom call was supposed to come in. That would give him three hours to get the check deposited and then get over to the client's place. He also wanted to run a quick background search on David and Marianna Watts. Just to see if what the guy had told him about himself was true. Stafford contracted an internet service that could pull docs from all fifty states. It usually was pretty thorough. He was billed on a monthly basis for the service and had actually been thinking of canceling it, but he'd gone ahead and paid the bill anyway when the last statement had come in. He was glad he had kept it going, the service was a useful tool. He'd log on and do the Watts search shortly.

But right now he just wanted to get to the bank and put the money into his account.

"Wow, five thousand dollars." It was a lot of money.


Detective Stokes entered Lieutenant Thibeut's office and sat on the leather couch across from his commander's desk. The Lieutenant was on the phone. It quickly became obvious to the detective that even though his boss had ushered Stokes in, the man intended to finish the conversation in which he was already engaged. It sounded to Stokes like the Lieutenant could be talking to payroll, the frivolity of that that was annoying. Stokes had something important going on and he wanted his boss to hurry. He was anxious to get moving on whatever was going on back at the duplex. It had already been five hours since he'd seen the woman and child being led into the residence. Anything could have happened since then.

Just as Thibeut seemed about to hang up, something the person said on the other end of the phone riled him up, and the conversation sprang back to life. The Lieutenant was leaned back in his oversized leather office chair with the phone in one hand. In his other hand he worked a ballpoint pen. The man was dressed in a suit; his hair slicked back showing just a touch of gray at the temples. Thibeut liked to take care of himself; he always gave a good appearance. And from what Stokes could tell, the women in the office seemed in full appreciation.

Thibeut finally concluded his business; he put the phone down and straightened the oversized chair. Then he leaned forward and clasped his hands together on his desk. The pen stuck up from between his palms.

"So you got the warrant?"

"Yeah." Stokes held the document up for display.

"Great. It's a knock warrant I presume?"

Most warrants that got approved were of the knock variety. A knock warrant just meant that you had to give notice before entering a property. The other alternative was a no-knock warrant. With the no-knock you could enter without notice, usually not busting the door down like they frequently suggested in Hollywood, however.

"Yeah, it's a knock. I started to ask about a no-knock, but the judge pretty much cut me off before I could even ask. But I didn't think that was really an option."

"It wasn't," Thibeut replied, the obvious implication being that his boss possessed superior knowledge of the vast workings of the justice system to that of the detective.

"So where do we stand?" asked the Lieutenant.

"Well, we've got two pairs of detectives staking the place out now. I'd like to be able to cover the front and rear of both residences. If I could get four uniformed officers to go along with the plain clothes already on scene that should be sufficient. And we'd need at least one female officer of course."

"What about Evans? This is his op. Is he along with this?"

Evans was the detective in charge of the surveillance. He'd been the one who'd registered the original tip, so it was his case. Thibeut was really the boss, but Evans needed to be kept informed of everything that concerned the stakeout. Stokes had tried earlier, to no avail, to get Evans when he had asked for the back up at the duplex that morning. However, he hadn't really tried since that time, and five hours later Stokes still hadn't given his fellow detective the heads-up.

"I haven't seen him. I tried to reach him this morning, but he wasn't around."

Thibeut opened his palms, the pen clutched behind his thumb, "So find him now. We've got to all be coordinated on this. This is his baby, he needs to be there."

Stokes thought maybe this part of the operation had become his "baby". After all, he was the one who had seen the women escorted into the residence. Being the witness, he was also the one who had been required to go get the warrant. But now he had to find Evans and bring him in on it.

"All right." Stokes rose from his seat.

"But what if I can't find him. We need to move on this."

Thibeut spread his palms again, this time shaking his head a little as he spoke, "That's fine, but at least give it a shot. I'll be here, I'm not going anywhere."

Detective Stokes dismissed himself from the Lieutenant's office. He headed back down the hall to the cubicled offices. If Evans wasn't at his desk, he'd have to search around the whole damn building.


David felt extremely relieved. He now had someone in his corner who maybe could help him. Jim Stafford hadn't been the exact picture of a private eye that David had in mind, but at least the guy looked to be old enough that he'd bring a lot of experience to the table. It sounded as if the man had maybe even worked a couple of kidnappings before, too. And Stafford was a big guy. Even though the man didn't necessarily inspire confidence, the PI himself appeared confident. And that seemed to rub off on David.

David had just picked up some fast food. It was the first thing he had eaten all day. He had been so worried regarding the day's events he hadn't even noticed the hunger pangs. But the interview with Stafford had made him feel better. The burger and fries were just what he needed. He ate as he drove, the car's air conditioner on full blast.

It was a little after two, plenty of time before the call; so things were shaping up. The money was on the way, and now he had gotten some help. It appeared he might actually have covered all the bases. David and Marianna's bank account had taken a hit, but in the grand scheme of things that seemed pretty inconsequential. What was $5,000? Especially when compared to the fact that his wife and daughter's lives were at stake. And then there was the ransom. Five thousand dollars was a drop in the bucket compared to the $120,000 he was going to owe Reed. That was another worry. So what, he thought. He'd figure all that stuff out later.

David made his way through the narrow winding streets of his Silver Lake community. He turned on to his road and headed uphill about two blocks before he came to his driveway on the right. He turned in. The house looked just as it had before. David stepped out of the car and glanced around for any suspicious observers, but there didn't seem to be any sign of trouble. He'd finished the burger already and took the trash and what was left of the fries with him. The drink was long gone.

The handle of the home's front door bobbled around in his grasp as he turned it and stepped through the entryway. Inside, everything appeared just as it had when

he left. He threw the trash and the fries away and opened
the refrigerator and got out a bottled water. It was a hot
day and his thirst had begun to catch up with him. The
cold water tasted good. David sat down at the kitchen
table. He saw his cell phone on the counter; it was still
plugged in from that morning. The green light was on,
indicating a full charge.

David tried to relax a little. He leaned back and put
his head against the kitchen wall. It had already been a
long day, but maybe things were starting to look a little
brighter. In front of David a baker's rack stood against the
opposite wall. Most of the shelving contained various pots
and pans and other cooking tools. The upper shelf
however, served a different purpose, it held only family
photos. There was a photo of Marianna and Julia, and one
of all three family members, and then still another of just
Marianna and himself. The last photo had been taken at
the beach. Marianna looked a little plump, but she wore
her weight well. David was wearing shorts and an open
shirt, his belly kind of stuck out. David didn't like that
picture. He always thought of himself as better looking in
person than he appeared in photos. Inwardly, he knew the
camera's view might actually be the correct depiction,
and his view the distorted one. But picturing himself as an
overweight, balding man on the latter side of middle age
was not something he wanted to think about.

David looked at his watch again. He knew he was
obsessing, but he couldn't help it. It was 2:24PM. Two
and a half hours and Stafford would be there.

The house was hot. It occurred to him that he had
turned the air conditioner in the bedroom completely off
before he had left for the appointment. He got up and
went to the bedroom and turned the window unit on, this

time he put the fan on medium. Then he lay back on the bed and tried not to think, of anything.


Stokes found Evans in his cubicle; the fellow detective had taken the morning off for a dental appointment. So Stokes spent ten minutes bringing the man up to speed on the latest developments at the stakeout.

"So we need to see Thibeut now so we can get this thing rolling. He's waiting in his office." Stokes was worried Evans might try to stall a bit in an attempt to assert some authority over the operation.

"All right that's fine," the man said rising from his rolling office chair. "I just wish you would have called me on my cell or something."

Stokes realized Evans was right, he'd probably tried to exert a bit too much authority himself.

"Sorry, I just didn't think of it. And I wanted to get that warrant as soon as I could."

The two men exited the room, Stokes led and Evans followed him into the hallway. They were headed back in the direction of Thibeut's office.

"So a woman and a girl, huh? Is that right?" Evans asked as they walked at a brisk pace.

"Yeah, the woman was definitely an adult, and the girl couldn't have been more than four or five."

Evans made an ugly face as they walked. "That doesn't make much sense. Doesn't really fit the profile for what we're looking at. I mean, unless the woman is a handler. And the girl's way too young, of course."

Stokes let Evans think.

"And you say it was at the location next door, not the address that we made."

"Yep. I had the one residence under surveillance when I saw this car pull up. At first, I thought the car was going to pull into our location, but then it turned into the place next door."

They were nearing the Lieutenant's office now and the two men paused to wrap up before entering.

"And you said there was a lookout at our location. Did the guy talk to the heavies with the women?"

"No." Stokes hadn't thought of that.

"No signals of any kind? Any eye contact?"

Evans was scoring points. Good thing the real game hadn't started.

Stokes shook his head.

"Well, goddammit, that doesn't make any sense. I mean maybe they're not related."

The two detectives stared at each other a moment before Evans continued.

"Or maybe they are. But I don't want to blow my investigation over some bullshit sideshow that may be a domestic or something."

Stokes didn't consider Evans any more accomplished than himself, but right now the other detective was getting the best of him. The suggestion that he might have misinterpreted the situation actually had some weight to it. But then Stokes thought of the woman and child back at the duplex. That hadn't been any domestic squabble. They needed help.

Evans was looking at Stokes, waiting for him to defend himself.

"OK, I see your point. If this isn't part of the juvenile trafficking then we don't want to blow the whole thing up with this. But I'm telling you, that woman and child were under duress. And four males escorting them from the car into the house is not gonna be a domestic."

Stokes looked to see if Evans showed any sign of agreement. He couldn't tell, but it didn't matter. He had the warrant, and unless Evans somehow convinced Thibeut to overrule the operation, the thing was going to happen. But it would be better to have Evans on board than to have him lobbying against him.

"Look, maybe what we should do is just go for the one address. We can make it quiet and try not to let the whole street know we're there." That was all he was going to offer. "But we're exercising the warrant. That's the best I can do."

Evans stuck his tongue into his cheek and eyed Stokes. He was a little shorter than Stokes, but the man didn't let that stop him.

"OK. We go after only the one address, and you've got a deal. But you're not in charge. Understand. We do this as a team."

What the hell, thought Stokes. At least he would be getting co-billing.

"OK. I'll go with that."

Stokes put his hand on the doorknob to Thibeut's office and tilted his head toward the door.

Evans nodded and fixed his tie.


Stafford waited while the search engine scanned through the records. It usually took almost a minute for the results to come back. Not that bad, considering. After all, fifty states worth of data was a lot of information to sort through. The service would bring up any records found in either the state court systems or the various motor vehicle departments. Jim tapped his finger on the table. It took only a moment longer and the results flashed up on the screen. He had narrowed the search of the numerous David Watts' to just his one particular person of interest by using his client's social security number. He'd obtained the number from the front of the personal check the man had given him. Stafford found it hard to believe anybody was stupid enough to still have that information on their checks, but then nothing had suggested to him he was dealing with a world full of Einsteins.

The data for the particular David Watts of interest, established two areas of residence during the man's life. According to DMV records, Watts had been born in Riverside, California and had then moved to New York City when he was around twenty-five. Then, eight years ago, he had moved back to California, this time to the Los Angeles area. There was no criminal data, only the DMV stuff. That pretty much coincided with the information that the client had disclosed. Records from the public school system could confirm the man's employment, but that data was a little trickier to obtain and would require a few phone calls. Stafford didn't have time to get into all that right now.

Marianna Watts was going to be a little more difficult. Stafford didn't have a social for her, but really, he thought, how many Marianna Watts could there be?

Stafford entered the name and waited.

The a/c unit in the front window was going full steam. Stafford had been surviving the heat pretty well until he had made the run to the bank. It was goddamn hot out. He was wearing khakis and a Hawaiian print shirt. He preferred shorts, but thought the khakis looked a little more professional. The loose fitting shirt was usually pretty comfortable, no matter what the weather, but right now it felt sticky on his back.

The screen refreshed in front of Stafford and the requested data popped up.

Florida, California, Texas, New York, Arizona … hell, even Minnesota. It looked like there were a few Marianna Watts' out there, or at least one or two who moved around a lot. It was impossible to tell which portion of the data might be relevant and which might not, not without more information about the particular woman he was searching for.

"Shit," thought Stafford, "that isn't going to help a bit."

The criminal records data appeared below the numerous DMV entries. There were two listings. One of the entries stemmed from Florida for a drug possession charge. The other was from California, for check fraud. Neither listing stated whether there had been a conviction in either of the cases. But that was typical; once the data got entered, it generally wasn't updated that frequently and could often even be entirely incorrect. Incorrect or not, without better info on the client's wife, the mess of data on the screen wasn't going to mean anything.


Harold Reed was ready to go home. It was almost 6:30 PM in New York and he hadn't left the office yet. Not that it was unusual for him to work late, but he wanted to get home at a reasonable hour tonight; he had a

busy day scheduled for tomorrow. He'd waited as late as
he could to call his brother-in-law.

"Ex-brother-in-law, that is," he reminded himself.

Harold had considered surprising David and just
showing up in LA at the man's house. But now, upon
further consideration, he'd decided to get David to pick
him up at the airport. His flight was scheduled to land at
LAX at 9:45AM the next morning. The first class ticket
had set Harold back $1,200. But that was OK. The ride
from the airport together would give them a chance to
chat about what the hell was going on and what David
really needed all that money for.

Harold reached for the phone and shook his head.

"Stupid asshole."


Detective Stokes had what he wanted. It was just
after 4:30PM and he was finally on his way back to the
crime scene at the duplex. Well, actually so far it was
only a possible crime scene, though Stokes felt pretty sure
it would prove out that something of a criminal nature of
some kind was under way at the location.

In addition to himself, three other plain clothed
detectives were in route, along with four uniformed
officers. With the four plain clothed officers already on
site, that would make a total of twelve law enforcement
types. That would be plenty, maybe even a little overkill.
Of course, if they entered and found a bunch of young
women being held, then that would be a different matter.
Thibeut had managed to round up two female officer's in
the group, too; one detective and one uniformed officer.

They were ready to move in, finally.

It took only a few minutes to get over to the Boyle Heights area. Stokes and Evans rode in the same car, with the other detectives together in another cruiser. The uniformed officers paired in two marked LAPD cars.

As they arrived on the scene, Evans had the marked vehicles park half a block away on Cesar Chavez, out of sight of either of the duplexes. One of the unmarked cruisers parked on the intersecting street where Stokes had earlier relocated for the rendezvous with the other undercover officers. With the two cruisers already on site, they now had the location of interest flanked on all four sides.

Stokes and Evans exited their vehicle, taking two of the uniformed officers with them and maneuvered to a location across the street from the front of the duplex in question.

Stokes noticed the tattooed lookout that had earlier been next door was no longer out front. The officers' positions were pretty well concealed anyway, but it was definitely better that the man was not present. When they moved in for the bust he would be an added impediment and would have to be taken down first. And that, depending on how it went, could alert the heavies holding the women at the residence next door.

In the street, traffic was starting to back up. It was rush hour and, apparently, more than one commuter had been convinced utilizing the smaller side road was a better course of action than dealing with the gridlock confounding the main boulevard.

"Man, this sucks," said Evans, standing beside Stokes looking at the traffic.

It had become apparent to Stokes from their conversation on the way over, his fellow detective remained un-persuaded blowing their cover, at this point, was the most prudent course of action.

"You know, it could be that those two women you saw this morning are the only female types in there. And they don't even fit the MO," the detective continued. "I know we gotta go in there, but it just pisses me off that we're gonna get made on this."

Stokes understood the man's frustration. Nabbing a forced prostitution ring would be a good bust. Not to mention that they'd be taking a bunch of young girls off the street and, hopefully, placing them back at home with their families, where they belonged. Of course, Stokes had been at this long enough to know that some of those homes would actually constitute the sort of environments the children would be better off not going back to. Hell, sometimes it was even because of their families that the girls found themselves involved in prostitution in the first place. But, none-the-less, any other outcome would likely be better than a brothel.

"Yeah, I hear ya," answered Stokes. Maybe they could just wait a little longer to see if anybody else might show up. But then nightfall would be coming in a few hours and it would be safer to get the bust done during daylight.

"Why don't we just wait until the traffic settles a bit, then we can take em? Maybe we'll see something in the meantime."

Evans didn't really have a choice; that was the best they could do. "I guess. But we've got a lot of manpower to just be sitting here."

Stokes turned and informed the two uniformed cops that were along that they would sit tight a while. Stokes knew both of the officers. Trujillo was a two-year guy and

Martin, the female officer, had been with the force something like four years. When the bust went down theses same two uniformed officers would be taking the front, along with the two plain-clothes officers, Arnold and Mendez, in the cruiser already in place. Brudzinski and Jackson, the other two uniformed cops were going to cover the north flank, while Detective Wystrom and Detective Garcia, the other female officer, moved in from the South. They were going to go for a static holding situation with the two detectives to the rear of the buildings. That would cover all of the bases.

Meanwhile, however, the traffic still sat in the street. Stokes looked at his watch, it read 5:05PM. All dressed up and nowhere to go. They could wait a couple of hours, but not much more.


David Watts pulled the curtains to the side and looked out the front window. Still nothing. He pursed his lips and made a pained expression. The private investigator he had hired was supposed to have shown up over ten minutes ago. Watts needed to discuss the upcoming phone call from the kidnappers scheduled for six o'clock. David's arm had begun hurting again and he let go of the curtain and stepped away from the window.

More medication was in order.

He made his way to the bathroom and opened the medicine chest and pulled out the bottle of aspirin. He opened the bottle and put two of the pills in his palm before closing the container and placing it back on the shelf. He downed the two aspirin with some water from the faucet. Surely that would make him feel better soon. The whole thing was becoming very stressful.

A little over an hour earlier David had received a phone call from his brother-in-law. It had come in on his cell phone and had almost, literally, scared the shit out of him. He had been sure it was going to be the kidnappers, but as it turned out it was only Harold. However, even though it had ended up only being Harold Reed on the phone, the call had brought somewhat unsettling news. David had expected that the next time he heard from his brother-in-law it would be when Harold called to give him the bank account information for withdrawing the funds tomorrow morning. However, Reed hadn't given any instructions on how to withdraw cash. Instead, his brother-in-law had called with instructions for David to drive to the airport in the morning and pick Harold up. Reed was going to be doing the cash withdrawal himself, to make sure it went smoothly.

That was terrible news.

David was grateful that his brother-in-law had voluntarily come through with the ransom amount, but David didn't want Harold getting personally involved in the situation. Reed was the kind of guy who wanted to take control of everything. He'd insist on getting full details of what had transpired and David would have to tell him. Harold would probably want to get the police involved, or, at the least, he'd demand to take over the negotiations with the kidnappers. And all this just as David thought he was getting things worked out, too.

"Damn it," he muttered aloud.

Then an even worse thought came to mind. What if Harold decided to renig on the money? What if when his brother-in-law found out that the cash was to be used for a ransom, Harold simply backed out? David could just hear it; "Sorry David, I'm not handing $120,000 of my money over to a bunch of criminals." It could happen.

In the midst of this horrible thought the sound of a car door slamming came from out front. That would probably be Stafford, David thought. David would have to worry about his brother-in-law later. For now he had to proceed as if the money would be there. He really had no other choice.


Jim Stafford had hurried the best he could. He was running ten minutes late, and the stupid winding streets of Silver Lake had kept him from being able to make up the time. As he approached the front door of what he hoped was his client's house he looked at his watch. It read 5:17PM; OK he was fifteen minutes late.

Before Stafford could reach the front entranceway the door opened and David Watts stepped outside. Watts had a look of incredible relief, like maybe he was going to cry, Stafford wasn't sure. But the man smiled at him and stuck out his hand.

"Man am I glad to see you. I thought maybe you got lost or something."

Stafford hadn't been lost, he'd just gotten a late start; shit happens.

"Yeah, I had some business to finish up from another case I'm working," Stafford lied.

"That's OK, at least you're here. Come on in."

As they entered the house Watts closed the front door and Stafford noticed the latch didn't seem to catch quite correctly.

Once inside, the investigator briefly looked around the immediate interior for any clues as to his client's life style or potential income. The place was clean and well kept, but the furnishings were less than impressive. The kitchen appliances were older and the carpeting in the living room looked as if it were nearing retirement age.

"Can I get you something to drink?" David opened the refrigerator door and peered inside. "We've got iced tea, beer, water. Oh, and juice…but it's in those little boxes." He held one of the little children's boxes up for Stafford to see.

Stafford wanted to say "Yeah, like I want a friggin juice box," but he passed on that and asked for the beer. Watts grabbed one of the little boxes for himself.

"So let's go over this stuff again," Stafford said as he pulled out a chair and sat down at the kitchen table. After getting seated he glanced up and immediately noticed the photos on the baker's rack.

"OK, is that her, there in the pictures?" He pointed at the framed pictures on the shelf.

David grabbed the one photo of Marianna and Julia together and handed it, along with the beer, to the investigator before pulling out a chair at the table for himself.

"Yeah, that's Marianna and Julia. It was taken about six months ago, I think."

Stafford studied the photo. The picture was of a woman and a child and looked to have probably been taken in a professional studio. The woman was approaching middle age, with olive skin and appeared of obvious Hispanic descent. The young girl looked to be four or five years old and had a similar dark complexion. The woman was dressed nicely, but had fairly average looks, and from the other photos on the baker's rack it appeared that she was probably a good deal over weight.

The only thing Stafford could see that a man might find attractive about the woman was she had a fairly large bust line. Otherwise, she appeared no real catch. But then, hey, beauty wasn't everything.

"And so you've been married two years. Is that right?"

"Yes, as of September, two years."

Stafford was curious as to the attraction. The woman had come with some baggage too; it seemed obvious that the kid in the picture was of no blood relation to his client; she certainly predated the marriage anyhow.

"So tell me how you met."

David went over the story of how he had first come to meet Marianna in the school cafeteria and how they had subsequently dated. He then explained how Marianna had revealed to him that she had a daughter already, though David tried to improve the story a little because it sounded a bit bizarre in the re-telling. He hurried through the whole thing, too; after all, his relationship with his wife wasn't the real point of the meeting.

Stafford was somewhat surprised at how little his client actually knew about his own wife. The man had never even met any of the woman's family. He wanted to know more about the relationship, however they were nearing the time of the ransom call and Stafford decided he'd have to leave that for digging into later.

"OK. Also, remind me before I leave, I want to get your wife's social security number. I just want to do a routine background check."

"Yeah, sure," David answered, even though he didn't think the investigator seemed to be focusing in on the immediate problem. "We need to talk about the kidnappers and the ransom call." David glanced at the kitchen clock. It read 5:31PM, half an hour to go.

Stafford humored him.

"All right. Well, there's really not that much we're going to have to do." Stafford leaned back in the chair and took a swig of his beer before continuing. "The call will come in. They'll ask if you have the money. Then you tell them that you have it, in cash. Don't volunteer that you won't actually have the cash until tomorrow unless they try to set up the swap for tonight. Then, obviously, you'll have to put them off until tomorrow afternoon or whenever."

Stafford looked closely at his client. The man looked worried as hell.

"Then you'll arrange for a drop location. They'll probably want you to take the money to some obscure place." It was always an industrial area it seemed in the TV shows. "But try to suggest a more public place, like a park or something. And also try to not let them get the money without handing your wife and kid over. They may say for you to leave the money and then they'll release them later. Try not to let them get away with that. Tell them you want to see your family or you won't give them the money. Otherwise, when they see that you have the ability to pay, then they might just hold on to them and see if they can get a second ransom out of you."

"Geez," thought Stafford, "there's a hell of a lot of shit to remember." It would have been helpful if he'd actually worked a kidnapping before.

"Oh, and see if they will let you speak with your wife when they call. Like to prove she's alive. You know?"

"My God," thought David, "prove she's alive?" David's arm hurt worse than ever now, but he tried to put the pain to the back of his mind.

"OK, so there's a couple of important things I have to remember." David tried to prioritize the list in his head. "First, I tell them I have the money. Second, I try to speak with Marianna. Third, I make sure Marianna and Julia are at the drop site." He looked to the investigator. "Is that right?"

"Almost. You have to set up the drop site, in a public place. That would be third. Then tell them you have to have your family back at the same time as when you bring the cash, or you won't leave it."

"So that's four things," answered David. "The money, speak with my wife, set the swap up for a public place and then make sure Marianna and Julia are there."

"You got it."

David had to make sure he remembered everything. He was going to be really nervous when the call came in. He told Stafford to hang on a moment and went into the office and retrieved a pen and a yellow note pad before returning to the kitchen.

"OK, I'm going to write this down."

Stafford studied his client as the man jotted down the four items. The guy was kind of a goofball. They'd be lucky if the guy could get through the upcoming call without having a nervous breakdown. "Geez," thought Stafford, "if he's having problems now, the guy's never gonna make it through the ransom delivery tomorrow."

"All right, I feel better having that written," said David as he set the pen down and looked over the list.

Stafford asked to see the paper and David handed it to him. The list looked like it covered the major points.

"Oh, where should I suggest we do the swap? Where would a good public place be?"

"Good question," Stafford said before finishing off the bottle of cheap beer that Watts had given him. He drained the last swallow and set the bottle on the table. "Let's see," he added, wiping his mouth with his forearm. "How about Dodger Stadium? That would definitely be public. And easy to locate them in the parking lot, at least in the daytime on a weekday. Otherwise there might be a game scheduled."

"That sounds good," replied David. It was certainly a very public place. "But what if they want to do it at night? The gates could be locked if there's no game on."

Stafford thought a moment, there were a million places one could chose from. "How about Griffith Park? Fern Hill Drive is open until pretty late. Yeah, suggest that. At the first loop within the park." Stafford looked at his watch; it was 5:48PM. "Where's the phone?"

David got up and went to the kitchen counter. The phone was on, but it still sat plugged in to the outlet. He picked it up.

"Is it charged?" the investigator asked.

"Yeah, all the way."

"Well then unplug it and bring it over here. It's almost time."

David did as Stafford told him and brought the phone over to the table and sat down.

"Don't worry it will be OK."

That was easy for Stafford to say, it wasn't his wife and child.

The call came in at 5:59PM. David answered it on the first ring.

"Hello."

There was silence.

"Hello."

"Is this the man with the pretty wife and daughter?" The voice sounded the same as David had heard in his bedroom that very morning.

"Yes, yes it is."

"Good, I'm glad to see you were waiting for my call."

David was eager to speak with Marianna. "Are they OK?" he asked, completely forgetting about the scripted items.

"Yes. They're fine."

"Can I speak with them?" David looked down at the note pad on the table. Number one read: Tell them I have the money.

"Maybe, maybe not. Do you have the money?"

"Uh…yes." David found it hard to lie when his wife and daughter's lives were on the line.

"In cash?"

"Yes."

"So when I walk in the door in a moment you will be able to hand it to me? All $120,000 of it?"

"Oh my god!" thought David. He was going to blow it. He looked at the door; the kidnappers could be right outside and the lock was still broken. Was Marianna here and he didn't have the money? What should he say? He looked at Stafford for help, but knew the investigator didn't know how things were proceeding on the phone.

Stafford saw his client's pained expression and knew something was going wrong. He stood up and moved to listen in on the conversation but Watts spoke before he could get there.

"No…well no, I don't actually have it here. I mean I have the money, but it's not here in cash."

There was a silence on the line.

Stafford looked down at his client; what the hell was he doing?

"Hello," David pleaded into the phone.

David placed his hand over the receiver and whispered to Stafford, who was now standing over him. "They want the money right now! He says they are out front!"

This wasn't something Stafford had bargained for. He went to the kitchen window and looked out. It was still daylight. No cars were out front of the residence save for Stafford's automobile and the client's. That didn't mean that the kidnappers couldn't be out there, however. And, of course, Stafford's handgun was in the trunk of his car. It hadn't even crossed his mind that he might need it at the client's house. He had gotten caught with his pants down.

The line was still silent when David removed his hand and tried again.

"Hello, please."

After a moment the voice responded, slower than before. "So you lied to me. That's not good."

David was beside himself, "Only that I had the cash right here. I didn't know I'd need it already; it hasn't even been a full day yet. But I have the money!"

"You have the money, you don't have it. Which is it?"

"It's just that's a lot of money. It takes a little while to be able to get that much together. It's not like I have that much sitting in my checking account. But I'm getting it."

There was a pause on the line and then, "Are you for real?"

David was confused, what did the guy mean? "It just takes a couple of days to find that much money."

There was another pause. The man on the other end of the phone was well composed. "Either you're playing me or you're a bigger idiot than I thought you were mister."

Now David was really confused. Stafford was over him again, motioning for him to let the investigator listen in, too, but David didn't react. There was a snicker on the other end of the line.

"Have you looked at your wife's bank account?"

"What?"

"Look at your wife's bank account. You might find what you need there."

What the hell is the guy talking about, thought David? "I don't understand."

"Look, for now, this conversation's over. I will call you back at eleven o'clock tomorrow morning. That will give you time to get to the bank. You better have the money then."

David was absolutely confused as hell. And it sounded like the kidnapper was hanging up. "Can I talk to my wife? Please."

"No! Eleven o'clock. Have the money then or else. There won't be a second chance."

And then the line went dead.

Stafford saw his client take the cell phone away from his head and place it on the table. What the hell had the guy been thinking? He hadn't followed the script at all. Watts had admitted he didn't have the cash yet, just as Stafford had told him not to. And there wasn't even the remotest discussion of a drop location. Were the kidnappers outside? That didn't seem likely if Watts' reaction to the end of the call were any indication.

"What the hell happened?"

Watts appeared stunned.

Stafford bent over so as to be in the man's line of sight. "Are they outside or not?"

"No. They're not outside," David managed to get out. He was lost in thought and suddenly the investigator seemed like a nuisance.

"Well then what the hell happened? You didn't follow any of the stuff we wrote down."

That was easily explained. "Yeah, they said they were outside. Well, actually the man asked if they came in right now would I have the money right now. And I was afraid they really were outside, so I told them I didn't really have it yet."

"Yeah I heard, and?"

"And they said they would call back at eleven o'clock tomorrow morning and that I better have the money then. Or there would be no second chances."

"Well, that is friggin fortunate, isn't it? Your brother-in-law will have the money at the bank for you by that time, won't he?"

"Yeah, that's why he said he was waiting until eleven; so I could get to the bank."

David's head was still spinning. He was having a conversation with the investigator but at the same time he was thinking about things he didn't want to let the P.I. in on, like things about his wife's bank account.

David had looked at Marianna's checkbook that morning when he had been adding up their financial resources. There was hardly anything in the account. But then the kidnapper had told him to look precisely there. It was as if the man was telling him there would be a lot of money in the account. There wasn't. But where would the kidnapper have gotten the idea that there was? His wife had no money; neither did David.

David heard Stafford still berating him with questions, but he didn't want to let the investigator in on the bank account thing, at least not just yet.

"So they want to make sure you have the money before they discuss the swap location and time?"

"Yeah, it sounds that way. Oh, and by the way, just so you know, my brother-in-law is flying into LAX in the morning. He's going to withdraw the cash himself."

"You're kidding."

Stafford considered that another fly in the ointment, but a least the presence of the brother-in-law would probably up the odds of successfully withdrawing the money.

"Glad you decided to let me in on that. What time's his flight?"

"Nine forty-five."

"That's cutting it a little tight." That was just an hour and fifteen minutes to get from the airport to the bank. "You better make sure you bring your cell phone with you. I assume you're picking him up?"

"Yes," answered David. "You probably should come too."

"OK, I think so too. From nine forty-five till eleven is just over an hour. We have to get out of the airport and to the bank by eleven. Or, of course, we could lie and say we have the money."

"No. I don't want to do that again." David wasn't going to chance the kidnappers catching him a second time. That could mean death for his wife and daughter.

Stafford shook his head, "Well, let's just hope the flight isn't late."

"Yeah, let's hope."


David watched Stafford's car disappear down the road. He took one last look around before retreating inside, he still felt a little unnerved by the kidnapper's assertion that the criminals had been right outside David's home.

David was going to meet the investigator at 8:30AM the next morning at Stafford's office off of Wilshire. Then they'd make their way through rush hour traffic to LAX. Even though they would be only about ten miles away from the airport, it was probably going to take at least forty-five minutes to get there in the congestion. And then they'd hope that the plane was on time.

There was plenty to worry about for the ransom drop tomorrow, but David had another consideration on his mind, too; that thing with Marianna's bank account. He hadn't mentioned to Stafford about the kidnapper bringing up the account. Apparently suggesting that there might be $120,000 in there. Was that what the man had been trying to tell him?

David threw his now empty juice box in the trash and made his way back to the office bedroom. He pulled open

the desk drawer where he had located Marianna's
checkbook before. He found it right where he had left it.
He opened the register and read the balance, $247.15. Just
as he had thought. David thumbed back through a couple
of pages of balances to see if he could notice any
irregularities. He didn't see any. There were regular
payroll deposits from the LA unified school district, along
with regular withdrawals to David's checking account.
David's account had been the larger of the two accounts
when he had been working, and they still paid the rent
from that account. Otherwise, all the other transactions
were minor amounts. As a matter of fact the account
probably hadn't balanced at over two thousand dollars
within the last year. But just as David was about to toss
the checkbook back in the drawer he noticed a peculiar
marking in the margin. He took a closer look. On the left
side of the register there was a number one with a dash in
front of it. The marking was very small, but it definitely
appeared to be a one, probably a negative one. The mark
was located next to an August 3$^{rd}$ entry of several weeks
ago. The line item was for a small withdrawal. The
subtotal to the right ran unaffected by the negative one
mark, however. David flipped the register back one page.
Sure enough, on the left side of the journal another small
number was entered. This time the mark was a number
two. However, this time there was no preceding dash
mark before the number. David flipped back another
page. There were two more similar entries in the left hand
margin, both twos. Proceeding back through the rest of
the register he found three more entries of these small
numbers. They were all twos. The entries went back to
April, with three marks having been entered in the month
of June and two in July. David tried to see if the small

marked numbers affected the subtotal to the right, but just as with the negative one, there was no effect on the running total.

These numbers probably didn't mean a thing, he told himself. Marianna could have been keeping track of any number of things with those marks. The kidnapper had probably just been throwing him a red herring. The account held two hundred forty-seven dollars, just like the register said. Tomorrow he could call the bank and verify the balance anyway. But then David remembered that he didn't have to wait until the bank opened to get the balance. He and Marianna now had access to the bank accounts through the computer. Something like a year ago he had signed both accounts up for on-line banking. They didn't use the service, at least not regularly, but David had tried to check on his account once and it had worked. They supposedly could even pay bills that way, but David hadn't tried that. He hadn't actually been interested in the on-line banking service at the time. Frankly, he had signed up only because of a free promotional offer. He had gotten two discount coupon books by signing both accounts up.

So there was probably nothing to it. He could clear up the issue in no time.

David pulled the computer keyboard over and double clicked the mouse. The screen illuminated after a momentary pause. David found the internet icon and opened up a browser window. He typed in the address for SoCal Trust Bank and waited. The site popped up and David logged on using his name and the password that he used for all his financial accounts. A screen came up for David and Marianna Watts. In order to look at the individual account information he needed Marianna's account number. He transcribed the ten-digit number from one of Marianna's checks. David took a deep breath and then pressed enter. The account information sprang up. Lots of entries were lined up on the left, but what David was looking for was a total. Then on the upper right of the screen the word "Balance" caught his eye. Below the word there was a box registering the total account value.

It read $110,247.19.

It was nearing seven o'clock and traffic was at last clearing from the side road in front of the officers. Detective Stokes had already become tired of waiting. He needed to find out what was happening inside the duplex.

"Let's do this thing."

Evans wished that the whole possible kidnapping scenario had not occurred in the first place. But he had finally resigned himself to the fact that his surveillance situation was going to be compromised. There was no other choice. "OK. I agree; we've waited long enough. Let's go in there and get those women out."

Stokes thought it was about time. He moved down the sidewalk to where Detectives Arnold and Mendez sat in their unmarked car.

"Let the other units know. It's a go, right now. And we'll need you guys," he told the detectives. Then he crept back to where Evans and the two uniformed officers were waiting. In a moment Stokes saw Wystrom and Garcia approaching up the street, on the opposite side, from the South. Then Jackson and Brudzinski appeared from the North, where their patrol cars were parked on Cesar Chavez. Evans motioned to Arnold and Mendez, who were now exiting their vehicle too.

"OK, let's go," said Evans to Stokes and the other two officers. "It will be the four of us at the door."

With that, the four officers crossed the street; the two uniformed cops, Trujillo and Martin unholstering their weapons as they moved. All totaled, ten officers now approached the front of the duplex.

The duplex was an attached two story side by side, with the second unit behind the first. There was a door to the front of the first unit and also one to the side, where it faced the driveway. It was the side door to the first unit where Stokes had seen the women entering that morning. The officers decided to make entry through this door, with Wystrom and Garcia focusing on the front exit.

Six officers made their way down the twin driveways between the duplexes, which formed a sort of alleyway. Stokes' group led, with Arnold and Mendez immediately behind. Jackson and Brudzinski were out front of the adjoining duplex and Wystrom and Garcia watched the front of the subject.

They had a good seal.

Martin and Trujillo moved up and flanked the subject door.

Evans motioned to Stokes, "You do the honors."

Evans stepped to the side as Stokes sidled up to the doorway. Fortunately, there was no screen. He knocked on the door.

They waited a moment and he knocked again. "Police! Open up!"

Nothing came from inside. Stokes looked back at Evans who shrugged and nodded toward the door. Stokes tried again.

"Police! Open up, we have a warrant!"

Still there was no response

"Let's kick it." Evans motioned to Trujillo. The patrolman was the biggest of the four officers at the door, even a little larger than Stokes, which was saying something. Stokes stepped back and Trujillo moved in front of the door. This was a dangerous position, because the officer was now directly in the line of fire should someone shoot from inside. Trujillo kicked the door with the sole of his shoe. The door budged, but it didn't break. His second attempt sent the door swinging inward, however. Trujillo immediately jumped out from the doorframe opening. Stokes had already taken the patrolman's position beside the door and he now yelled into the open doorway.

"Police! Come out with your hands up!"

There was no response at first. But then a faint noise came through the doorway and movement could definitely be heard inside the building. Evans motioned to the two uniformed officers to lead the way in. Trujillo stepped to the doorway and entered in a crouch, followed by Martin and then Stokes. Stokes immediately moved past the female officer. He knew it was chauvinistic, but he didn't like putting female officers in the line of fire, at least not ahead of himself. The doorway they had entered led into the kitchen. The room was empty, but food sat cooking on the stove with the burner still on. Only one exit appeared to leave the room, and it opened to a hallway toward the front of the house, immediately beyond was a stairwell upward. The officers moved into the hallway to the bottom of the stairs. Stokes motioned to Trujillo to check the front room. Stokes watched the stairway with Martin beside him, leaving Evans behind in the kitchen.

Trujillo returned in a moment. "Nothing," he said, shaking his head. "There's only the one room."

That meant whoever was in the residence was upstairs. And stairways were no fun. However, Stokes reminded himself, they had yet to determine the exact nature of what was transpiring, and therefore what level of resistance they might yet be up against. But the fact that the subjects had retreated upstairs instead of coming to the door certainly suggested they needed to exercise caution.

"Police! Come down with your hands up! We have a warrant." Stokes yelled up toward the second floor.

Again, there was no response.

Suddenly, three loud pops echoed from outside. Then the sound of a couple of rounds being fired from a police issue sounded from out front, followed by a couple of more pops, and then a plethora of bangs.

"Goddamit, what the hell was that?" Stokes looked to Trujillo, "You wait here!"

Stokes turned and headed back into the kitchen. Martin was already ahead of him and placed herself at the side door exit beside Evans, who was crouched and looking outward with his weapon drawn.

From behind the other two officers Stokes couldn't see what was going on outside, but he didn't want to put himself directly within the doorframe. "What is it?" he yelled to Evans.

"I don't know. But Arnold is down."

Martin rose partially from her crouch and exited the doorway. Stokes moved into where the uniformed officer had been positioned.

In the driveway area two men lay on the ground. Mendez had his weapon drawn and was crouched over one of the forms, who appeared to have fallen face down. Martin was moving forward in a semi-upright position toward the second figure, which lay further away, across the second of the driveways in front of the duplex opposite. It was hard to tell right off, but it looked to Stokes like the second prone individual across the way was wearing a white wife beater tee. The figure lay on the ground right in front of the side entry to the other duplex. Patrolman Jackson came into view, moving along the side of the facing building. He, too, had his weapon drawn. He reached the further prone figure, arriving just after Officer Martin. Jackson took a look at the individual and then turned his attention toward the doorway through which the man had apparently exited. He pushed the door open and peered inside. Meanwhile Martin, after briefly examining the body in front of her, turned back towards Stokes and Evans and made a slashing motion across her throat.

The man was dead.

Stokes heard Wystrom's voice from out front calling for an ambulance. And then he heard another voice, which he assumed was Brudzinski's. Officer Martin rose and spoke with Jackson before turning and coming back into the duplex with the two detectives.

"Looks like just the one guy," she said, addressing both men. "But Arnold's down and so is Garcia. Mendez says the perp came out the side door behind them and just started blasting away. Garcia had a sightline from out front and exchanged fire with the shooter before being hit herself."

"Shit," growled Evans. "How bad are they hit?"

The officer shook her head, "Don't know sir. Arnold took one, maybe two in the back of his vest before one got in under his arm, and Garcia got hit in the throat."

"Are we sure it's only the one guy?"

"So far. But we need to enter the residence to be safe." Martin looked at Evans. "I'll go in with Jackson and Bruzinski if one of you two will cover us for a moment. It should only take a couple of minutes."

Evans thought for just a few seconds. "OK, I'll go with you. Stokes, you stay here with the other uniform." Evans motioned for Martin to exit and the detective followed her out. Stokes watched a moment as Martin headed back to Jackson's side and Detective Evans stopped and checked on Arnold.

"Detective Stokes!"

Stokes looked back and saw Trujillo standing at the hallway entrance to the kitchen.

"Detective, we've got a talker!" Trujillo motioned for him to come to the stairs.

Stokes ran over to the stairwell. "What is it?"

"There's people upstairs. They want to talk."

Stokes was surprised by the speed of the development. He actually wished that it had come slightly later, after the chaos outside had a chance to subside.

Trujillo was wondering about the events outside himself. "What happened out there?" he asked, nodding back toward the kitchen.

Stokes quickly explained about the two officers down and the one probable shooter. "They're clearing the building now. And I don't know if it's related to what we're doing in here or not."

"Well I think that's what got these guys talking. As soon as the shooting stopped they started yelling down the stairs."

That made sense. They probably thought the police were coming down heavy and didn't want to end up like the perp across the way.

Stokes yelled up the stairway, "So you want to talk?"

"No hablamos ingles! Espanol solamente!" came the reply.

The detective looked at Trujillo.

"Sorry. I forgot to tell you they only speak Spanish," said the officer.

"Great."

Stokes spoke a little Spanish, you had to if you worked East LA, but his language skills weren't good enough for a possibly complex negotiation session.

He thought a moment. Trujillo spoke Spanish, fluently, but he couldn't have a uniformed officer conduct a kidnapping negotiation.

"Tell them to wait a minute," he said to the larger man. Stokes would have to go out and get Mendez. He'd of preferred Garcia, but she was down. Stokes thought Garcia was an excellent officer; he just hoped she was only down, and not out.

"Escuche! Un momento. Tenemos un policia espanol que viene," Stokes heard Trujillo yell up the steps as he left. As he reached the kitchen he could make out the reply from above. "Quiremos un abogado tambien!" He'd heard that before; they wanted a lawyer.

Evans and the other officers were now all within the driveway area. The group also included the two plain-clothed detectives who had been stationed out back.

Jackson and Martin had apparently cleared the duplex opposite.

"Nobody other than the stiff?" Stokes inquired.

"No its clean," Martin replied, meaning no one else had been found.

The plain wrapper from across the street had also come to the scene, having been moved into the second driveway. Arnold was still down, but he was conscious, and Garcia had actually gotten to her feet and was now being helped into the back of the unmarked car by Wystrom. A couple of sirens could be heard closing in on the location. One was clearly the sound of an ambulance.

Mendez remained huddled over his disabled partner. Stokes hated to pull him away, but he needed the man's services.

"We've got these guys ready to talk inside. Looks like it could still be a hostage situation, but the perps only speak Spanish."

Mendez realized that Stokes meant he was needed in the residence. The detective said something to Arnold before patting the man on the hand and rising. The ambulance siren now blared loudly and the vehicle suddenly appeared on the street out front. Brudzinski was waiting for it and waived the driver into the first driveway.

Stokes also needed a female officer inside, so he called to Martin, yelling over the sound of the siren, which abruptly cut off.

Evans came over to Stokes and got the lowdown on the situation in the duplex before following Mendez within. Being free from any other immediate duty, Stokes went over and checked on Arnold, who was now being tended to by officer Jackson. The detective appeared coherent. He had a bullet wound in the side and, from what little Stokes knew of traumatic injuries, the man probably had a collapsed lung. But he'd probably make it.

Stokes had to stand away as the paramedics moved in. Two more black and whites pulled up alongside the curb and cut their sirens. The alleyway was now full of flashing lights. In the driveway, Garcia was apparently down in the back seat of the unmarked cruiser. Wystrom was signaling for the paramedics, and one of the men left Arnold and rushed over to the car before leaning into the back door over Garcia.

Stokes saw that there was little he could do now to assist his fellow officers, so he turned and headed back toward the duplex. The last rays of the sun still illuminated the top third of the southeasterly building. Evening was quickly approaching and the detective had already had a long day. Stokes just hoped they would be in for an expeditious negotiation, not one of those protracted ones. That could make for a really long night.


David's head swam. Where on earth would Marianna get one hundred and ten thousand dollars? It befuddled his mind.

There were a myriad of equally unlikely possibilities, of course. However, one of those possibilities kept pushing to the forefront of David's mind. He didn't want to admit it, but in reality, there was only one way for someone of their means to get that kind of money, and that was by doing something illegal. David tried to interject other answers, like maybe Marianna had won the lottery, or maybe she had come into an inheritance. But, cruelly, the reality was setting in; Marianna was involved in something criminal.

David walked into the bathroom and turned on the sink faucet and splashed some water in his face. The water trickled down his jaw. He couldn't believe it; he wanted to cry. So was this kidnapping thing all a hoax? No, not if Marianna already had the money. But somehow the kidnapping was tied in with his wife's large bankroll. The kidnapper had told him to look there for the money. And sure enough, there it had been. So the kidnappers had known about the bank account already. That would explain why they had asked for the unusual amount that they had, $120,000 instead of just $100,000. Of course Marianna's account only had $110,000 in it, but that amount could prove out the arithmetic of the little marks in the margin of his wife's checkbook. There were six entries of the number "2" and then one entry of "-1". Multiply all that by ten thousand and you get the current total. So that meant, not only had Marianna deposited twenty thousand dollars six different times, but she had also recently withdrawn ten thousand dollars.

"Wow."

David went back into the office and took his wife's checkbook back out of the desk. He went over it one more time. He looked for any additional anomaly he could find in the math, any other additional figures in the margins or any checks or withdrawals made for reasons he might be unaware of. He scrutinized every detail. There was nothing.

So where had Marianna gotten the cash in the first place? What kind of illegal activity was she involved in? He had so many questions. And how had the kidnappers known about the money? Were they part of whatever criminal scheme his wife was involved in? Hell, had his wife even really even kidnapped? Maybe she was just pretending to be held against her will. But then David remembered the dawn intrusion into their home. Marianna's fear had been real, that had not been faked. And what about Julia? Marianna would never subject Julia to such treatment, at least not on purpose. If there was one thing David was sure of, it was that Marianna loved her daughter.

Unfortunately, after that, David wasn't sure of much anything else.

The negotiations took nearly two hours to conclude. At 9:35PM the two kidnappers finally released the woman and young girl over to the custody of the police. The ordeal had obviously been traumatic for both the woman and the child, though both individuals appeared physically unharmed. Stokes helped with the arrest of the two perps who had held the women captive. The kidnappers were the same two Hispanic men whom Stokes had seen escorting the victims into the duplex that morning. A search of the premises turned up little additional information as to the exact nature of the crime. The two men had cooperated in releasing the women, but they were still demanding an attorney before they made any statements to the police. At least an "abogado" had not been required at the crime scene, thought Stokes.

Thibeaut was off duty now and Evans went in and reported to the night duty Captain, Richards, about how the bust had gone down. Stokes and Evans still had to debrief the kidnap victims before they could be released.

Then the victims would go to the hospital for a quick exam before getting a ride home. Tomorrow they'd be required to give a more lengthy statement to the detectives, at least the woman would.

Stokes intended to volunteer to take the ladies to the hospital himself. He wanted to check up on the condition of his fellow officers anyway. Apparently Arnold was coming around fine, but Detective Garcia had, according to Wystrom, lost a lot of blood due to her neck injury and was now listed in serious condition.

With regard to the shooter, as Stokes had expected, the man looked very similar to the tattooed man he had spotted outside the duplex that morning. A cursory inspection of that residence had found no other individuals inside, but may have brought to light some evidence of the prostitution ring that they had been trying to identify. Evans would return to the location tomorrow to do a further inspection of the premises. So far, they didn't have enough information to determine if the shooting and the kidnapping were interrelated. But that could probably be answered in the next day or two.

Evans stuck his head into Stokes' cubicle where the detective was trying to enter a preliminary report.

"Ready to go? The female officers are done with them," he asked.

"Yeah, just give me a minute." Stokes wanted to call Debra and let her know he was running late.

"OK, I'll see you in there."

Stokes picked up the phone and punched an external line before dialing home. The phone rang a couple of times and then Debra's voice came on the line. Stokes looked at his watch; it was almost eleven.

"Hey it's me," he said softly.

"I figured," she replied. Her voice sounded tired. "Why aren't you here?"

"Working late. Sorry."

"When will you be home?"

"Soon. I just have to question a couple of women that we picked up."

"A couple of women? Are you sure you're at work?" Stokes knew she was kidding. Debra absolutely trusted him. It made him trustworthy.

"Yeah, I'm at work." He didn't like being at the office this late, leaving her alone, but it was part of the job, and she accepted that. And she was proud of him.

"Well come home soon. I'm waiting up."

"I will…and honey."

"Yeah."

"The good guys did a real good job today."

There was a pause.

"Of course you did Bren, that's what makes you all the good guys, isn't it?"


Two aspirin and a sleeping pill, that was what he needed. David set the alarm on his digital clock for seven AM and then went back to the bathroom and opened the medicine chest. He took a couple of aspirin with a cup of water and then found an old prescription for diazepam. He had almost thrown the prescription out a couple of times, but now he was glad he had kept it, it would come in handy. With his mind racing there was no way he was going to be able to sleep without help and the diazepam would put him out for hours. He just hoped he wouldn't sleep right through the morning alarm. But that was eight hours away and worth the chance, he needed to be rested for tomorrow. So he downed one of the tablets and went back into the bedroom.

Inside the house the heat of the day had not relinquished to the slightly cooler night air and David turned the window a/c unit to medium. He lay down and tried to quiet his mind.

Tomorrow.

Tomorrow he'd borrow $120,000 from his brother-in-law. Marianna's bank account didn't have all the cash that was necessary anyway. He'd save that money to start paying Harold back. Maybe a little at a time. And what had Marianna done with the other ten thousand dollars? Where could that be? Really, what the hell had his wife done?

There were just too many questions.


Detective Evans was already in the interrogation room when Stokes entered. A female officer also remained present, as required, just as a precaution against possible litigation.

The woman they had rescued earlier had identified herself as Marianna Espinoza and the young girl as her daughter, Julia. There were no known missing persons cases for either individual however, though tomorrow they'd do a more thorough background check on each. Mrs. Espinoza had also confirmed that the two Spanish-speaking individuals, who had earlier been taken into custody, had indeed, detained her and her daughter against their will. The two male suspects had been unwilling to corroborate that story, however, having been, so far, completely uncooperative.

Evans was in the process of questioning Mrs. Espinoza when Stokes entered.

"So what did the two men want from you? Did they demand a ransom?"

The woman seemed to squirm in her chair. "I don't know, they didn't say. They kept us in the dark about everything. I'm just so glad you were there to rescue us."

"And they took you from outside your home in East Los Angeles?" Evans continued.

"Yes, that's right."

Stokes looked at the little girl for a reaction, but the child was looking down and playing with her hands.

"And your husband was inside asleep?"

"Yes, like I said. I can call him and he will come pick us up."

"That won't be necessary just yet, first we're going to get you over to the hospital for a quick exam; make sure you're all right. But I can have an officer call him now and let him know you two are OK."

The woman squirmed again, "Oh no, you don't need to do that. That would just scare him. I mean he doesn't even know we got kidnapped. He probably just thinks we're out or something. I'll call him to come get us from the hospital."

"Sure," replied Evans. He didn't seem to be getting much useful information from the woman. He looked at Stokes. "You got any questions for the lady, Detective?"

"Yeah, sure." Stokes thought a moment. Something about the story seemed a little odd.

"What about the other men?"

Mrs. Espinoza looked a little surprised. "What other men?"

Now it was Stokes' turn to be surprised. "The men in the car that dropped you off at the residence. The muscular guy with the tattoos on his arms. And the driver; I didn't see him. But there were four men who dropped you off."

The woman got a sort of funny look on her face. "Oh, you mean those guys! Yes, there were four. I wasn't sure who you meant."

"Yeah, those guys. Do you know anything about them?" Stokes felt the woman's casual attitude starting to irritate him.

"No. You know they drove off and didn't really say anything to us."

"Did they speak English?"

"No, not that I heard."

Stokes glanced toward Evans and then looked back to the woman. "So you have no idea who these people were or why they abducted you? Is that right?"

"No. That's right."

Stokes wondered if the woman were holding out on them. And if she was, whether it was from fear of the kidnappers, or for some other reason. Sometimes victims in poorer neighborhoods were loath to identify criminals. This was usually due to fear of retribution, but other times it was due to a bizarre respect for the criminals themselves. Criminal activity sometimes was the only source of obvious wealth in a poor area and then the bad guys were looked upon as something like Robin Hood types; at least robbing from the man, even if they wouldn't share with the poor.

"So what was your husband's name?" Evans continued with the questioning.

"Francisco Espinoza."

"And what was your address and phone number again?" Without a purse or any documentation on the woman to verify her identity, Evans was trying to insure that the lady had given them legitimate information. If she had lied, then there was a good chance the woman would trip up when trying to repeat the make believe data.

Mrs. Espinoza answered the question and let out a heavy sigh. Evans looked at the data sheet the woman had filled out earlier. Stokes could tell from Evans' reaction that the woman had succeeded in repeating the information back accurately; it was either her real address or a really well prepared lie.

"Are we almost done here?"

"Not quite yet," Evans answered.

"Sheesh ..." the woman moaned.

Evans stood up from where he was seated at the table with the lady and her child.

"Can I get you some more water?"

"Actually I'd just like to go. It's been a long day."

The detective took the paper cup from in front of her anyway and through it in a trashcan in the corner. Then Evans left the room, mouthing to Stokes that he would be right back.

Stokes tried to fill the void.

"Sorry to keep you here so long. But we just need to make sure we have all the information straight before we let you go. The more information we can get, the better our chance of building a case against these guys. And the other two from this morning."

"Yeah, but I told you everything already. You're acting like I'm the bad guy or something."

Stokes needed to ease the situation down some.

"So how old is your little girl?"

The Espinoza woman smiled and ran her hand through her daughter's hair. "She's four and a half. Right honey?"

The little girl nodded her head a couple of times but didn't look up, obviously intimidated by the officer and the whole situation.

"She's my pride and joy," the woman added.

"Yeah, that must have been quite scary this morning, huh?"

The little girl nodded her head again.

Stokes wasn't sure where to take the conversation next. But before he could think of another question the door opened and Evans re-entered the room. The officer had a glass of water now and Stokes saw that it wasn't the paper kind this time, it was an actual glass. The detective set it down in front of the woman.

"There you go," he said. "So let's go over the whole scenario one more time."

"I already told you! What more can I say?"

"So some guys kidnap you from in front of your house, you don't know who they are, nobody knows you were taken and they don't want anything. Is that your story?"

Mrs. Espinoza shook her head. Even Stokes was beginning to think that maybe Evans was pushing the questioning a bit far.

"I only can tell you what I saw," she answered. "Why are you keeping on asking me the same questions?" Then she reached out and took a drink of the water.

Stokes looked at his watch, it was approaching midnight. He was ready to let the two women go home. They could be questioned more thoroughly tomorrow. But Evans didn't seem quite ready to give up yet.

"Yeah, but look at our position. We have a crime committed and two officers get shot. We just need some answers as to why it happened."

"Look I just want to go home now, my daughter's tired."

As if on cue, the little girl leaned over in her chair and put her head in her mother's lap. The woman stroked the child's forehead. It was obvious that the girl was the older woman's daughter, or at least some close relation. It was also obvious that it was late and the two women had been through a long ordeal that day. And they still had to be driven to the hospital for their medical clearance.

"I mean do I have to get an attorney or something?"

Evans and Stokes looked at each other. Each had performed plenty of interrogations before. Suspects were one thing, but when you were questioning the victims you had to tread lightly, and sometimes enough was enough; especially when the subject of attorneys came up.

Stokes spoke toward his fellow detective. "What say we let this go for now and resume tomorrow?"

Evans nodded slightly, "Yeah, I guess that's what we'll have to do. I guess the ladies have had a long day." The words were sympathetic, but the detective's face did not convey compassion.

"Thank goodness," replied the woman.

"But we'll need to see you in here tomorrow," Evans added. "Hopefully in the morning."

"Yeah sure. But now I want to go home and see my husband."

Stokes volunteered to escort the women to the hospital, but Mrs. Espinoza chose to have the female uniformed officer drive them over. Before leaving with the policewoman, Marianna Espinoza added her gratitude one last time, but it was mainly directed toward Stokes.

"I just want to thank you again. I think you saved my life and my little girl. Who knows what those men would have done." She gave him a big smile and then turned and left with the female officer.

Evans let out a long puff of air and turned toward Stokes.

"That's a bunch of bull shit if I've ever heard it."

Stokes wasn't quite as convinced as Evans seemed to be. "Yeah, there sure is something fishy with the whole story. She repeated her address correctly I take it?"

"Yeah, but that could just have been rehearsed."

"Pretty good rehearsal, though."

"Yeah, maybe," said the detective.

"I guess you were looking for some prints with the glass trick?"

Evans looked at the glass of water on the table. "Yeah. I didn't want her walking out of here with no way to ID her."

"Good idea. Just don't let the Lieutenant know you're fingerprinting victims now."

"Say, you think you could pull the prints and run them for me?"

"Yeah, sure. I can do it in the morning. And I'll keep it under the table."

"Thanks," said Evans. "Look I'm going home. I'll see you in the morning. It's been a long day and I want to be back over to the shooting site early."

"OK, I'll see you then," replied Stokes. "I was thinking of stopping at the hospital and checking on Garcia and Arnold on the way out."

Evans' jaw dropped a little. He paused a moment, his mouth opening still further before he spoke.

"I thought you'd heard…Garcia didn't make it."

# Wednesday, August 24<sup>th</sup>

Marianna Hernandez Espinoza Watts said goodbye to the female officer in front of the hospital and headed for the green Honda Accord parked at the curb just beyond the admissions area. She had her daughter, Julia, by the hand, dragging her along. The little girl teetered forward beside her mother, the child obviously half asleep. When they reached the vehicle a man inside reached over and pushed the passenger door open. The car was a two-door model and Marianna leaned the seat forward and bundled Julia into the back before climbing into the front seat herself. The driver looked at Marianna a moment before turning back toward the young girl and addressing her.

"Hey Chiquita, how you doing? Long time no see, huh?"

But the child just made a hushed affirmative noise and immediately appeared to fall asleep.

The man turned back to Marianna. "What the hell happened?" he asked, as he pulled the vehicle away from the curb, looking back toward the uniformed officer in the entryway.

"What happened? Ferdie is what happened!" Marianna looked over her shoulder at her child to see whether the girl might only be feigning sleep, but it looked like the little girl was really out.

She swung back to the driver and continued, trying to be a little quieter. "That son of a goat kidnapped us!"

"What?"

"He and that cholo of his, Marcelo, came right into my house and took us. They tied up David and told him he needed to pay to get us back. Hell, they even hit him!"

Wow, that was unbelievable. "So they know about the money?"

"Of course they know about the money!"

"Did they say how much they wanted? I mean, did they tell your boyfriend how much you took?"

Marianna looked at the driver and then sneered at him. "You are so stupid! They asked for the whole thing of course. One hundred and ten thousand dollars!"

The man driving the car leaned back a little and shook his head, his mouth open in amazement. He was silent for a moment.

"And the cops came in and got you?"

"That's what I told you on the phone."

"So what? Did your David man call the cops to come get you?"

Marianna made another farcical face. "Are you kidding? He couldn't track down caca in a bowl of rice. He had no idea where we were."

Now she paused a moment. "It seems like they must have just got lucky or something."

The driver let out a muffled laugh. "Sounds like you're the lucky one, bitch!"

"Fuck you Paco!"

"Hey at least they got Ferdie and Marcelo. Ferdie's a bad hombre."

"They didn't get Ferdie, you stupid pendejo!"

A high-pitched sound came from the back seat and Julia shifted to her other side.

"Shut-up, your gonna wake the girl," Paco whispered. They came to a stoplight and he leaned toward Marianna. "What the hell do you mean they didn't get Ferdie?"

Marianna rolled her eyes and turned toward the window, moving away from the driver's glare. She turned back, but kept the increased distance. "Ferdie wasn't there when the cops came, neither was Marcelo. They left us with two cholos I'd never even seen before. I'd guess they were part of the Tijuana thing, but they didn't even speak English. Maybe they're Juarez puntas or something."

Francisco "Paco" Espinoza wasn't happy with that news. But he wasn't sure yet whether he was actually implicated in the whole mess with Marianna or not. Maybe Ferdie wouldn't guess that he might be somehow involved.

"So what did Ferdie say to you?"

"What do you think?"

"I don't know."

"He said he was going to kill me if he didn't get his money, of course." Marianna stared forward a moment. "And take Julia and have her make him some of his money back for him," she added in a whisper.

Paco turned onto Eastern Avenue; they weren't but a few blocks from his row house. He was trying to remember if any of the Tachos gang knew of his address.

"So what are we gonna do?" he asked.

"We're gonna do the only thing we can. We're gonna go to the bank in the morning and take all the money out and get the hell out of here."

Paco wasn't too keen on "getting the hell out of there," but he was interested in withdrawing the cash; he'd been itching to get his hands on that ever since the spring.

"OK, sounds good." At least for now. "So where we gonna go?"

Marianna shook her head again, "Geez, I don't know. We'll decide tomorrow. Maybe we'll go to Saltillo or something. With that money we can go anywhere we want."

Well almost anywhere, thought Francisco. They'd just need to avoid Ferdie; and the cracker, Paco had almost forgotten about him.

"So where's your husband? You called me to come get you. Does he even know you got away?"

"No he doesn't know. I used our name. I didn't have my purse or any ID, so I just told them I was Marianna Espinoza. That way they couldn't call David, and then if they asked for your ID when you picked me up, we'd match."

Paco realized sometimes he didn't give Marianna enough credit. She could be pretty shrewd.

"Smart thinking. You really got the cops fooled."

"Only until tomorrow. They want me to come back in for more questions. Then they'll find out I lied. So we gotta be on the move by then."

Paco made a right from Whittier onto McBride. They were only a couple houses away now. The streets were dark, but there was still a lot of activity about; mainly teenagers, causing trouble. Paco guessed it had to be around one in the morning. Where were the parents nowadays, he wondered? He hadn't been allowed to freely roam the streets when he was a kid. What were things coming to?

"So, one thing. Why don't you want David knowing the cops got you out? He doesn't know about the money does he?"

Francisco turned the Accord into a driveway that led to the rear parking area for the group of row houses where he lived. He then pulled into one of the many empty spaces, choosing one near the house. Several of the units were foreclosed, and with so many tenants gone, parking was no longer the problem it once had been.

With the engine off Marianna dropped her voice to a loud whisper. "No, he doesn't know about the money. But with the kidnapping and all it wouldn't take a genius to figure out something was up. Even he isn't that stupid."

Paco opened the driver's door and stepped out of the car. It was still a warm night, but a little breeze had begun to develop. Marianna got out and turned to retrieve her daughter. Paco looked at her over the roof of the automobile. He nodded his chin into the air and addressed the issue of the current husband one last time.

"So no more gringo."

Marianna lifted the still sleeping Julia into her arms and closed the door. Then she said matter-of-factly, "It would be better for both of us if I never laid eyes on David Watts again."

Paco took that in. It was kind of funny. He even grinned. The guy would never even know what had happened. It just reminded Francisco of how glad he was the woman was now David Watts' wife and not his.

She could be one cold bitch.

"Man I need a beer. How about you?"

Brenford Stokes depressed the button on the coffee pot and turned and looked at the clock on the wall; it read 6:37AM. He wasn't yet fully into detective mode, but he was beginning to get there and the coffee would help. Sometimes he liked to keep thoughts of his professional work away from his home life. He needed time to just be a regular guy, like a husband and a son, and whatnot. But this morning was different, after the events of yesterday he had a lot of workplace thoughts in his head. The death of Lourdes Garcia lay especially heavy on his mind. Stokes had known the detective for something like a dozen years, almost since she had broken in as a rookie cop. The woman was personable, attractive, and well liked by everyone. She was good at her job, too. She was actually one of the best police officers that Stokes had ever met.

And she had a husband and three kids. And now she was dead.

Stokes went over in his mind again what had transpired at the shooting site. After further investigation of the crime scene and interviewing the witnesses later today, surely more would come to light. But right now, the officer's death seemed like a pointless tragedy. By the time Stokes had headed home, the department still hadn't ascertained whether the dead perp was connected to the kidnapping victims or not. Stokes had taken the opportunity and confirmed the deceased's identity as being the same man he had seen at the lookout the prior morning. In his mind, the scenario didn't seem to add up. Any lookout would surely have communicated with the heavies when they brought the two girls in, wouldn't they? That's what would have been logical. But not this time. And then why did the idiot open fire? The man had shot Arnold directly in the back, and, according to Mendez, the man had fired at him too, but the officer had reacted quickly enough that he had been able to veer out of the way. Apparently, Garcia, having been out front of the subject duplex, had an angle on what was transpiring and fired at the perp. Unfortunately, the killer was able to get a single shot off before being struck by Garcia's rounds. Mendez had then finished the suspect off.

Below him Brenford felt a pressure on his calf. He looked down and saw that two of the cats were trying to ingratiate themselves, hoping for some half 'n half or at least some milk. Curly was being more aggressive, while Larry waited patiently, like always. Larry was actually a female, but you couldn't have three stooges with one having a woman's name, so the cat had been anointed Larry while she was still a kitten.

Stokes heard a noise from behind; he turned in time to see Debra enter the kitchen. She came to him and planted a kiss on his cheek.

"Good morning," she said, reaching into the cabinet to get a mug, taking care to avoid stepping on the cats.

"Morning," Brenford answered. His wife had just showered and smelled great. But neither the feline company nor Debra's radiance could pull Stokes away from his current melancholy.

"Do you remember Detective Garcia? Mexican lady. I think you might have met her at one of the Christmas parties," he asked as Debra poured from the carafe.

His wife shook her head, "No." She sipped the steamy liquid and looked over the rim of the mug. Her husband wasn't immediately forthcoming so she raised her eyebrows.

"I thought maybe you had met her was all," Stokes continued, his voice sounding a little dejected. "She was killed yesterday."

Debra pulled the mug away from her mouth. "Oh, honey I'm so sorry." She tried to give him a look of sympathy. "Did you know her very well?"

"Yeah, I did," Stokes said, nodding his head. "She'd been around the department a long time. Really nice lady. She was a really good cop, too."

Debra reached out and took his hand. Brenford, however, only looked down at the floor. She moved closer and put her free arm around him. She placed her cheek against the middle of his chest, where it naturally rested, her husband being a good foot taller than herself. "I'm sorry honey."

They just stood there a minute, Debra doing most of the embracing, even though she still held her coffee mug in one hand. Then Brenford put his arms around his wife and pulled her close a moment before finally releasing her.

"She had three kids, too. It's a shame."

Debra went over to the cabinet and pulled out a second mug before filling it and handing it to her husband. "Was that why you were working so late?"

Stokes didn't really want to get into all the details of what had transpired yesterday. "Sort of," he answered. "There was a couple of things going on, the shooting, and also a kidnapping."

Brenford looked at his wife. She was so beautiful. With her mid length blonde hair she had that unusual combination of being both cute and sexy at the same time. She was everything a man could ask for.

"Sounds like a busy day." Debra took another sip of her coffee and then set the mug on the counter. "Look, if you need to talk, just call. I've got to go. I know it's selfish, but I'm just glad you're safe." She reached up and kissed him on the cheek and then left the kitchen. Stokes could hear her retrieve the car keys from her purse in the entryway.

"Call me," came through the opening to the hallway.

There was brief silence as his wife waited for him to respond.

"OK!" Stokes finally replied.

"Love you!" And then the front door closed.

"And I love you, too," he thought.

David Watts reached over and turned the alarm off on the nightstand before looking at the clock; it read 7:00AM. He swung his legs onto the floor and thought about standing up, he needed to get moving. But for some reason he just sat there, a feeling of extreme lethargy weighing him down. He tried to shake the cobwebs from his head, but it was of little use. He needed some coffee badly.

It took a couple of minutes but he finally motivated himself into action and made it to the bathroom. Some cold water in the face helped and, after using the facilities, he trudged into the kitchen and put on a pot of coffee. He wouldn't have much time to enjoy it, however. He needed to be in the car by a quarter till eight if he was going to get to Stafford's by 8:30AM. That was when they had arranged to leave the investigator's office for the airport. At least so David thought he remembered, he was having trouble thinking clearly. He wondered if maybe his lethargic state had something to do with the medication he had taken the night before. It must have, he thought, because he had never felt quite so out of it as he did this morning. He needed the coffee and considered waiting for it to brew, but decided he couldn't put off getting ready, so he headed back to the bathroom.

After a quick shower David felt a bit more awake. He dressed and sat down at the kitchen table for a moment with a cup of the strong coffee when it was done. He tried to get his thoughts together about what he needed to remember for the day. He was going to meet Stafford and, together, they would make their way to pick up Harold. Then they'd go to Harold's bank and withdraw the cash. The call would come in to his cell phone, which he made a mental note to be sure to remember. Then, either they would go directly to the ransom drop, or they would come back here and wait for whenever the ransom drop was scheduled. And, hopefully, Marianna and Julia would be delivered safely back to him right then and there. That would just leave the question of the other money; David still wasn't sure what to do about that. Should he withdraw it? Should he use it to repay Harold? What in the world had Marianna done to get a hold of that much cash? David was still flabbergasted.

At any rate, sometime during the day, he wanted to get to the bank and double check whether the balance shown on the computer was correct. He thought about taking Marianna's checkbook with him so he would have the account information, but he didn't think it would be wise to go to the bank with the investigator and his brother-in-law along. He didn't want to let them in on that secret just yet. So he decided to leave the checkbook at home for now.

David glanced at the clock; it was almost time to go. He went to the refrigerator and took out an ice cube from the freezer and placed it in his coffee. He waited a moment and then took a sip. After a couple of swallows he poured the rest down the sink.


Marianna Watts watched from just up the street as her husband backed out of the driveway and headed southward down the residential lane. Francisco Espinoza, or Paco as he liked to be called, sat beside her at the wheel of his old Honda Accord. It was 7:50AM and, so far, everything had gone to plan. The only problem she'd encountered so far that morning was Paco's smelling of stale beer from the night before; she'd had a hard time getting him moving out of bed. "The only thing worse than a current husband," she thought, "is an ex-husband."

"Should we wait or just go ahead?" the ex-husband asked.

Paco was always impatient. "Let's just give him a minute to make sure he didn't forget something and have to turn around and come back."

"I thought you said he doesn't have a job. Where's he going so early?"

Marianna looked at him incredulously, "How the hell should I know? Maybe he's going to the police."

The sun was already well into the sky by this time. In fact the front of the house was brightly illuminated from the East. Having been pulled from bed without her purse, Marianna now had no way to get back into her home. It wasn't going to be easy explaining Paco if the two were caught breaking in. It would probably be better if just she went to find a way, Marianna thought. That way, if she were caught, she could just say she had forgotten her keys or something.

"Maybe he's going to meet Ferdie with our money."

"You idiot, he doesn't know about the money."

Paco liked giving her a hard time and wasn't going to be defeated that easily. It was fun antagonizing his ex-wife.

"Well maybe Ferdie told him about the money," he said with as much of a smart-ass tone as he dared.

"Shit, Ferdie wouldn't do that. He wouldn't even know where the money was anyway." But Marianna wasn't as sure about the situation as her words indicated. Could it be that Ferdie knew the money was in a bank account? Well, somehow, he had found out she had been siphoning off cash from the drug deliveries. So maybe he knew about the bank account, too. But would he tell David? Of course he would. How the hell else would David come up with that kind of money? And Ferdie would know that would screw up her little marriage thing, too. So David knew; he had to. Then the worst possible thought of all came to mind; maybe David was on his way to pay Ferdie, and to pay Ferdie with her money.

"Shit, let's go. What are we waiting for?" Now she didn't care who saw what at the house. They needed to hurry.

Marianna opened the passenger door and exited. The suddenness of her departure surprised Paco, but he jumped out and followed her toward the residence.

Marianna went to the front kitchen window to see if it might be open a little. She doubted it, what with the heat, David probably had been running the window air conditioner and had the house sealed up. Paco went to the front door and raised the mat.

"You guys keep a spare key?"

"No," Marianna answered as she headed for the corner of the house, but she hadn't gotten far when she heard Paco's voice from behind.

"Hey!"

She turned and saw Paco with his hand on the front door knob. He faced her and put his other hand out to the side, toward the door.

"It's open!"

Marianna rushed back to the entryway, and, sure enough, the front door stood open. The front latch looked to have been broken.

"Ferdie must have done that when he came and got us."

Marianna entered and looked around. There was no reason to yell "Hello"; she knew no one would possibly be there with David gone. Paco moved in to the kitchen and opened the fridge. "Hey there's a couple of beers." He reached in and pulled one out, "Damn, it's just the cheap stuff though. Pendejo can't even buy decent beer."

Marianna had no time for Paco's shenanigans. She made her way directly to the family office. She opened the desk drawer and saw what she was praying would be there. She grabbed the checkbook and opened it. She didn't know what the heck she might find inside, but upon inspection everything appeared to be just as she had left it.

"Is it there?" she heard Paco yell from down the hall.

"Yes!" It was there all right, thank goodness. She turned with her prize and headed back toward the kitchen.

"Now I just need my purse," she said turning the corner from the hallway.

Immediately she found the item, right in the same spot she always kept it. She grabbed the bag and sat down at the table. Paco watched as she opened the purse and sifted through the contents. She pulled out a wallet, which she immediately flipped open to her driver's license. She also checked to make sure she had a couple of credit cards for additional ID.

"Is it all there?" Paco asked.

"Yeah, it's all here," she said with a smile. "All we gotta do now is get to the bank." There was still a possibility David could get to the money first; really all he needed was the account number.

Then it dawned on her; hadn't she left the checkbook in her purse and not returned it to the desk? She wasn't sure. But if she had failed to return it to the office, then that meant David had purposely removed the checkbook from the purse. Did that mean he was on to her? It didn't make sense; he hadn't even taken the thing with him. Maybe her code had fooled him. It was just hard to tell; maybe she'd returned the checkbook to the office after all and just didn't remember doing it.

"What other stuff you got in here? Anything worth taking?"

Marianna dismissed the checkbook confusion as paranoia and turned her thoughts briefly to Paco's question. There were a couple of things she'd like to have, like maybe some of Julia's clothes and maybe some jewelry. But, really, they needed to rush if they wanted to secure the money, and besides, trashing the place would just leave obvious evidence that they had skipped town.

"No, we gotta go. Don't mess with anything."

"Oh come on. Remember when you left me? And you stopped up the toilet and shit."

Marianna didn't care to remember anything about her marriage to Francisco Espinoza. "Look just leave everything alone."

She put the checkbook and her wallet into the purse and headed for the front door. Ferdie really had done a number on the lock. She entered the front yard and saw that the neighbor across the way was staring in her direction. Paco followed her into the yard.

"Man, you know, I still owe you for that one."

"Come on!" she called back to him as she increased her gait. Paco had to run to catch up to her, which he did right as they arrived at the automobile.

They got in and Paco immediately started the engine. The pair couldn't help noticing the neighbor still had an eye on them, though it was apparent he was trying to not be too obvious about it.

"What about that white bread?"

"Just drive," answered Marianna. "Forget about him. We're going to be long gone with the money before he ever talks to anyone."


Jim Stafford exited the front of his office and locked the door behind him. A warm gust of wind swept by as he turned to head out to the curb to meet his client. David Watts had arrived late and Stafford didn't think they had any time for an office visit. They'd have to do their talking on the ride over to the airport. It was already hot out, but the gusty, Santa Ana conditions that had developed made it a little more bearable. The investigator was wearing his customary khakis and Hawaiian shirt, but today he was also outfitted with a light colored sport coat.

Not too many people went in for the sport coat look in Southern California, not even businessmen. Sometimes you might see an exec in a suit, but that was about it. This was partly due to the laid back style, but the weather was also to blame; it was just too hot to warrant such an additional contrivance. But Stafford persevered, at least occasionally anyway, because he liked wearing a sport jacket when he was carrying a weapon. It easily concealed a shoulder holster and he could enter pretty much anywhere without suspicion. Besides, the sport coat only added to the mystique; it looked very private eye.

David Watts was exiting his vehicle as Stafford approached. He immediately noticed the investigator walking towards him.

"Mr. Stafford."

"Yeah, hey. How you doing?"

His client began to answer in the affirmative, but Stafford spoke right over the man. "Thought I'd come out and meet you. We're running a little late. I don't think there's any reason we need to go up to the office, do you?"

Watts shook his head in agreement and looked at his watch. "OK." Then he started to get back in his car, but Stafford stopped him.

"Let's take my car. I got some stuff in there maybe we could use. Besides, it's a little bigger." Stafford hated those tiny econo-boxes; he could barely fit in them.

"Yeah, sure," David replied. "I got a little bit of a late start. Sorry."

"That's OK. I'll just drive a little faster." Stafford smiled, but his client didn't seem to get the humor. He turned and walked down the sidewalk a half a block with Watts following after him. He stopped at a late model Dodge Charger; it was dark blue with black trim. Stafford opened the passenger door for his client and then stepped around to the driver's side.

Stafford thought the car was pretty impressive, but Watts showed no sign of particular interest in the vehicle.

"Maybe the V8 will impress him," thought Stafford, though he still regretted not having opted for the high output version. He looked at the fuel gauge; it read full.

"Ready to go get that brother-in-law? Or should I call him the money man?"

"Yeah, let's get going," David answered. He still wasn't amused.


Detective Stokes stared at the computer screen. He was having a hard time coming up with credible information on Marianna Espinoza. The address she had given for her residence was coming up as being owned by Paolo Martinez, and he couldn't find any records of a marriage certificate being issued in the victim's name in any of the fifty states, at least not in the woman's age range. Of course, if the woman were a renter, then that would explain her name not coming up and wouldn't preclude her from residing at the Martinez house. Even so, the detective was starting to think the woman had not told the truth. It was, in fact, beginning to look like she might be an illegal. That would be a typical scenario. In that case the supposed kidnappers would actually be smugglers, bringing illegal aliens across the border. She was probably being detained for failing to pay for their services, which was a common occurrence. The smugglers, or traffickers as they were sometimes called, would offer to bring people into the U.S. for a certain fee. Then once the individual arrived on American soil, the fee would suddenly go up, like double or triple the original agreement. Knowing little about the new country they were in and not wanting to be deported, the illegal immigrants were at the mercy of the traffickers. So the smugglers would detain their clients until the destitute people could get their families to send enough money to get them released. They really had the illegals over a barrel. Typically, the individuals came from Mexico, or some Central American country and didn't speak any English either.

That was the one thing that differed in this case, Stokes realized; Marianna Espinoza had a good command of the English language.

The detective was startled by a knock on the partition behind him. He swiveled around in his chair and saw that it was Evans.

"Hey. I'm getting ready to head over to the shooting. You interested in going along?" the Detective asked.

Stokes looked at his watch. It was a couple of minutes after nine. He wasn't sure what he wanted to do.

"Have you gotten anything on the kidnapping victims? I'm not coming up with anything on the info the lady gave us last night. She gave a bad address, and there's no marriage cert, no nothing."

Evans gave him a perplexed look. "It's not a rental?"

"I haven't confirmed that yet. But why wouldn't I find a marriage license? I mean I'm getting nothing."

"I knew something stank with that woman's story. You think she's an illegal?"

Stokes shook his head, "I don't know. The scenario is right, but something tells me that's not it." The detective thought a moment. "Have we tried calling her yet today?"

"Not that I know of. I mean it's still early. We were up pretty late. Besides, I got the impression you wanted me to go a little easier on her."

"Yeah, well I think maybe we're being too kind. I'm going to give her a call."

"OK," Evans raised his eyebrows, "but I wouldn't pussy foot around with her."

"No. I won't."

"Were you able to pull a usable print from the glass?"

Stokes pointed out the glass behind his phone. "Don't know; I haven't tried yet. I still have it here. Guess that should be next on my list before I call her."

"Yeah. Maybe that will turn something up. Looks more likely than the information she gave us. Anyway, I'm going to head out." Evans wanted to check that he understood what Stokes meant. "So you're not coming."

"No. I'm going to work on this end." Stokes leaned back in his office chair and put his hands behind his head. "I hope you find something. I'd like to piece this thing together and figure out what the hell happened. And just who it is that we're dealing with."

Evans smiled; he appreciated Stokes commitment, especially in light of the death of Garcia. "I hear ya." He paused a moment. "Oh, by the way, a Detective Padron from Homicide will be looking to ask you some questions, if he hasn't already."

"Great. Thanks for the heads up."

"No problem. He's in with Thibeut now, so I'm sure you'll be hearing from him soon."

Evans turned and half waved goodbye as he left for the corridor. "Good luck."

"Yeah, you too."

Stokes swiveled back to face the computer, but he stayed in the same position; it was a good thinking position.


When Harold Reed rode down the escalator to the baggage claim at LAX his ex-brother-in-law was waiting for him. Harold immediately picked the man out of the crowd; David Watts was as dumpy looking as ever. If anything, Watts was even heavier and more balding than the last time Harold had seen him. Before reaching the bottom of the escalator it was apparent to the insurance executive that Watts had recognized him, too. Watts approached him through the sparse crowd and met Harold before he could get half way to the baggage turnstile.

"Harold!"

Watts stuck out his hand and kind of bowed at the same time, as if groveling before the taller, better dressed man. Harold took his brother-in-law's hand while David patted him on the shoulder with the other.

"Wow, it's good to see you."

Harold had a large briefcase with him and David tried to take it. "Here, let me get that for you," but Harold pulled it away.

"No, I've got it," he said brusquely. "Let's just get my bag."

"OK," David replied.

Harold headed for the baggage claim drop and David accompanied him.

To David's side, Harold noticed that another individual followed along. It was obvious to Reed that this third man must also be in their company. Harold turned and pointed to the third wheel while aiming an exasperated look at his brother-in-law.

"Oh, I'm sorry. This is Jim Stafford, he's a private investigator."

Reed almost didn't believe what he was hearing. He looked at the man.

"I'm sorry, a what?"

"A private investigator," David repeated.

Stafford stuck out his hand to the guy in the business suit. "Yeah, Jim Stafford."

Reed let the man's hand hang in the air. He turned back to David. "What the hell are you doing?" There wasn't going to be any interloper in the chain of command; Harold wouldn't stand for that.

"What do you mean?" David answered, as Stafford withdrew his offer of greeting.

"I mean, what the hell do you think you're doing hiring a private detective before we've even talked about this?"

Reed looked back at the investigator. He was actually a little embarrassed at not having taken the man's offer of a handshake. But that idiot ex-brother-in-law shouldn't have gotten the man involved in the first place.

"Look I'm sorry mister … Stafford was it?"

"Yeah, Stafford," the investigator answered without offering up his hand again.

"I think David here has over reacted. Whatever's going on here we can take care of ourselves. If he's hired you then we'll settle up for the time you've already put in. But we won't be needing your services."

Stafford looked at his client and then back to Reed. "Look Mr. Reed, I think it would be better if we discussed this outside. There's really a lot to this, and I think you should know all the facts before we rush off and make any decisions like that."

Harold looked at David and then back to the investigator. Stafford was a big fellow, and a little intimidating, but he was dressed like a used car salesman and looked somewhat disheveled. Reed could handle him. He turned toward David again.

"Well?"

David shifted uneasily but tried to meet his brother-in-law's gaze. "Well, Harold, I think Mr. Stafford is right, we should talk about it outside, when we get to the car."

"Wonderful." Just fucking wonderful.

Reed tapped David's chest with his index finger and addressed his ex-brother-in-law at close range. "If you want to see one dime of this money, you better have a really good explanation for all this."

With that Harold turned and walked over to the turnstile to wait for his bag. The clock in the terminal read 9:59AM.

The phone number was a fake. Detective Stokes got an unrelated residence when he called the number the Espinoza woman had given him. And when he checked the exchange he found that it was actually for Boyle Heights and not for East LA. The two exchanges were close, and it was possible that a digit had been transposed erroneously, but there was really no way of knowing. Even so, it was looking more and more like Marianna Espinoza, or whatever her name was, had lied to them.

That pissed the detective off.

Lourdes Garcia was dead because they had rescued a probable illegal and her child, and the woman didn't even have the common courtesy to tell them the truth. The detective tried to control his rage. He knew he should not have expected more. The woman had not given the truth, obviously, because she hadn't wanted to be deported. What else would you expect? Up to that point, Stokes realized, the woman and her child had probably been victims too, victims of the human traffickers. That was the reality of the situation, but it didn't really lessen his anger. The rescue had hardly meant anything, such a waste of a good officer's life.

Stokes's mood was also fouled from having to answer a litany of questions from the Padron detective from Homicide. The guy had acted like the department was almost as at fault as the shooter. After that interrogation, and before checking on the voracity of the phone number, Stokes had requested records pull up any matches for the Espinoza woman's fingerprints. He'd pulled a decent print from the water glass, but even so, he knew there was only a moderate likelihood a match would actually come up. However, stranger things had happened, and that was quickly looking like his only good lead on the woman.

In the mean time, now that the phone number had proven a dead end, and seeing as the prints wouldn't be back for a while yet, Stokes decided he would head back to the shooting scene. Stokes hadn't heard anything from Evans as to the progress of the crime scene investigation, but then Evans wasn't really in charge of the operation anymore. Homicide and the forensics guys would have the location sealed off, but vice would be allowed some limited access and Stokes knew he might pick up something if he just went over and nosed around a bit. Besides, unless he went to work on another pending case, which he felt completely unmotivated to do right now, there was really nothing else to occupy his time. So he headed for his car.

It was another scorcher of a day, and the Santa Anas were blowing like all hell as the detective pulled out of the station lot. The gusty conditions were typical for this time of year in LA. The wind patterns for the late summer and fall brought warm air from the high desert up north barreling down through canyon passes toward the Los Angeles basin. Somehow the combined effects of having to tunnel through the canyons and the compression caused by the lowering altitude not only sped the air up, but also super heated it, too. So you got these warm windy conditions, not every day, but they were frequent none-the-less.

Stokes looked at his watch; it would only take a few minutes to get to Evans' location. It was a straight shot up Soto to Cesar Chavez and then a couple of blocks over to the crime scene. The traffic was easing some from the morning congestion and the work crew had departed from where it had been the day before. So it wasn't long before he came to approach the side street.

When Stokes arrived at the scene there were still a half dozen official vehicles out front of the duplexes and in-between in the driveways. The units included several black and whites and unmarked cruisers, and the forensics team van sat in the entrance to the driveway of the first duplex. That was the unit where the perp threat had been eliminated in the doorway.

Stokes pulled up along the curb and exited his vehicle toward the forensics van. Yellow tape ran across the two driveways in front of the van, it then turned and covered the front area of the second duplex. A uniformed officer stood in the driveway as a couple of lab coat types moved around the scene. Toward the back of the second duplex Stokes could see Evans speaking with what looked like a couple of Hispanic kids. He headed that direction, ducking under the tape and flashing his badge to the uniformed cop. As Stokes approached, he saw that the youngsters he had seen from a distance were actually African American.

"Hey!" He yelled to the detective as he came closer. Evans greeted him in return.

"What have you got going here?" Stokes inquired.

Evans pointed to the two kids who were seated on the stoop of the second unit of the duplex, the unit that was located behind the one where the Espinoza woman had been held. "This young man and woman were just filling me in on some stuff. They live behind, in the second unit here."

The two kids looked warily up at Stokes. One of the kids was a young girl, maybe twelve years old or so, and the other child was a boy, he looked to be only about five.

"So you can't think of anything else?"

The two kids shook their head and the girl answered "No sir."

"All right, well when your momma gets home have her call me, OK?"

"Yes sir," said the girl.

Evans turned and stepped over to Stokes who was just a few feet away. The two children took the opportunity to hop up, before quickly opening the door and entering the house.

"I was just asking them what they knew of the neighbors. They live in the back unit here. Seems the only adult left for work early this morning. Don't know why the kids aren't in school, at least the girl anyway."

"Anything on who the occupants of the other units are?" asked Stokes.

"Well sort of. The shooter's duplex is owned by an Enrique Calderon. However, according to the owner, neither unit is currently leased. The second duplex owner is named Hobbs, Elias Hobbs. But we haven't been able to get in touch with him. So there's nothing on the occupancy information there yet."

"Are the kids named Hobbs?"

"No, Johnson, at least according to them."

Stokes thought he detected a bit of disbelief in Evans' response.

"What, you think they're lying?"

Evans shrugged his shoulders a little.

"Don't be so cynical, they're just kids, they've got no reason to lie to you."

"Yeah, I guess." Evans had been writing in a notebook and he scribbled down another thought before he flipped the booklet closed. "So, did you have any success getting a hold of our Mrs. Espinoza?"

"No. It was a wrong number, not even the right exchange. The number was for Boyle Heights and she gave us an East LA address."

"Could just be a mistake. Did you get anybody from the sheriff's department to run a make on the address?"

Stokes hadn't asked for that yet. East Los Angeles was not in the incorporated City of LA, so it was a county jurisdiction. "No. Not yet." He'd have to do that when he got back to the office. "So that's it? You haven't got anything else here?"

"Hell no, that's not it. I'm just waiting for the lab boys to finish up so I can get into the units. Homicide was already in. You know Jacobs, used to be in vice a couple years back?"

"Yeah, sure," replied Stokes. The guy was a character, everybody knew Jacobs; the man didn't need to have been in your department for you to know who he was.

"He was here and gave me a little heads up on what was in the north building."

"You mean the unit the shooter was in?"

"Yeah."

Evans paused a moment, for effect. It was annoying. "And?"

"And there's a lot of stuff in there that we were looking for. Like pics of young girls and stuff. Jacobs wouldn't get too specific though, we just got to wait and get the whole picture when we get in."

"So it may have been a warehouse like the tip suggested."

"Yup."

"And the other unit? Where the lady and the kid were."

"Jacobs didn't say anything about that one. I don't think they found anything in there."

Well, that was good news and bad news, Stokes thought. Even though they maybe had been right about the prostitution stuff, they had also probably blown catching the ringleaders in the act. Unless the Espinoza thing was related, and the two perps they already had in custody were their men. But that seemed unlikely, and besides, the apparent flight of their main witnesses would make convicting even those men pretty difficult. Of course, if they were able to tie the murder of officer Garcia in with the commission of any other crime, then they could insure that the two men in custody would be in for a long prison stay.

"So you may have been right. Moving in on my bust may have screwed us on the prostitution thing."

Evans pursed his lower lip, "Maybe. But at least we got some info in there. It might lead us to the guys we're after. I mean, it was a good lead, it wasn't a waste of time."

No, not a waste of time, thought Stokes, but so far the price had been pretty high.


It took about ten minutes for David to explain the entire kidnapping scenario to his brother-in-law as they drove. The man seemed to think the story was somewhat incredulous and he was blustering about how absurd he found David's actions. But at least, David thought, they were nearing Harold's bank and they'd soon have the money, if Reed would just cooperate.

"Well, why the hell didn't you call the police? You don't even know if these guys are going to hand over Marianna and Julia when you give them the money. Is there any guarantee of that?"

Of course there was no guarantee. "They said no police. They were very specific about that," replied David. "And I know there's no assurance that they'll do what they say, but we're talking about Marianna's and Julia's lives here. I can't screw around with them."

Harold Reed had a dilemma. Giving the money to the kidnappers was going to be like taking it and flushing it down the toilet. But not giving it to David meant his ex-brother-in-law would probably rat Harold out on his infidelity. Watts was serious about this; the lives of the man's wife and child were at stake. Of course, that begged the question, was being ratted out worth one hundred and twenty thousand dollars? If Harold Reed were a poorer man then it wouldn't be. But really, $120,000 was almost a drop in the bucket; it was really the principle of getting screwed out of it that was bothersome.

David studied his brother-in-law for some reaction to his plea. He could almost see the cogwheels turning in the inner workings of the great man's mind. He needed more ammo to convince him.

"There's even a really good chance I'll be able to pay you back soon, too."

David had turned and was looking at Harold in the back seat as he said this. He immediately noted the look of surprise on his brother-in-law's face. Stafford also momentarily turned his attention from the road and looked at his client. David suddenly realized he might have made a mistake.

"What in God's name are you talking about?" came Reed's response. "You told me on the phone you couldn't pay your way out of a phone booth. I don't need to hear this crap. You're about as likely to pay me back as global warming is to melt the ice in my refrigerator. How the hell did I get involved in this mess?"

David needed some damage control. Stafford was pulling the Dodge into the bank parking lot and David really needed his brother-in-law to go in and get the money.

"I just mean I'll work really hard and start paying you back right away." From the look on Reed's face that hadn't helped any; the man's face was so red he looked like as if he were going to burst. "And then there's a small inheritance I'm in line for," David lied on the fly, "It's not much but it would be a good start on paying you back."

From Stafford's viewpoint the whole scene that was now playing out in his car was almost comical. Here was this poor sap begging for money to save his family's life and this stuck up prick of a brother-in-law was worried about whether he was going to get his money back. And then there was the thing about his client insinuating that he had some sort of funding of his own, not from what the investigator had seen at Watts' home. But, never the less, funny or not, Stafford, from his own financial point of view, wanted the day's plan to proceed onward to a successful conclusion. So he turned to Harold Reed to help his client out.

"I think really, as you obviously know, the only real thing of importance here are the lives of Marianna and Julie. The rest can be hashed out later."

"Julia."

"Huh?" Stafford looked at David before it dawned on him. "Yeah, I mean Marianna and Julia."

Harold hated to face it but he had no choice, between Watts' leverage and looking like a schmuck if he balked on the money, he had no way out. He was also finding the Stafford fellow to be incredibly annoying.

"All right, I know. I'm here for Marianna and Julia, let's make that clear. And David, you'll owe me for this."

A rush of relief washed over David. He looked at his watch; it read 10:31AM.

Reed opened the car door and stepped out.

"I'll just be a minute. Then we'll need to go to another branch to withdraw the remainder of the money."


Detective Stokes knew it was out of the Los Angeles Police Department jurisdiction, but the duplex location was only a few blocks from the street that the Espinoza woman had given them as her residence. So he called back into headquarters on his cell phone and got one of the other detectives to look up the address on the computer. After getting the information he needed, Stokes pulled away from the duplex investigation and made a right on Cesar Chavez back into the traffic. After a few blocks the road bent to the left leaving the City of Los Angeles behind and entered the jurisdiction of the Los Angeles County Sheriff's Department.

A large portion of the County of Los Angeles was consumed by the incorporated City of Los Angeles and other surrounding cities. Here and there, however, small pockets of county land breached the megalopolis's hold and these areas came under the dictate of the Sheriff's Office rather than that of the LAPD. The two entities worked closely together however, being as the two areas of governance were so intertwined. But that didn't mean one policing force was allowed to operate on its own within the other's jurisdiction. That was only allowed when a case of hot pursuit crossed the two territory's boundary line. Otherwise, you just didn't go commando into the other guy's sandbox; it wasn't cool.

Before crossing under the I-210 freeway the detective made a right onto Eastern Avenue and made his way down to Whittier, where he turned left. Stokes immediately passed under the interstate, whereupon he began looking for the cross street he wanted. Before he located the road however, he found his path blocked by a pool of water. On the sidewalk, a fire hydrant gushed openly out into the street. There wasn't much depth to the water, so it appeared the hydrant had probably only recently been opened. A couple of small children were racing through the spray along the curb, enjoying the cooling vandalism, which had, undoubtedly, been perpetrated by older youths. Stokes called the break into central dispatch to have a county fire department crew come out and seal it up.

After fording the intersection, Stokes found the street he was looking for. Two blocks down he came to the address that he had been given. The residence was near the end of a section of row houses. The units were lacking in curb appeal and similar to the other residences in the area, which was kind of run down. A few for sale signs dotted the street and a couple of the houses appeared boarded up.

Stokes parked along the curb and exited his cruiser. A few younger Hispanic men were out front on the sidewalk and gave him some notice. At first there appeared to be some inclination for the youths to approach the detective, but then they backed off, having probably made him as a cop, Stokes figured. The street kids were pretty savvy when it came identifying law enforcement.

Stokes stepped up to the front of the particular row house he was interested in and looked at the mailbox nametag. Usually, the nametag spot would be found empty, but this time the detective found himself in luck.

"Easy enough," thought Stokes; the name read "Espinoza". He tried ringing the doorbell, but didn't hear any sound inside when he pushed the button, so he opted for knocking. There was no response. He knocked again, and then looked through a narrow side window beside the door. He couldn't put his hands to the glass to shield the glare because there were security bars protecting the window. Stokes knocked one more time before deciding to head around to the back of the building. As he turned from the door he saw that several of the youths were now nearby, taking particular notice of the detective's activity. A couple of the young men looked fairly muscular. Stokes wouldn't have wanted to find himself in the present situation were it the middle of the night. But right now, in the daylight, he didn't feel much danger.

"You guys know the people who live here?"

The young men looked at each other for an indication on how to respond. Then one of the bigger guys took a step forward. "What's it to ya man? They done something wrong or somethin'."

Stokes tried to keep the smile to himself as he thought of how to answer; the street dialect always cracked him up.

"No, no my man. I just wanted to get a word in with them."

The youth now tilted his head and swung his shoulders forward, letting his arms hang in a kind of apeish fashion. "Well you a cop, ain't ya?"

Stokes moved slowly toward the youths, it was best not to seem intimidated.

"Yeah, I'm a cop. But I'm not here to arrest them." He smiled and pointed over his shoulder, back at the row house. "The lady who lives there, and her little girl, they got into some trouble and I wanted to see if they were all right."

The youth now turned and looked at the others, they passed a snicker back and forth before one of the other guys spoke up.

"Man, there ain't no lady lives there, no little girl either. What you tryin' to feed us?"

Stokes wasn't really sure how to respond. The news that the kids thought there was no woman or child living there was surprising, especially since the residence was tagged "Espinoza".

"So there's no lady who lives there?"

"Not unless you call a ho a lady." It was the big youth in front again. There were a few snickers from the crowd.

"Your saying there's no woman living here. Kind of heavy, big chest," the detective palmed his hands in front of his pectorals. "And no little girl?"

"That's right man," the big guy answered. "Just a skinny little chiclit that sometimes comes by and drops him for some dinero."

The big kid smiled and the other youths laughed at the disparagement.

That would be some interesting information, if true, but maybe the kids were just trying to blow wind up his ass and really didn't know anything about the residence. It wouldn't be the first time that had happened.

"By the way, shouldn't you boys be in school?" Stokes asked, changing the direction of the conversation in an attempt to remove the gathering crowd. "You're not out here working are you? Maybe making a little money from the cocaina, huh?"

The group immediately took a step back upon hearing the drug assertion. They most likely wouldn't want to get frisked. Probably at least one of them would be carrying some sort of contraband.

"Hey muchacho, don't be hatin' on us," the big guy replied, also stepping back as he spread his arms in the universal sign of "Hey, I ain't got nothin'."

"Well then you better get moving before the rest of the cops get here and we pat you all down."

The youths slowly turned, muttering insults under their breath, and headed away down the sidewalk. It took a minute for them to get any distance as they kept spinning back around to show the officer that they had no real fear of him.

After they'd gotten about a half a block down the road Stokes turned and made his way back past his cruiser in front of the residence. He wanted to swing around the rear of the buildings and check out the parking lot. But as he started past the front of the Espinoza residence, a blur of movement caught his eye. The movement appeared to come from the doorway of the row house he had just approached. The door was still closed, but Stokes focused in on the area just to the right of the entryway. When he did, he saw that the motion actually came from within the lower portion of the vertical glass window beside the front door. Someone was inside. Stokes hurried toward the door and up the short stairway. However, his arrival was a little late, and he only caught a glimpse of a shadowy figure moving away. The view to the inside was still obscured, but there was no doubt in the detective's mind as to what he had seen; a little girl had been at the window.

    Paco Espinoza sat in the car waiting. It was hot and the air conditioning no longer worked in his vehicle. Just sitting there sucked, but at least a breeze mitigated some of the discomfort. He had been meaning to sell the vehicle, get one with a working a/c, but he just hadn't gotten around to it, and now the summer was almost over. But soon, he hoped, he'd be able to afford a better automobile, maybe a new Honda, or maybe even a BMW or Lexus, it just depended on how things worked out for him.

    Once again, as twice already before, he had parked across the street to keep his car, and himself, out of the view of any security cameras that might be in operation. This was the third branch of the SoCal Trust bank that he and Marianna had been to that day. At the first branch they had found out some shocking news; banks didn't keep loads of cash around for people to come in and take. Paco had known one or two guys who had actually knocked off a bank, and they both had, apparently, per their retelling of the stories, come away with less than they expected to. Paco had thought that his friends had probably just been stupid, or that banks must have a secret place where they keep the really big money, like for the important white customers to withdraw or something. But the bank lady had explained the situation to Marianna at their first stop. With everything being done electrically today, the banks didn't need to keep as much cash as they used to. So they didn't get robbed so much, they had a limit on how much you could come and take out, at least in cash anyway. You could call ahead and they would get more from the reserve bank if you just let them know a couple of days in advance. But, of course, if you didn't have a couple of days, like Marianna and Francisco didn't, then you had to go to more than one branch to withdraw large amounts of cash.

So at that first branch they had gone to, where the lady had been so helpful, Marianna had withdrawn $35,000. That was the normal maximum cash withdrawal allowed without special permission. Unfortunately, when they went to the second branch, they had not called ahead to see how much money was in that particular bank. So when Marianna went in she was told that they only had $32,000 that she could have without going below their minimum money for little stuff. But there, another helpful lady called around, and found a branch where they had the other $43,000, and even got them the special OK to take that much.

And now, they'd had to drive all the way up to North Hollywood to get it, but that was all right, so long as Marianna hurried back out of the bank soon with the money, because Paco was fucking hot. He glanced out the passenger side window at the strip mall where he was parked. A cold cerveza sounded good, but all he saw was a Laundromat and an auto parts store. He'd have to wait on the beer.

Soon enough, the door swung open, and Marianna exited the bank. She looked both ways, but then crossed the street illegally. That was stupid. Paco could see that her purse was swelled to popping from the large amount of cash inside. He looked down at the paper bag in the floor of the passenger seat; it was filled about a third of the way with stacks of one hundred dollar bills. He wanted to make sure all the money would fit; however it looked as if that wasn't going to be a problem. That was too bad Paco thought; they should have gotten the money in fifties and then they could have had a whole sack full.

Jim Stafford stood in front of the Fiduciary Federal Bank and waited for Harold Reed to come back out with the cash. On the way out of the car Stafford had asked the man in the suit why they would have to be stopping at a second bank location. The man had looked at him with a combination of superiority and disgust and explained, "No financial institution is going to have $120,000 just sitting around waiting to be withdrawn." According to the insurance exec it was highly unusual to find more than $40,000 available at any one location. Apparently Reed, however, had the clout to get the amount they needed in two withdrawals of sixty thousand dollars each. "Well ain't you just the second coming," the investigator had thought upon hearing Reed's explanation.

Despite the man's acrid self-importance, however, Stafford remained anxious for the man to come back so the group could get going to the next branch location. The investigator paced back and forth in front of the bank. He wasn't sure why he had gotten out of the car himself, except that he figured maybe he needed to protect the money. After all, sixty thousand dollars was a large sum and Stafford had that thirty-eight under his jacket. So he stood guard. What the hell.

It wasn't long before the glass door swung out and Harold Reed finally exited the building.

Stafford made eye contact with the swiftly moving executive. "Got it?" he asked.

"Of course," Reed answered, as if it were the stupidest question he had ever heard.

Reed climbed in the rear seat followed by Stafford into the front. David looked to either of the men for a clue as to how the trip inside the bank had gone. Stafford started the car.

"Did you get it? Did you get the money?"

Reed pursed his lips and folded his hands on the briefcase in his lap before turning and gazing out the window. Stafford looked in the rear view mirror and saw that the suit had no intention of answering. He turned back to move the car from the parking space while he answered his client's question. That also served the purpose of speaking the answer so Harold Reed could hear it. "Of course he got it. His high and mighty wouldn't be put off by a little thing like sixty thousand dollars."

"Just drive and leave the thinking to me," Reed replied.

David felt relieved to hear that they now had at least half the ransom amount, but he didn't like the bickering that seemed to have developed between his brother-in-law and the private investigator. They all needed to be on the same page. Though, at the same time, David couldn't help but appreciate, at least just a little, Stafford getting a bit of a jab in on Reed. After all, the man was full of himself.

"How far is it to the other branch?" asked David.

Stafford didn't wait to see if Reed would answer, being from New York there was no way the man would have known anyway. They were in the Century City area and needed to get to downtown. "Almost half an hour."

David looked at his watch, it was a quarter till eleven; they only had fifteen minutes. "We've only got a few minutes. Drive as fast as you can."

"You got it," Stafford answered. He hardly slowed the car for the immediate turn, and the tires squealed, breaking their grip on the pavement as they exited the parking lot. "We may get lucky and the traffic won't be too bad. You never know."


Detective Stokes knocked on the door again. There was still no response, and the form didn't appear back in the window. "Damn," he thought, "if that kid would just come to the door I could get this thing straightened out."

Realizing that pounding on the door wasn't working; Stokes reverted to his earlier plan and moved to find his way around the buildings via an alleyway to the rear parking area. Behind the row houses, in the back lot, there were a number of empty parking spaces, as well as quite a few broken beer bottles and other various items of discarded trash. None of the spaces were numbered, however, so it was impossible to see if maybe a vehicle was in the spot for the Espinoza address. All Stokes could do was to try the rear entry of the row house where the little girl had appeared. He found the correct door and tried the knob; it was locked. He gave another attempt at knocking. He waited and then knocked again. After a third attempt he decided it was to no avail; the kid just wasn't going to answer.

So there wasn't much else he could do, he wasn't in jurisdiction and he didn't have the authority to call in a surveillance team. Besides, the fact that the little girl was here, at the location that the Espinoza woman had sited, and the fact that "Espinoza" was on the front of the residence, kind of gave credence to the woman's story. But that still didn't explain why her name hadn't come up in the computer system or why the lady had apparently given them a bogus phone number. There were a lot of unanswered questions as yet. All Stokes could do, at this point, would be to head back to the station house and track down a couple of the loose ends that he had dug up. First off, he would call the LA Sheriff and see what they had on the Espinoza residence. He could also request that they place a unit outside to see if the lady actually showed up here, and if she did, they could detain her. Then maybe he could get the Espinoza woman back in for questioning. After the phone call to county, he would go down to records and see if the fingerprint sample had come up with a match.

Stokes hoofed it back to the front of the row houses and climbed into his unmarked car. Down the street the group of youths were slowly making their way back in his direction. He was glad he was leaving and not tempting fate with the muchachos twice. He started the car and immediately reached for the fan switch and turned it on high. He had been so lost in thought about the investigation that he'd temporarily forgotten about the heat. Sweat was now running down his brow. As the compressor unit kicked in, the air began to cool and Stokes stuck his face close to one of the vents. "Thank God for air conditioning," he muttered as he sat back and put the car in gear. It would suck to not have a/c. Even worse, he thought to himself, imagine getting broken down in this heat, and in this area; now that would really be a bitch.

The call came in right at eleven o'clock. If there were one thing you could say about the kidnappers, thought David, it would be that they were prompt. Harold Reed had just disappeared into the First Street branch of Fiduciary Federal Bank and there was no way that David was going to be able to procrastinate on the phone long enough for the man to return. He was going to have to lie, again. This time, however, he wouldn't be so easily fooled by a simple trick like the kidnappers had pulled on him the evening before, when they had told him they were right outside his house.

Stafford apparently heard the phone ring and had rushed back to the driver's seat from his position in front of the bank. "So? Answer it!" he yelled at Watts.

David took a deep breath and pushed the "talk" button on the phone.

"Hello."

"Watts?"

"Yes, I'm here," David replied.

"Look, I don't know how you found out about your wife. Maybe that smart ass PI guy's helping you out or something. But you owe me $120,000. And if I don't get paid then I'll come and get you and your wife, and everybody else you love. We won't be talking about just two dead bodies; it'll be more like a dozen. And you won't like what I do to you before you die, not one bit."

David was a little confused, it was the same voice as before, but this time the man's warning seemed more ominous than ever. And how did he know about Stafford? Did he even know that David didn't quite have all the money yet? And what did the kidnapper mean by finding out about Marianna, did he mean the bank account?

Because the man had clued David in to that himself. There was a lot of pressure to answer correctly and David could feel the pain returning to his arm and chest.

"But I have the money. I mean I've got it right here."

There was a pause on the other end of the line.

"You've got the money?"

"Yes, I've got it all." David tried to remember the rules for the phone call. "Are my wife and child OK? I want to know they're alive." There was another pause and no response from the other end, so David tried again. "Can I speak with them?"

Then the voice came back, "Not right now."

"When? Please I need to know that they're all right."

"Look, you'll get to see them when I get my money."

David couldn't control himself, "Please, please I just want to know that they are OK."

"You can see them at one o'clock. You bring the money and you'll get them back then. But not before I get the money."

David thought about the offer, one o'clock was only two hours away. He could do that; he was aching to see his wife and child.

"OK, one o'clock, that's fine. Where?"

Out of the corner of his eye David could see Stafford shaking his head and making some sort of hand gesture. But David didn't focus on what the investigator was trying to relay to him, he was concentrating too hard on the conversation.

"Good answer. Where is simple. You know where Lincoln Park is on Valley Boulevard?"

David tried to picture the place, he couldn't really, but he had a general idea of the location.

"Yeah, I think I know where that is."

"Good. There's a bus stop on Valley right in front of the park."

"OK."

"You go to the bus stop and at 1:05PM the 35L bus will come by. You get on that bus with the money in a nondescript container, like maybe a suitcase or a briefcase or something. Then you go to the back of the bus and leave the container on the floor. You go one stop and get off the bus. If no one follows the bus then I'll get on the bus and get the money, and we'll be home free. Then I'll let Marianna and the kid go. But only after I have the money."

David thought that didn't sound too complicated. He also remembered Harold was carrying a black briefcase. "OK. I've got a briefcase with me, it's black."

"Good. And remember, get there before one o'clock," the voice continued, "the bus could be early or something. Got it?"

"Got it," David replied. "The 35L at 1:05PM. Drop the case in the back and then get off."

"That's it. And don't blow it by trying to do some hero bullshit or something."

"No, I won't do that."

"Good. See you soon," the man said, finishing the conversation, and then the line went dead.


As long as they were in North Hollywood, Marianna figured the pair could swing by Van Nuys and empty a small deposit box that she kept in the SunTown Bank and Trust. There wasn't much in the box, just the remains of the ten thousand dollars that Marianna had withdrawn from her and David's co-checking account, and a few other odds and ends of a personal nature that she didn't care to have David know about.

Paco was being a pain in the ass however. She could have told him about the little bit of money in the box and it might have motivated him, but Marianna could tell that Paco was going to get stingy with the loot and so she wanted to keep as much to herself as she could.

"This is stupid. We got no business going to Van Nuys. There's a bag in the car with a hundred grand in it and we're gonna go up to Van Nuys so you can get some pictures and shit."

"Yeah, that's right!" Marianna answered. She was quickly tiring of Paco's company. "And my passport's there, too!"

Paco gave her one of her own sneer faces, "So what you want with a passport anyway? I ain't got no passport. You going somewhere without me?"

"Stupid pendejo," Marianna thought, but kept it to herself, she needed Paco a little longer.

After a few more miles passed in silence the SunTown Bank and Trust appeared on their left.

"There it is. See, that wasn't so bad, was it?"

Paco kept the look of disgust on his face.

He turned into the bank and parked in a regular spot, forgetting to avoid the view of the security cameras this time. Marianna started to get out of the car, but then turned back.

"Give me the keys," she said to Paco, and extended her open palm.

"Huh?"

"I said give me the keys. I don't want you driving out of here with my hundred and ten grand." She gave him the come hither signal with her fingers. "Fork 'em over."

Her co-conspirator was obviously annoyed by the request, but he pulled the keys from the ignition and placed them in Marianna's palm.

"Geez bitch, what you got no trust for your own?"

"Not when it comes to you," she replied before exiting the Honda. "I'll only be a minute."

Paco watched Marianna walk into the bank. She used to look kind of thin when they had been married, but now she had really packed on the pounds. She was just a lot of dead weight. Hell, he wasn't even sure if he was going to be able to stuff the woman in the trunk.

Paco reached over and opened the glove compartment and pulled out a shiny silver object. He wiped it in his shirt once and then smiled at it before placing the object under his seat.

Marianna would fit; Paco would make her fit.


It was ten minutes past eleven when David's brother-in-law finally exited the bank. He had a pissed off look on his face. Reed got in the back seat of the Charger and slammed the rear door closed. Stafford and David both looked at the man and wondered what could possibly make such an angry man even angrier.

"What's wrong? Didn't you get it?" asked David, fearful of Reed's answer.

Reed's head swelled up a little bit before the answer to the question came bursting forth. "They didn't have the whole damn thing. All they keep at this branch is the standard $40,000. Frickin imbeciles! What kind of a bank is that? I pay plenty in their fees to get service like that?"

"Wow," thought David, with the sixty grand they already had, that only made one hundred thousand dollars, which left them twenty thousand short. How the hell would they make up that amount? "Can't we go to another branch?" he inquired.

"No," replied his brother-in-law, "they only have two branches in the Los Angeles area."

"And you don't have another bank to get money from?"

Reed looked at David like he was an idiot. "Not in Los Angeles I don't!"

Well, that left only one alternative. David had hoped he wouldn't have to divulge the information about Marianna's possible account balance. But now he decided he had no choice but to let Stafford in on the news.

"Can I see you outside?"

"Me?" replied Stafford.

David nodded an affirmative and the two men climbed from the car.

"Where the hell are you going?" Harold yelled from the back seat.

David held up an index finger in Reed's direction and said, "Just a minute, I just want to say one thing to him."

Stafford was curious as hell as to what his client wanted to discuss out of earshot of the insurance executive.

"We've only got $100,000 and we need $20,000 more," stated David.

That was pretty obvious to Stafford. "Yeah. And?"

David tried to keep his voice down, "I think I can come up with the rest of the money."

Stafford raised his eyebrows at this.

"I could go to the bank right now and get it, but I didn't bring the checkbook."

The investigator shook his head, "You don't need the checkbook. If you've got two forms of ID and a photo driver's license then they can't refuse to release the money to you."

"Oh," David hadn't realized that.

"But I thought you told me you only had a little bit of cash. So what's up now, suddenly?"

He went ahead and let the bomb drop on Stafford. "I think Marianna may have hidden some money away in one of our accounts."

"Hidden away money. What do you mean?" This was quite a surprising development. "Like how much?"

David really kept his voice low now and moved closer to the investigator, "Like maybe $110,000."

Stafford was blown away, "One hundred and ten thousand dollars? Where would your wife get that kind of money?" Hadn't Watts told him the woman worked in a school cafeteria?

"Geez, it's almost as much as the ransom they're asking for." Then it hit him. It suddenly all made sense. Stafford didn't know why he hadn't at least considered the possibility before. There was a reason for the odd ransom amount; the kidnappers just wanted their money back. So the wifey had ripped somebody off to the tune of a hundred and twenty grand. There was no other explanation.

"How long have you known about this?" Stafford questioned Watts.

David tried to think of a good answer, but the truth, well sort of the truth, seemed like the best course. "Just since the phone call. The kidnapper suggested I look in our bank account for the money."

"So what are you stringing this guy along for?" Stafford asked, pointing back toward the interior of their car.

"I don't have enough to cover the whole ransom, and besides, I'm not even sure that the money's really there." David gave him a sheepish look, "And, anyway, Harold was already on his way out to get the cash for me. It just seemed like the right thing to do."

Or a good way to rip off your brother-in-law, Stafford thought. Suddenly the investigator was not so sure about the appropriateness of indulging his client in his efforts. Apparently, the man's wife was a crook, too, and David Watts wasn't much higher on the honor scale than his spouse. And the money Watts had in that bank; it was probably dirty. What was the guy intending to do with it, keep it? And then use the brother-in-law's cash for the ransom? That didn't seem right. Then Watts would be as big a criminal as the kidnappers. Of course Stafford could understand wanting to rip off the brother-in-law, Harold Reed was no daisy himself.

"Hey, what are you doing out there?" the suit yelled from inside the Charger, just to prove Stafford's point.

"We'll be right there," David shouted back to the man. Then he returned to Stafford. "So, what do you think? We should go to my bank and get twenty thousand?"

The investigator ignored his client's question. He had suddenly come up with an idea and he didn't want to lose his train of thought. What was the point? Oh, yeah. Adding together Watts' newfound fortune and the Reed guy's briefcase full of cash, there was something like $200,000 about to be turned over to a bunch of criminals. All that money was about to get split up between the kidnappers and the two assholes currently accompanying Stafford. That didn't seem like a good idea, especially considering they were all pretty much equally nefarious.

"Mr. Stafford?"

David Watts was right in his face now; Stafford had to answer. "Yeah, yeah. We should go to your bank," the investigator replied. But then he paused a moment, fomenting the last thread of the beginning of what seemed like a plan of action.

"Yeah, you know, David, I'd be a little careful about just leaving that money in the bank if I were you."

Watts gave him a funny look.

"If that money's in there, then, really, it should be given over to your brother-in-law after we get Marianna and Julia back. If he pays the ransom, then you need to pay him back right away."

Watts started to say something but Stafford held up his hand, he had a more important point before his client tried to argue his way out of the plan.

"But, more importantly, if the money is there now, there's no guarantee it will be there later. If Marianna was holding out on you, then when she gets released, how do you know the first thing she won't do is run to the bank and take out all that money? You don't know that do you?"

David didn't want to think about that. Ever since he had heard about the inflated bank account balance he had been trying to avoid contemplating what that might mean regarding Marianna's loyalty. But Stafford was right, he had to at least consider whether Marianna would up and run as soon as the ransom was paid. And while he didn't want her leaving home at all, it would be worse if she up and fled with all that money, too.

"I guess you're right. I should probably take it all out when we get there."

Stafford had made his point. But then he remembered the party would need to go to at least three banks to get all the cash out. "Shit," he accidentally said aloud. They'd just have to get the first, what was it, $40,000 out and then get the rest later. Or maybe he could make do with $140,000. Either way, it was getting toward eleven-thirty and they needed to hurry.

"Damn it! What are you doing out there?" came Reed's voice again.

"Keep your pants on!" Stafford yelled back, suddenly no longer a bit concerned about what the old blow hard thought of him.

"You ready to go?" he asked, a bit more kindly to the man he still needed.

"Yeah, we better hurry," David answered.

The two men hustled back to the car and jumped in. Stafford roared the engine to life and then headed off in rush out of the parking lot, though he had no idea which direction to go.

"Hey Reed," the investigator called to the suit in the back seat. "You got one of those fancy phones with internet?"

"Of course."

"I need you to look up the nearest SoCal Trust Bank. I've got some money in there for your boy David here. Get us up to that $120,000."

Stafford suddenly realized he felt good. Like he'd received a rush of adrenaline. Yeah, baby; he felt really, really good.

"Kidnappers, here we come!"

Detective Stokes finally got through to the LA County Sheriff's data desk. He'd already been on hold about ten minutes when the clerk came on and took the address information for the Espinoza residence in East LA.

Now he waited again. After a bit he glanced down at his watch, it was 12:02PM; it had been another seven minutes.

"Detective?"

"Yes," Stokes replied, a little surprised, assuming he'd actually be on hold a bit longer.

"Yeah, we've got that address registered for Paolo Martinez as the owner, not Espinoza." Stokes already had that information, he figured most of the units in that section of town would be rentals.

"You don't have any way of checking on who the property might be rented to?"

"Well, since it didn't come up with the name you inquired about, I did a quick DMV check and came up with a record match that way."

Wow, that was some thorough work. "What record match?"

"The address is listed in DMV as the residence of Francisco Espinoza. He's listed as thirty-six years of age, five foot six, and one hundred and fifty pounds. He has dark hair and brown eyes."

"No record for a Marianna Espinoza though?"

"No sir."

"Hmm. Is Espinoza a resident?"

There was a pause before the girl answered, "Yeah, he's legal, a U.S. citizen even. You want me to fax over the DMV sheet?"

"No, that's OK, I can pull it," Stokes answered. "But hey, thanks, you were really a help."

"No problem Detective. Goodbye."

"Bye."

Stokes leaned back and put his hands behind his head to think. So, that now made three links to the East LA address for the kidnap victim. First, the woman had offered the address as her residence, second, there really was an Espinoza renting at the location, and third, the woman's daughter was currently inside the residence. That was good. But they still hadn't located the woman to bring her back in for further questioning, and further, they had yet to even verify the existence of anyone named Marianna Espinoza. Stokes just wished the fingerprint lab would get back to him. He had recently called down to records and found out the system was temporarily out of service. That happened now and then.

A few years ago, the fingerprint system had been nationalized and it was much more effective today. The way it used to work, you'd be looking for a match in California, say, and your search would come up empty, as a non-record. So you'd think your suspect had no criminal history. The problem was, over in another state, say, Arkansas, there'd be a dozen fingerprint matches for the same guy and you'd never even know it. So your suspect would walk, even though another jurisdiction might be trying to find the very same guy. It had really been frustrating. Murderers had walked out of jails all the time, just because the states hadn't shared information. So today's database was much better, it included all fifty states and the District of Columbia. The only drawback was that the system had now become much more complicated. So sometimes when you called records you were informed that "the system was down". It was the price you paid for having a more thorough search.

When the system came up, however, Stokes would soon know if Marianna Espinoza, or whoever she might be, had ever been convicted of a crime, anywhere within the United States. And if they got a match, then he'd also know if Marianna Espinoza was really Marianna Espinoza.

Stokes' phone rang.

He picked it up immediately, "Stokes."

"I wanted to give you an update on the County stakeout for your East LA row house." It was Thibeut. Stokes had asked the Lieutenant to see if he could use some leverage to get a County unit or two out to the Espinoza house.

"Great."

"They won't be able to get over there for a couple of hours. Seems they've got their own hostage thing going on right now in Florence and they don't have any units to spare."

"Damn. That's too bad," the detective replied. It looked like the Espinoza lady would be able to come and go as she pleased for a while.

"Yeah, well I tried."

"And I appreciate it Lieutenant. I guess we'll just have to wait. But thanks for giving it a shot." The detective was about to hang up when Thibeut interjected and spoke again.

"Stokes."

"Yeah?"

"It's nearby, why don't you swing over to the place at lunch. Bring a sandwich and check out the beautiful landscape on your own time."

Stokes chuckled a little, the landscape didn't sound appealing, but he might drive by anyway. "I might just do that."

"OK, well, your choice."

"Thanks," Stokes answered and Thibeut hung up the phone.

He looked at his watch again; it read 12:14PM. It was about time for lunch. He'd considered going back to the East LA location, but he'd already decided to wait and make up his mind once he stepped outside. It had been stacking up to be a brutally hot day.

They didn't have to drive too far to find a SoCal Trust Bank; there was one just to their North in Echo Park, near Dodger Stadium. It was not the branch that David normally used, but it was still not far from his home in Silver Lake.

After pulling the Dodge into a space out front, Stafford shut off the motor and turned to Harold Reed in the back of the car.

"We're going to need the briefcase."

"The briefcase?"

"Yeah, we got to have something to put the money in. Take what you've got in there now and set it on the seat, it won't go anywhere. Then we'll put it back in when we get back here with the cash."

Harold was pissed off at this, but it made sense. They couldn't just carry the money around in the open. He opened the case and started setting the bundles of one hundred dollar bills on the seat beside him.

But he couldn't resist getting a dig in on the seemingly inept investigator, at least inept in his eyes anyway. "It's like amateur hour here. Keeping $100,000 on the back seat. Where'd you learn your craft? Romper Room?"

"Yeah, Romper Room," Stafford replied, taking the briefcase from Reed as the man held it up, the case now empty.

Stafford opened the driver's door and exited the car. David took this as his cue and also got out. In front of the vehicle the two men met and exchanged a couple of words before Stafford handed the briefcase over to Watts. Watts then turned and went inside the building.

Reed was aghast. What the hell were they doing? He opened the rear door and stood out, one foot inside and one foot out. He was hit by a wave of warm air.

"What the hell's going on?" he yelled at Stafford. The investigator had now stationed himself in front of the bank, like some sort of security guard or something.

"Just sit tight. We're getting the rest of the money."

"I thought you said this was your bank! Why the hell is David going in there?" He pulled as sarcastic a tone as he could, "Shouldn't you be in there if it's your money?"

The suit was a frickin, pompous pain in the ass, Stafford thought again. But he realized he needed to placate the man a little longer.

"Actually, this is really David's bank. I just told you it was mine because I thought you'd blow your stack if you found out he had twenty grand available." Stafford looked at the older man; he was turning red in the face again. "So, was I right?"

"Of all the bullshit," thought Reed. "You'd like that, wouldn't you?" The investigator just smiled at him. "Don't worry, I've dealt with your kind before," Reed added, and then, after shaking his head to convey his disgust, he sat back down in the car and closed the door.

Harold couldn't believe the disrespectful attitude of the private investigator. Watts had really picked a winner. When this was over he was going to look into taking legal action against the man. Reed had some powerful friends; maybe he could even find a way to have the guy's license revoked or something; that would fix him.

And what about David? The twerp had been holding out on him. He had twenty thousand dollars in the bank and didn't even breathe a whiff of it to Harold. Well this was going to be the last time his ex-brother-in-law ever did something like that to Harold Reed, it wouldn't happen again. He was sure about that.


It was just too hot out to contemplate driving over to the Espinoza residence, only to have to turn around and come back again, leaving the situation probably still in limbo. Stokes figured the LA County unit would be over there soon enough anyway; there was no reason for him to go wandering around outside his jurisdiction again, at least not just yet.

So the detective had picked up a burrito, to go, from the Mexican restaurant just across the street from their headquarters building. It was a good burrito, and really big, but the price was pretty high; the restaurant owner had apparently realized there was a buck to be made given his opportune location so close to all the working blues.

Stokes was about halfway through the massive wrap when his phone rang. He lifted the receiver and found his wife on the other end of the line.

"Honey?"

"Debra," he attempted to reply, trying to swallow the mouthful of carnitas he had just bitten off, but the sound came out nothing like his wife's name.

"Brenford?"

Stokes got the bite to a manageable size before he answered again. "Debra, yeah it's me."

"Oh, sorry. You sounded funny."

"Yeah, no problem. I was just getting some lunch."

"Oh … sorry to interrupt."

"That's OK." Stokes swallowed the last of the bite. "I can talk now."

"Where'd you go?" she asked.

The Detective assumed his wife was asking where he'd gone to get his lunch.

"Oh, just that little Mexican place across the street. You remember we've eaten there before."

"Yeah, I remember it." She paused for just a moment before continuing. "Hey, I thought you said you were going to call me."

Oh yeah, Stokes thought, she had told him to call her. She had been worried about his mental state given the events with Lourdes Garcia.

"Sorry honey, I've been busy. Besides I knew you'd call me if I didn't try you soon enough."

"Very funny. So how's it going?"

"It's going OK. To what in particular are you referring?"

"I don't know," Debra replied with a sigh, "I guess the kidnapping thing. Homicide would have the Garcia case, right?"

Stokes didn't want to have to keep rehashing Detective Garcia's death. It was better if he just concentrated on the work he needed to do instead.

"Yeah, homicide's got Garcia, I'm still working on the kidnapping case though."

"Any luck?"

"Not much so far." Stokes looked at the phone on his desk, another line had lit up and begun flashing. "Hey honey, can you hang on a second?"

"Sure."

Stokes punched hold and then pushed down the button for the other line.

"Stokes."

"Detective, this is Capelli in records."

"Oh, yeah…Capelli."

"We've got a match on the prints you sent us."

"Really?" Stokes was anxious to get the information, but he wanted to be able to devote his entire attention to the matter. "Hey, hold on one second," he told Capelli. Then he put the man on hold before getting back to the line where Debra waited.

"Debra?"

"Yeah?"

"Hey, I've got another call, I've got to go."

"OK," Debra replied. "But there's one thing I need to ask first."

"OK, make it quick."

"Did you see Moe this morning before you left?"

"Ah honey." Stokes paused, remembering how important the animals were to his wife. "No I didn't see Moe this morning. Is he missing or something?"

"I don't know. I just haven't seen him today that's all; maybe yesterday either, I can't remember."

"I'm sure he'll turn up. He always does. I've really got to go."

"All right. I love you."

"Love you," Stokes answered and then punched into the other line. God, that was all he needed, to have to worry about a cat right now.

"Sorry about that."

"Uh, no problem," Capelli answered, his voice coming back to the phone.

"So you got a match."

"Yep."

"Is it Espinoza, Marianna Espinoza?"

There was a slight pause before the records man answered, "Uh ... no. It's a Marianna, but not Espinoza. The file shows a Marianna Watts, Marianna Hernandez Watts of Silver Lake. Married to a David Watts. One child."

"Marianna Watts?"

"Yep."

"How did the ID come up? Probably a criminal charge, right?"

"Uh, yep. You got it. Extortion conviction; right here in California."

Wow, thought Stokes. Now they were getting somewhere. The woman had lied, but she was probably still right there in the area; if not with her daughter in East LA, then maybe Silver Lake, which, he reminded himself, was LAPD juris territory, even his own bureau.

"Hey, Capelli."

"Yeah."

"You're not about to leave for lunch are you?"

"No I brought it. Why? You buying?"

"Not today. But I need that record sheet. Can I come down and get it, like right now?"

"Yeah, sure," Capelli answered. "So you're buying another day?"

Stokes laughed to himself, "You got it. I owe you one." The detective rose from his desk. "Don't move, I'll be right down."

"I'm not going anywhere, I've got lunch to eat."


David Watts turned from the teller's window at the Echo Park branch of SoCal Trust Bank; he was white as a ghost. He had an oversized briefcase in his hand, but there was no money in it. There was no money in it because the account, from which he had expected to withdraw cash to fill the case, had been depleted of funds. His wife of two years had just emptied out the account. The very account David, himself, had established for her a little over a year ago. Not only had she taken some of their family's combined funds, but she had withdrawn an additional one hundred and ten thousand dollars from the account, too; money that Marianna, had apparently secretly deposited into the bank herself.

David Watts was crushed.

If Marianna had withdrawn the funds only earlier today, and the teller had confirmed just that fact, then that meant she was no longer in the clutches of the kidnappers who had broken into their house that morning. So if his wife was free to move about, and hadn't contacted David, then the next conclusion was almost inescapable – Marianna had been in on it the whole time. The whole kidnapping had been a fake. And now? Now Marianna had escaped with almost all their money. The implications were staggering.

David felt the pain in his chest travel down his left arm and upward into his neck. But the worst thing, the really cruelest part of all, was that she had played him. He had thought he had a wife, a home, and even a child; they were a family. But no, in reality he had been played, there had been no love. His wife was, at the least a con artist, or, and more likely, maybe even the most cunning of criminals.

David Watts had no wife, he had no daughter and he had no money, even his home had been violated.

David pushed the glass door of the bank branch building open and stepped into the heat. In front of him sat the blue Dodge Charger. His brother-in-law was leaning down and looking through the front windshield of the fancy car in front of him. There was a look of scorn on the man's face. Was it always there? Or was it just reserved for David? David wasn't sure and he didn't care. To his right David saw the investigator walking toward him with a look of concern. The man's hand seemed to be reaching for the briefcase, but David pulled it closer to his side.

He felt light headed. David tried to breathe, but nothing came. A wave of pain swept over him and David felt his strength give way. His legs gave out from under him and he fell. Even as he collapsed, however, he continued to try to protect the empty case in his grasp.

Detective Stokes looked at the data sheet in front of him as he walked. Unfortunately, there wasn't that much on it. The information began with the woman's birth. Marianna Hernandez had been born in Satillo, Mexico in 1970. Then there was a big blank spot, probably because the birth info had been all the data available from Mexican records. The next thing on the list came from 1995, a possession charge in San Diego County. The charge had been dropped, but the woman had been deported back to Mexico because she was in the U.S. illegally. In 1997 Marianna Hernandez was convicted of extortion in Los Angeles County. She served six months of a nine-month sentence in the North County Women's Detention Center before being deported, again. There was nothing on the sheet as to the specifics of the extortion conviction. There was one last line item, and this last bit of data really caught the detective's attention. Stokes stopped to read it outside Thibeut's office. He wanted to stick his head in and tell his boss they'd ID'd the kidnap victims.

In September 2007 Marianna Hernandez had married a certain Mr. David Watts of Silver Lake, California, instantly making her a legal permanent resident of the United States of America. In addition to the bride and groom, a two-year-old daughter of the bride was noted as being granted permanent residency due to the discourse of the marriage. The daughter's name was Julia Espinoza.

Jim Stafford was standing to the side of the entrance to the bank when he heard the sweep of the seal and the door swung open. He turned in time to see David Watts, his soon to be former client, exit the building. The first thing Stafford noticed was that Watts had the oversized briefcase clutched in his right hand. It was a welcome sight. The second thing Stafford noticed, however, was that the man carrying the satchel looked white as a sheet. His client also appeared like he might be lost as to exactly where he was. Stafford started for the man, but before he could get there Watts began a swoon to the ground. The investigator reached for the big black case, but he somehow missed it as Watts landed in a heap on the ground.

"Dammit!" he muttered. What the hell was wrong with the man?

"David!" he yelled at the now prone figure. Stafford made another attempt to get the briefcase, as he looked for some sign of recognition in Watts' face. The man looked like he was practically dead, and Stafford suddenly realized what the trouble could be; Watts was having a heart attack.

The ailing man, despite his condition, continued to have a grip on the briefcase however, and Stafford had to use two hands to pry Watt's fingers from the handle of the case. This was fucking everything up, Stafford thought. Stafford wanted the case, but not right there, right now. He'd intended to take it from Watts, at gunpoint if necessary, but at a more secluded location.

Just as the, soon to be retired, investigator began to free the money from the dying man's grasp, Stafford heard the suit start up again behind him.

"What's wrong with David? My God, what are you doing?"

Stafford turned and took a step back toward the driver's side door, case now in hand. Reed was part way out of the car again, with one foot on the asphalt.

"Here, we gotta get the money in the car," Stafford told him and handed the briefcase to Harold before pushing him down by the shoulder, back into the rear seat. "Put all the money back in the case. We don't want to lose any."

Harold did as the investigator asked, and pulled his foot back in as Stafford closed the rear door. The investigator then hopped into the driver's seat himself.

"What about David? We can count the money later." Harold couldn't understand why the other man had left David on the sidewalk.

Stafford slid the key into the ignition and started the motor.

"What are you doing?"

The investigator put the car in reverse and turned to see where he was headed as he moved the vehicle from the space.

"I'm afraid David has had a little set back. He won't be accompanying us any longer."

Reed was almost at a loss for words. Furthermore, the faintest hint of fear now crept into him. He almost didn't recognize it.

"I don't understand."

"I think he's had a heart attack. I'm sure somebody from the bank will be able to get some help," Stafford explained, as he put the car in drive and headed for the lot exit. "They'll call an ambulance for him, that's all we could do. Right now," he added, turning onto the busy boulevard out front, "right now we gotta get this money over to the ransom drop. We have to make sure we get Marianna and Julie back."

Harold couldn't believe it, David having a heart attack? And this guy just left him there? The story about getting the money to the bus stop made some sense, but there was something really fishy about what had just transpired. Harold wasn't sure what to do. He looked at his watch. It was 12:46PM. They probably had just enough time to get to the drop location, he thought, though Harold really wasn't even sure where they, or the location, might be.

"Do we even know what bus? David had the bus number," Reed asked.

"No, I got it," replied the driver.

Stafford, of course, did not know the bus number; he had no intention of even finding a bus in front of a park. But he had decided a park setting might not make a bad locale for his plan. So after turning onto Sunset he headed north for Griffith Park. The park was big and had lots of hidden drives and parking areas; it would be perfect. He'd almost opted for Elysian Park, it was pretty big, and closer. But then he'd remembered the academy was there, the LAPD Academy. That wouldn't be a good place to throw the old fart out of the car; he wanted a private setting, where no one would see him.

Harold didn't like the vibe he was getting. But for the time being he had little choice in the matter. All he could do was to sit back and enjoy the ride. Harold looked down and saw the stacks of one hundred dollar bills sitting beside him. He picked the case up from the floor where he had set it and placed it in his lap. He'd arrange all the cash neatly inside, like a civilized person would. With a flip of the front switch he popped the case open; to his amazement, it was empty.

Reed's mouth opened just a bit, and he started to say something, but then thought better of it. He needed to think a moment. Why was the case empty? As much as he'd like to accuse Stafford of taking it, he knew the investigator didn't have it. He'd seen David come out the front door of the bank with the briefcase. Then Stafford had taken it and handed it to directly to Harold. The case had never opened. So where was the money? Had David kept it? You could almost stuff twenty thousand dollars in one hundred dollar bills in your pockets. But that didn't seem likely; there would be no reason for David to do that. Stafford had acted like the money had been his, and then "surprise, hey David has twenty grand, not the P.I. asshole." Was it a game? Maybe the money hadn't been in the account. Harold could believe that. It would figure that Watts had been broke; hadn't the man admitted that very thing when he'd asked Harold for the money? So why would they say David had the money and then drive all the way over there when they were so short of time. It didn't make any sense. Then another thought came to him; was this all some sort of ruse? Was somebody trying to put one over on Harold Reed?

"OK, we're almost there," Stafford said from the front seat.

Harold suddenly felt a twang of anxiety. He didn't want to part with his $100,000; not until he was absolutely sure he wasn't being set up. He thought about only putting part of the money in the case, but then thought of the possible consequences of such an action. If the ransom drop was legit, and Marianna and her daughter's lives depended on the money, then that would be a disaster. He couldn't chance keeping part of the money.

"Hey," the investigator said into the rearview mirror. Harold looked up and saw the man's eyes looking back at him in the glass. "What are you doing back there? You got the money in the case?"

Harold picked up a couple of the stacks and started placing them in the briefcase. "Yes, just about done."

"Good cause we're there; it's just in the park here." Stafford turned off Feliz Boulevard on to Fern Dell, which led into the park. Unfortunately, Reed saw the Griffith Observatory on the hill adjacent just before the car ducked onto the low-lying drive.

"Isn't that that famous observatory?"

"Which one is that?"

"The one on the hill there."

"Lead the guy on," Stafford thought to himself. If he could keep the man talking, maybe the blowhard wouldn't figure it out until it was too late.

"Oh yeah, that one. You know the name of it?"

"The name?"

"Yeah, the name. You're a smart guy, you must know the name of it."

Harold really detested the investigator, partly because he was arrogant and rude, but also partly because he made him afraid for some reason. Not many people did that.

"I can't remember the name and I don't care. But I do have a question. Who's going to put the money on the bus, you or me?"

Stafford chuckled to himself; he tried to not let the suit see. "I don't care. You want to do it?"

Harold was up for it. At least that way it would get done right. And he'd also get to stay with the money till the very end. He thought again about whether to mention the twenty thousand dollar shortage to Stafford, but decided against it. At this point $100,000 would be all they were going to get their hands on anyway. They'd have to negotiate the remainder of the payment with the kidnappers.

Stafford turned a corner and saw a secluded parking lot a little to their right. There was only one car in the lot, a mini-van, and it appeared un-occupied. The site was far enough off the road that it would not draw much attention, either. Stafford could make Reed walk down the hillside a ways, too. It was perfect.


They had stopped and eaten some lunch at a cheap taco joint. Paco had wanted to pay with one of the new one hundred dollar bills from the bank, but Marianna hadn't let him. She was always such a wet blanket.

It was a little after noon or thereabout and Paco had the green Honda headed East on the I-10 freeway in the direction of his East LA row house. He was trying, however, to come up with a location for a brief side excursion. It was really hot out though, and the sweltering conditions were making it hard for him to think. They had the windows down, in an attempt to alleviate the heat some. But once the temperature reached over one hundred degrees, and Paco was sure it was well over that, the hot air blowing through the car didn't really seem to help much.

Marianna was finishing up her horchata drink beside him. She'd eaten two tacos and a burrito while they had sat outside the restaurant. She was really turning into a pig, thought Francisco. He needed a place to turn her into bacon.

"Why you driving so slow?"

Paco thought a moment for a response. "Don't want the cops to pull us over, do you? Not with all that money in here."

"Yeah, well if you drive too slow they'll pull you over, too."

Paco pressed on the accelerator a bit just to humor her. He'd take it back off shortly.

The question kept running through his mind; where to do it? Where, where, where? He realized with the lack of any rural area within the middle of the LA sprawl the only out of the way place would be an industrial location. Fortunately, there was a good industrial area, just to the south of where they lived, in City of Commerce. There were plenty of warehouses and railway lines and what have you. But he needed to figure out the best route, and then, also, a reason for taking Marianna down there with him.

The I-5 exchange exit came up momentarily and he had to make a decision. He turned off. Paco glanced over at Marianna. She didn't act like she had even noticed. Of course, it wouldn't be completely irrational to be taking the I-5 south at this point; they could always head into East LA via the 60 freeway a little further on. After that, he'd have to do some explaining.

"Can you imagine? One hundred thousand dollars," Marianna said, thinking about what she might do with the money. Of course, she'd been thinking about what to do with the money for months now, ever since she had started skimming $20,000 at a time off of Ferdie's coke deals. But now she'd have to share the money with Paco.

That stank. But, she reminded herself, had it not been for Paco introducing her to Ferdie, she wouldn't ever have had the opportunity to lift the cash in the first place.

She still wasn't sure what had prompted her to go looking for her ex-husband. Had it been that she still loved the man? Marianna looked over at Paco while he drove. Hell no, she thought, that hadn't been it.

A Mercedes pulled up along side their car. Inside a dark haired, dark skinned woman was at the wheel. The woman had too much makeup on for Marianna's taste.

"Fuck you lady", she thought to herself. "I've got one hundred thousand dollars in here and could buy two of those lousy cars." Though when she thought about it, she realized two Mercedes would probably be more than the amount she had. "Whatever." Then it hit her. That's why she had looked Francisco up again. She wanted a Mercedes, she wanted nice things. It wasn't so much that she wanted what Paco had; it was more that she didn't want what David Watts had, which was nothing. She had thought Watts had a career, and money. But then it turned out the old gringo hadn't even been employed full-time.

What a gyp.

Marianna thought marrying an educated white American would lift her up to a whole different economic and social status, but it hadn't. David Watts had been a fraud. Marianna still had to work in that shit hole of a cafeteria, while David sat at home and did nothing. Marianna had expected that she and Julia would be catapulted into a life of luxury, well at least semi-luxury anyway. But it hadn't worked out that way at all. So she had found Paco. And then he had told her about working for Ferdie. Then Ferdie had employed her. But that had been a rip off, too. He didn't pay her nearly what he had said he would. So she had ripped him off. And now she had what neither David, nor Paco, nor Ferdie could provide her; she had one hundred thousand dollars.

Marianna saw the exit for the 60 freeway fly by, but it took her a second to realize what that meant.

"Hey, where you going? That was the exit."

Paco just looked ahead. "Yeah, I know. I got a errand to run before we go home."

"An errand? What kind of errand?"

Paco now looked at Marianna, seated beside him. "I gotta pick up some stuff. The man's waiting for me."

"Paco this ain't no time to be picking any shit up! What are you thinking?"

"Hey, I owe the man, too."

"What difference does it make if you owe the man? We're getting the hell out of here, today. Remember that?"

Paco was looking forward to getting Marianna out of the car. "Hey, the man's a good hombre, I don't screw him over like you do."

Marianna was pissed, but she didn't see the danger; for her, Paco was just confirming once again what an idiot he was.

"You know we got a daughter at home, too. She's only four."

"She'll be all right. She's a tough kid."

"Easy for you to say," thought Marianna. "You're not four."

That was the one real regret that Marianna had in this whole affair. Francisco Espinoza had never been a real father. He had always taken Julia for granted. It was almost as if he didn't care.

Not like David.

David Watts loved Julia, Marianna was sure of it. And she also knew her daughter loved David in return. The little girl had even recently taken to calling the man daddy. That was too bad. Julia deserved a father; but then Marianna deserved a life. And just because Watts loved her daughter didn't mean he could provide for the child. Julia would get fed all right, get the basic stuff. But she'd probably never rise above some sort of domestic position or something. She'd certainly never have an opportunity to go to college what with that stupid punta Watts never making any money.

Marianna could make the money; she'd be the one to make sure her daughter got a good education. She didn't need a man for that.

Fernando Alba sat in his car alongside Valley Boulevard, just north of Boyle Heights. He was waiting for the 35L bus to appear. It was a couple of minutes after one o'clock in the afternoon and he expected the bus to pull up to the metro stop any minute now. He needed to be ready when the vehicle approached, because he intended to board with the other waiting passengers. But Fernando, or Ferdie as he was better known, was only a matter of yards from the embarkation spot and, besides, he had the comfort of the air conditioning while he remained in his vehicle. After only another minute or so Ferdie saw, what had to be, the bus he was looking for, approaching. He shut off the motor and exited the car into the heat. He approached the stop slowly, moving in behind the other waiting passengers so as to remain out of sight. Ferdie was expecting David Watts to disembark and he didn't want the man to notice him. He didn't think Watts could ID him from any brief glimpse the man might have possibly gotten the previous morning, but you never knew. Besides, Ferdie had one distinguishing feature that the man might have been able to identify; both of Ferdie's arms were tattooed; full sleeves. If Watts had seen his arms, then he'd recognize the myriad of tats if he saw them again. So he waited behind the other people.

The bus pulled up to the stop and the doors opened. The front display read "35L – Downtown". Several people poured from the bus. Ferdie thought he saw the Watts fellow, but then realized it was another Caucasian and not Watts; everyone else was Hispanic. The waiting passengers began to board and Ferdie suddenly realized he wasn't sure what to do. Had Watts not left the briefcase? Maybe the fool had already gotten off, but Ferdie had checked, there were no stops between their present location and the park. Maybe the guy was still on the bus. If he were, then when Ferdie boarded, Watts would have an opportunity to identify him if he saw the tats.

The last waiting passenger boarded and Ferdie decided he had no choice. If Watts had delivered the briefcase, then he had to enter the bus and retrieve it; otherwise some punta would pick up the case and later find that he had become $120,000 richer.

Ferdie hurriedly entered right before the doors closed. Once aboard, the Tachos leader realized he didn't have correct change and had to beg a woman in the front row to break a twenty-dollar bill for him.

The bus was about half full and Ferdie quickly made his way to the back of the vehicle. On one side of the very rear seat sat an elderly couple, on the other a young man leaned against the opposite window. There was no briefcase to be seen. Ferdie stepped back and looked at the next pair of seats; two young women occupied one, the other was empty, but still no briefcase. He stepped back another aisle; again, nothing.

Ferdie advanced back to the elderly couple in the rear. "Buenos dias," he announced.

The man returned his greeting, "Buenos dias, Senor."

"Has visto un maletin?"

"No. No he visto nada." The man grimaced a little, obviously worried that the tall man with the tattooed arms might accuse him of stealing something.

Ferdie turned toward the teenager against the window who was apparently listening in. "Y usted? Un maletin?"

But the young man shook his head and answered no.

Neither of them had seen it. It was obvious they weren't lying, either; there was nowhere they could have been hiding a container with that much money.

Ferdie couldn't believe it, had Watts backed out on him? Maybe the guy hadn't made it in time for the bus. Actually, the better possibility was that that bitch Marianna had finally decided to let her husband in on what she had done. It didn't matter; Ferdie still wanted his money.

He turned and walked back toward the front of the bus, examining each seat and every occupant as he went. When he reached the front he turned and addressed the whole crowd, virtually all Hispanic.

"Hey! Hey, escuche!"

Ferdie yelled it loud enough that he immediately gained the attention of everyone on the bus.

"Alguien ha visto aqui un maletin?" he asked.

A couple of the people shook their heads, but many of the others just looked to their neighbors to see if anyone knew why there was a man yelling at them.

"No briefcase? With money. Maletin con dinero!"

Still no positive responses came from the captive audience. It just wasn't there.

Ferdie turned to the driver, who was already paying close attention to the loud and slightly threatening looking passenger just behind him.

"Let me out."

The man got a scared look on his face, but bravely tried to maintain some level of control. "I can't, you'll have to wait until the next stop," he replied.

"You'll let me off right here, or I'll fuckin' rip your balls off and feed them to my dog. You understand?" Ferdie had a finger in the man's face.

The driver only hesitated a second before deciding the prudent course of action was to do as ordered. "OK, ok," he said, raising his hand as if to tell the passenger to remain calm.

In a moment the driver had the bus pulled to the curb.

Then he cranked the lever and opened the door.

As he stepped out Ferdie could hear someone behind the bus honking his or her horn. He didn't care. He had two blocks to walk back to his car in the heat. Then he'd call David Watts on his cell phone and ask him what the fuck was wrong.


Harold Reed looked at his watch; it read 1:08PM. They were late.

Stafford had pulled into a small lot and parked behind a mini-van, the only other vehicle around. It didn't look to Harold like a very good spot for a bus stop.

"This can't be right. I don't know about California, but this would be a pretty screwed up place to put a bus stop in most parts of the country. I don't think you know where you're going."

Jim Stafford turned and looked at the man in the back seat. He was glad the guy was about to be gone.

"Actually, you're right. I just parked here so we would be out of sight. The stop is over there, down that hill." Stafford pointed to the embankment just south of them.

"Down that hill?" Harold looked toward the drop-off; it seemed heavily over grown with underbrush and a few overhanging trees. It also looked steep and a long way from any possible road below.

"Yeah, down there," the investigator answered. "Come on, I'll go with you. I won't make you go alone."

Harold looked at his watch again. They were already late; there would be no way to traverse the embankment and make it to the bottom with any chance of catching a one o'clock or one o' five bus, or whatever it was. Something wasn't right. Then he thought of how Stafford had left David out in front of the bank. When you added all the odd occurrences and behavior it spelled that something really, really wasn't right. A wave of fear swept over him; he felt nauseous.

Stafford looked at the suit in the back seat, he didn't look well. Maybe the guy was on to him.

"Come on, let's go. We're late."

Reed just sat there.

"What the fuck is your problem buddy?"

"I'm not going down there. We're too late, the bus will already be gone." Harold watched as the anger grew in the investigator's face. "Let's just go back and check on David and see if he's all right. We can try again, later, to get the money to the kidnappers."

We'll that's it, thought Stafford.

"That's fine. You do what you want to do. I'm going to take the money to the drop. It'll be good riddance to have you out of my hair. David will be real happy when he hears about how you behaved, too."

Harold tried to answer, but Stafford wouldn't let him.

"Get out of the car," ordered the investigator.

Reed didn't move. "Damn it, I said get your ass out of the car!"

The suit looked dumbfounded, but then reached for the handle and started to open the car door. The problem was, he still had a hold of the briefcase.

"No. The money stays here. You idiot, how am I supposed to pay the kidnappers if you take the money?"

Harold didn't know what to do. He wanted out of the vehicle, badly, but he also couldn't bring himself to leave $100,000 of his hard earned money with a man who was, apparently, on some mission of his own.

"Well?"

"No. I can't leave you the money."

What the hell? Stafford was enraged. His on-the-fly plan to flim-flam the man into just handing over the case hadn't come off quite as well as he had hoped.

Stafford reached into his jacket and pulled the thirty-eight revolver from his shoulder holster. He pointed it at Reed.

"Look asshole, let go of the case and get out of the car."

Harold Reed had never had a firearm pointed at him in his life, at least that he could remember. And now that it had happened, he didn't quite know how he was supposed to react.

Reaching for the gun was the wrong idea.

As Stafford had the thirty-eight pointed at the obstinate asshole in the back seat, the man's left hand suddenly left the door handle and grabbed hold of the end of revolver. Stafford had no intention of actually shooting the man, but somehow the weapon discharged. It fired and the bullet went right through the palm of the man's hand.

Had that been the extent of the damage the suit would have been lucky, but it wasn't.

After passing through the man's extremity, the bullet penetrated the left eye socket of the, soon to be former, insurance executive. Both men froze at the sound of the gun going off. There was a momentary pause as the injured man's circulatory and nervous systems caught up with what had just happened. The circulatory system seemed to react first, possibly due to the trauma that the metal projectile had inflicted on the man's ability toward any form of cognitive process.

First, blood spurted from the open wound where Reed's eyeball had only recently resided. It shot forward and landed on Stafford, drenching his hand, and covering the thirty-eight firearm in warm, red liquid. Another glob of blood pulsed from the wound and fell down the front of the man's expensive, three-piece suit. Only then did a reaction finally emanate from what was left of the man's brain. The man's mouth opened and a medium pitched sort of shriek emitted from inside him.

Stafford was frozen in disbelief himself, the event, the grabbing, the firing of the weapon, the pulsing of the blood from the man's face; it all seemed to happen in slow motion. When the shock wore off momentarily, Stafford saw Reed sitting in front of him, oozing blood all over the car and making every sort of horrific noise imaginable. He realized he needed to do something.

Stafford climbed out of the car, opened the rear door and dragged the bloody man out by the collar. Amazingly, Reed appeared to be somewhat still functional, though Stafford couldn't figure out how. But, as the man fell to the pavement the investigator saw that Reed's head was still, surprisingly, intact. Apparently, the man's hand had impeded the bullet enough that it hadn't blown right out the back of his skull.

"Why the hell did you do that?" he yelled at the wounded man.

The suit was now on his knees, with one hand on the ground. Reed's other hand, and his face, were lifted up toward the investigator as if pleading with Stafford to help him, yet the demonic noises continued to spill from the man's mouth as blood oozed from what was left of the eye socket. It was repulsive.

"Why the hell did you do that?" Stafford yelled once again.

The investigator was beside himself. He hadn't actually meant to kill Reed; he had just planned on leaving him at the bottom of the ravine. But now the asshole had left him no choice, the man was as good as dead anyway.

Stafford looked around and found that no one was in sight; it was unbelievably lucky. The investigator raised the thirty-eight that he still had in his hand and pointed it at the dying man's temple. Nothing happened at first, but then Stafford thought about all that money, and the alternate possibility of all that prison time and it made the decision easier. He pulled the trigger.

The sound of the gunshot registered off the hillside to his north and blood again poured forth from the suited man's head, just not as much as before. Then the mortally wounded man's limbs gave way and he fell to the pavement.

"Fuck!" Stafford screamed again, angry that the insurance executive from New York had forced him into such a barbaric act.

Stafford had never really committed a serious crime before, at least not anything that you could do hard time for. But that had now changed.

Harold Reed was dead.


Francisco Espinoza finally found just the right place. It was off Washington Boulevard behind a row of warehouses and up against the railroad tracks. Unlike some of the other industrial buildings in the area, these buildings appeared to be unoccupied. They were ramshackle and a few were boarded up. He just needed a specific spot was all. He spied an alleyway between a couple of promising looking structures and headed for a service road that ran behind them.

"Who you gonna meet back here? Nobody lives here," Marianna complained, eager to get back to her daughter and on with the business of leaving.

"He doesn't live here. This is where he works. Don't be so stupid," Paco replied. He just needed her to go along with the plan for another minute or so.

"OK, this is it," he said as they rounded the last warehouse. He started to slow the car and then saw that the location actually wasn't suitable. At the building in front of them two men were loading a dually pickup truck with items from inside the rundown structure.

"Uh, no…this isn't it."

"You don't even know where he works?"

"No, no. It's right around here." Paco drove on past the men with the truck, down the service road a bit further.

"We can't fuck around on this all day. If you don't know where he works then we can't just drive around looking for him you know."

"No, it's right here. Just keep your pants on."

"Don't worry, my pants won't be coming off around you anytime soon."

Paco turned the corner on the last building; the road came to a dead end. But a berm for the railway tracks now bounded their location on three sides and was raised enough to provide some cover. The final warehouse looked empty, too; it would do.

"Yeah, OK, this is it."

"Here?" Marianna sneered and drew up her upper lip. "This don't look like no place to work."

"No, this is it." Paco opened the door and stepped out, but he left the door open. He needed to get Marianna to the back of the car, and he also had to retrieve the Saturday night special he had under his seat.

He walked to the rear of the vehicle and opened the trunk. There wasn't much in there. It would also be nice if he had a pillow, he thought. Then he remembered the grease towel that he kept on the floor of the back seat.

"Hey Marianna, come here!" He looked about the deserted area. It was still empty.

"What?"

"Hey, I need you back here. I want to show you something." But there was nothing to show her. He needed something. All he had in the trunk was a spare tire and an old hip-hop magazine. He'd have to make do.

"What the hell you want me to see in the trunk?" came the reply from the front seat.

"A letter."

"A letter?"

Paco heard the passenger door open, and in a moment Marianna was at the back of the vehicle beside him.

"A letter? What letter?"

Paco grabbed the magazine and set it on the spare tire. "In there. It's going to blow your mind," he said, and then began to move toward the front of the car. "I gotta go see my friend. But it's really gonna surprise you, look."

He slid into the driver's seat and pulled the firearm from under the cushion. He then quickly turned and reached for the towel in the back. It was right where he expected, and he yanked it forward. Paco glanced back but didn't see Marianna coming around the trunk lid. He wrapped the towel around the end of the revolver, leaving enough fabric loose, so that it hung down and covered the gun.

"What letter? There's no letter in here."

Paco rose from the seat.

Marianna was coming around toward the driver's side of the car now; she had the magazine in her hand.

"There's no letter in here. Who was it from?"

"Oh it must have fallen out," he replied, before moving by her, back to the rear of the car. She didn't seem to notice anything unusual about the towel in his hand.

"There it is."

Marianna moved back beside him again. "Where? Are you fucking with me?"

Paco pointed into the rear of the trunk, "There."

Marianna Hernandez Espinoza Watts leaned forward to peer over the spare tire. When she did, Francisco Espinoza, her ex-husband, placed his dime store handgun with the towel wrapped around it about an inch way from her head, just behind her ear. Then he blew her brains out.

She was only the second person that Paco had ever killed.

Fernando Alba stared out the windshield of his black BMW 740i as another bus pulled away from the curb. It was silly, he decided, to sit and look for the Watts man to exit from some random bus; he simply wasn't going to show. And now Ferdie couldn't raise the man on his cell phone either. What the hell had happened to the fool? All Ferdie could figure was that Watts must have hooked up with Marianna and now he didn't think he needed to deal with his obligations. But the man was mistaken if he thought that, because he did.

Ferdie had lost some muscle due to the bust at the duplex, and a couple of his other honchos were away on a pick-up in Suarez, but he still had one guy he could rely on; he had Marcelo. Marcelo was a loyal man and an extremely effective weapon. Ferdie decided he needed those services now.

The Tachos boss started the BMW's motor and turned on the a/c. The walk back to the car had left him dripping with sweat, which only added to his growing anger.

Then he dialed his man. Marcelo answered right away.

"Marcelo?"

"Oh, hey amigo. Que pasa?"

"Donde esta?"

"I'm at home."

Fernando thought a moment on how to phrase his discontent.

"That prick Watts didn't show for the money drop off."

"Wow..."

"Yeah. I think Marianna might have finally gone to him and fessed up or something. I just don't know. But we got to act now, before she runs with the money."

"What do you want me to do?"

"Since Watts didn't show, then maybe they went back to their house. That would be stupid, but you never know. So I'm going to go over there and check it out."

"OK, you want me to come, too?" asked Marcelo.

"No. I got another idea where she might go. Remember her old husband, that Espinoza guy that used to do some work for us? She was married to him in Mexico."

"Yeah, Paco. He's the one that got us to try her."

"Yeah, that's right, Paco. Well, she might just try hiding out with him. He's the kind of shit that would double cross me, too. Didn't he live here in the neighborhood?"

"Yeah, off Whittier."

"Cool. I've never been there, but didn't you like hang out with him for a while at his place."

"Man, for like a couple of days was all."

"Yeah, but you know where it is."

"Sure."

"I want you to go over there and see if you can find her; or Watts or Espinoza or whoever. That bitch and her husband owe me one hundred and twenty grand. There's a chance they have the money with them too, Watts said he had it and then didn't show. So, you know, it's got to be somewhere."

"If they got it I'll find it."

"And Marcelo, do whatever you have to do. These people are los muertos a me."

"Got it."

"Good."

Ferdie was about to hang up when Marcelo spoke back up.

"Hey, uh … Ferdie. Isn't there a kid involved? Doesn't Marianna have a little nina?"

"Yeah, she does. So?"

"So, I mean, what do I do if I find her there, too?"

"What are you, fucking loco or something? You don't hurt her; she's just a little kid. Geez, use your brain."

"Sorry. Just checking man."

"Just get over there right away and see if anybody's there. I'll call you in a little while." Ferdie pushed the red disconnect button on his phone.

Detective Stokes sat at his desk looking for his pen. The phone rang but he didn't answer it right away, because he had something he wanted to get on paper. He located the errant writing instrument and then picked up the receiver momentarily.

"Stokes, hang on."

He set the receiver back on his desk. Stokes looked at the screen in front of him. There it was, the address for David and Marianna Watts. They weren't too far away, either, only over in Silver Lake, like the lady had said. The detective jotted down the house number before picking the phone back up.

"Sorry about that. This is Stokes."

"Damn it man, don't put me on hold."

"Evans?"

"Yeah, it's me."

"Sorry." The guy was being a little touchy about being put on hold. "Don't be such a prima donna, I've got big news here I'm working on. I've ID'd the Espinoza lady from last night. Got a line on an address for her, too."

"Well that's good," Evans answered. "But I've got some news of my own."

"Yeah?"

"Yeah. After forensics finally let us into the shooter's unit, we found everything we were looking for. It was definitely a temporary warehouse set up, there was even a mini meth lab in there."

A methamphetamine lab, that might explain the shooter's ridiculous behavior, thought Stokes. Junkies high on meth always felt they were invincible, and would often take on the police, firing at officers even when it should have been obvious that to do so was simply committing suicide.

"But the best thing," Evans continued, "is that we got another address, and it looks like a big operation is going down there right now. Like it's the main thing."

"Wow, that is good." Stokes wanted the prostitution ring perps, if only for what had happened to Garcia. But if they could help out all those young women, too, that would be icing on the cake.

"I'm on my way to get a warrant. I figured you'd want to be there, too; when we move on it."

"Uh … yeah." Stokes suddenly had his plate full. "Where is it? In the city?"

"Yeah. It's even under Central Bureau, just north of Vernon. It's just a little south of downtown, on Forty-third Street."

That was a bonus, the address being located in the Central Operations Bureau region. The Los Angeles Police Department was divided into four regions, each administered by it's own Bureau. Each Bureau was then sub-divided into divisional jurisdictions. The Vernon area address didn't fall under Hollenbeck's purvey, but since it was still within Central Bureau the Hollenbeck detectives already working on the case would be able to participate.

"OK, I tell you what. I've got to run out and check the address for this Watts woman … uh, you know, the Espinoza woman, apparently Watts is her real name. But I want to be there when your bust goes down. Can you give me a call after you get the warrant signed?"

"Yeah, I can do that. But if you're off somewhere else, we're not going to wait for you buddy."

"I know, I would hate to miss it. But just call me first."

"OK," Evans replied. "Look, I gotta go."
"OK. Good luck."
"Thanks. You too."

It had taken all of Paco's strength to lift his ex-wife's body into the trunk of the Honda, and then, on top of that, she had barely fit. But he'd stuffed her down inside the best he could. Afterwards, standing up from wedging Marianna in, he suddenly felt something wet on top of his head. Paco touched his hair and discovered there was blood in it. It took him a moment to realize where the blood had come from, until he noticed the interior of the trunk lid. It was covered with brain matter. Paco had pushed the top of his head right into it. It was absolutely gross.

So after wiping Marianna's tissue off him with the grease towel, Paco headed home with his car stuffed full of cash and the remains of his wife. When he got to the house Julia was waiting for him and wanted to know where her mommy was. He just told the child they were going to meet her mother later.

In the meantime, he had to pack a few things. So far it looked as if he would get off without a hitch. Marianna was dead, he had the money, and best of all, nobody knew. After leaving town he'd have to ditch the Honda and steal another vehicle. That was no big deal, he'd hotwired plenty of automobiles before. He didn't have the expertise to steal a really late model car, they had better safety systems, but anything like ten years or older he could handle.

Paco already had two suitcases packed for himself. He was filling a gym bag too, when Julia entered his bedroom. He looked at the little girl and realized she had no clothing other than what she was wearing. That was all right, though. He'd pick her up some things on the way out somewhere. Maybe he'd get her some toys, too.

"Hey Chiquita. You ready to go on a trip?"

"Where's mommy?" the child asked.

Paco was getting a little tired of hearing about "mommy".

"She's going to meet us on our trip. We're going to see her. OK?"

"OK."

"What, your mommy didn't pack you any clothes? No toys either?" Paco thought he'd get a jab in for old times sake.

The little girl shook her head.

"Don't you have some special toys? Like dolls or somethin'?"

"No."

"No?" No toys? What was the kid lying?

Paco threw the now stuffed gym bag on top of the two suitcases on the floor.

"There was a man at the door."

Paco froze. What did the kid just say?

"What?"

"There was a man at the door," the child repeated, now rubbing one of her eyes with a little balled up fist.

A man at the door? Who the hell could that be, thought Paco? It could only be bad news. Paco knelt down in front of his daughter and grasped her by the upper arms.

"What man was at the door?"

"A man."

"You didn't let him in did you?"

"No."

At least that was good.

"Did you know the man?" Paco immediately regretted asking the question. Of course she didn't know him. The child didn't even live around here. Unless it had been Watts?

"Did you know him?" he repeated, this time shaking the girl by the arms a little.

"No!" she yelled right in his face.

"OK, ok." Paco thought a moment. "Was he a white guy or a Mexicano, like us?"

Julia shrugged and tilted her head. "I don't know," she said, drawing out the "know" in an effort at complaint.

"What do you mean, was he white or brown? Or maybe he was a black guy. Was he a black man?" Paco made the "black man" sound ominous.

"No. He was like in between."

"In between? Like sort of black and sort of white?"

"Like sort of white and sort of like us."

Geez, thought Paco, who the hell would that be, a part white guy? It certainly wouldn't be David Watts. Then a terrible thought came to him, it might have been Ferdie. He wasn't really in between, but he was kind of light skinned for coming from south of the border.

"So what did the man say?"

"Nothing."

"Nothing, huh. Did he walk away, or did he drive."

"He drove in the car."

That was good, so he probably wasn't waiting out front or something. Paco went to the front window. He didn't see anything out of the ordinary, at least he didn't notice any light skinned Hispanics hanging around.

It didn't matter; they needed to get out of there, and out of town. Paco was a little unnerved by the knowledge of a strange man's visit.

"Julia!" he said loudly to let the child know he meant business. "You have to go to the bathroom?"

The girl shook her head.

"We got to go in the car for a long trip, you sure you don't have to pee or somethin'?"

"No."

"OK."

Paco grabbed the gym bag in his left hand and one of the suitcases in his right and made his way toward the rear kitchen. Julia followed along.

"Wait here while I put these in the car, I gotta come back," he said to the little girl. Then he pushed the rear screen door open and stepped into the parking lot, the door slamming behind him.

He'd gotten a spot almost directly behind his unit and Paco only had to walk a few paces to set the bags beside the Honda's passenger door. He put his hand inside his pant's pocket to retrieve his keys and as he did so he became aware of movement to his left. Startled, he looked up. A fairly large man stood in front of him. Paco's first inclination was to make for the gun in the Honda, but that thought was quickly supplanted when he recognized the man's face; it was Marcelo, his old buddy.

"Paco!"

"Hey, Marcelo. What you doin' here?"

Marcelo reached out and cuffed him on the shoulder. "Just in the neighborhood man, I thought I'd stop by."

"Oh yeah? Great, man," Paco replied, as he placed the car keys in the door lock.

But he didn't feel all that great about it. Marcelo and he had been pretty friendly a while back, hell, Marcelo'd even stayed with him for a couple of weeks, but there was another side to the man, a dangerous side. What's more, the hombre worked for Ferdie. But Marcelo would not have been the man at the door, Marcelo was dark, and that gave Paco some latitude to believe that his old friend maybe wasn't a threat. Though he still wanted him gone.

"Well it's good to see you," Paco said, trying not to give away his fear.

"So what you been up to? You shackin up with anybody today? Anybody home in there?"

That was an odd question, thought Paco. "Uh, no. Not shackin up with no one."

Marcelo looked down at the bags beside the passenger door. "Well you goin' somewhere?"

"Uh, yeah. Just going on a little trip. Like a weekend thing."

"A weekend?"

"Yeah."

Marcelo peered inside the Honda; he seemed to notice the brown bag with the crunched together top on the floor. "Looks like your takin' a lot of stuff."

"Yeah."

The tall man looked Francisco in the eye from close range. "So you seen that ex-wife of yours, Marianna, lately?"

With that question, Paco was pretty sure now that he was being made. Marcelo wasn't on a personal call.

"No. I haven't seen her. Why do you ask?"

"She owes a friend of ours some money, a lot of money actually."

Paco needed to get around to the driver's side of the car. He had placed the revolver back under the driver's seat after cleaning it off from before. He just had to think of a way to get at it.

"Why don't you let me see what kind of clothes your taking on your trip. Maybe I can give you some suggestions on what to bring."

That was it; all pretense was off. Paco could even make out the bulge of the gun stuck in Marcelo's pants.

"Yeah, OK." Paco bent over and unzipped the gym bag before leaning the suitcase over and unzipping it. "Here you can have a look," he told the big man. Then he started around the front of the car, adding "I got another bag for you to see, too."

But Marcelo didn't fall for it.

"No, no, no. You show me," he said, pulling the pistol from under his shirt and motioning Paco back with it.

Paco stopped and slowly came back. He opened his arms a little.

"Hey what's this about?"

"It's about $120,000. Now come over here and show me you don't have it in these things."

It was decision time. Paco was one building away from the end of the row houses. If he moved back around beside the car he'd never get to the corner. As it was, he'd have to dodge back and forth as he ran in order to not get shot. Or, another option was, he could make for the driver's side of the car, then open the door, and get the gun out. Then he remembered the keys were still in the passenger door. He wouldn't even be able to open the driver's side. So that left the last option, he could go over and go through the suitcases with Marcelo. Then they'd finally get to the paper bag inside the car. Then that would be it. Then Marcelo would have the $110,000 or $120,000 or whatever it was, and Paco would be dead. Of course there was always the chance Paco might be able to wrestle the handgun away from the big man, somehow. It wasn't much of a chance, but given the options, it might have the better possibility of success.

But Paco's calculations were suddenly interrupted by voices coming from behind Marcelo.

"Fuck man, the hombre's got a gun."

Marcelo turned to see whom it was, commenting on his shake down, and when he did, Paco made his decision. Still standing close to the front of the car, he decided on flight toward the street.

Paco spun and ran; he ran with all the strength he had. After a few feet he darted to his right, then he darted to his left and, finally he headed back to his right for the corner of the building and the alleyway. He was only a few feet away. That was when he felt the first searing pain. It knocked his breath away and he stumbled. The first impact was followed by another, and then another. Paco crumpled face first to the ground. His whole torso was in agony and he couldn't breathe.

As Francisco "Paco" Espinoza felt his life ebbing away, all he could think was that he had been so close, so close. Not much else came to mind.

Meanwhile, Marcelo turned back to see if the two teenage boys, who had stumbled upon what was going on, had been macho enough to witness the killing and still remain to watch the aftermath; but they hadn't. The boys' presence at the crime scene could, of course, pose a problem. The pair obviously had seen enough of Marcelo to be able to ID him, but he didn't care. He wasn't the type of man to let little things like that bother him. Besides, when you walked the streets with a reputation long enough, you became invisible. Nobody saw you, nobody knew you. That was how it was for him; he was a ghost.

Casper, the brown fucking ghost.

Marcelo turned the key in the car lock and opened the passenger door. He reached in and pulled the paper sack out and unwaded the top of it. Inside were stacks of one hundred dollar bills. He didn't count it, but from his previous experience with sleeved bills, Marcelo knew there would be something like one hundred grand in the bag.

That was all he needed to know, he'd leave the exact amount for Ferdie to sort out.

Jim Stafford's car resembled a slaughterhouse. Blood lay spattered all over the back seat and the carpet; it even dappled the headrest of the front driver's seat. The car was trashed.

Having pulled into his apartment complex Stafford now looked down at his sport coat; it was a mess, too. When the blood had spewed forward from the Reed guy onto the car seat, some of it had even landed on Stafford's forearm. And then, without thinking about it, of course, Stafford had wiped the gun off on the jacket.

Jacket, gun, car, what did he care; he had a shit load of money in a briefcase and was going to skip town. The bills, the clothes, they suddenly didn't matter. Stafford owed the bank on the car anyway, so what did that matter?

He looked a bloody mess, but in the underground parking structure it was hard to make out much of anything anyway, and Stafford chanced stepping out of his vehicle before stripping off the soiled coat. He threw it in the backseat where it couldn't further contaminate the already sodden upholstery. He looked at the briefcase now resting on the floor of the front passenger seat. Stafford would have liked to bring it upstairs with him, but that would just be tempting fate he decided. He'd be back to the car in less than an hour. It would be better to leave it there.

He closed the door and locked it with the remote control fob. Then he tested the door, just to make sure.

"Safe and secure," he noted as he stepped away from the car and glanced around the lot. It didn't appear that anyone had taken any notice; the structure was virtually empty.

Stafford stepped into the elevator and headed for the third floor. It only took a moment before the doors opened to his hallway. Being overly cautious, he glanced up and down the corridor before walking a couple of doors down to his apartment. He inserted the key and turned the knob, then he stuck his head in; he didn't hear anything. He didn't know why he should have, possibly paranoia was setting in.

"Don't get that way," he thought to himself.

The incident with Watts' brother-in-law had really gotten to him, apparently. Stafford had never killed anyone before. He hadn't thought it would be a big deal. But the brutality of the man's death had caused such a great revulsion in him that Stafford couldn't even let himself think about it.

That was over, done with, he told himself. Time to compartmentalize it.

The investigator unbuttoned his shirt and headed for the kitchen. He wanted a drink of something cold and then a shower. A nap would have been a nice touch, too, but he really couldn't afford the luxury of taking that much time, he needed to get out of town. And he still had to swing by his office to get some things. When he'd closed up shop that morning, he hadn't realized it would be his last day at work; but then, how could he?

Stafford pulled a soda from the fridge and headed for the master bedroom. After stripping down, he climbed into the shower, not even waiting for the water to warm up. He needed something to wake him. Something to get him geared up for his new life ahead. The cold water helped.


Ferdie pulled up to the curb at the Watts home. He had thought about parking down the street, but then changed his mind. He decided he would park right out front; he was done screwing around.

The place looked similar to what Ferdie had seen the morning before, in the dim early light. Ferdie exited the BMW and strode right up to the front entryway. He was going to knock, but he happened to glance at the lock and saw that it was still broken. Marcelo had really smashed it before. Actually, it wasn't that surprising it hadn't been repaired; who would be able to get a locksmith that quickly?

Ferdie grasped the knob and pushed the door open; it swung freely inward.

"Hey!" he yelled.

There was no response, no sound of any sort.

"Hey! Anybody home?"

Ferdie stepped through the entry and into the kitchen.

The room was empty. Nothing seemed amiss, just a cheesy, average American, working stiff kitchen. He moved back into the hallway and walked to the rear of the home where the master bedroom was located. It, too, was empty. On the way back down the hall Ferdie glanced in the other pair bedrooms also; one looked like an office and the other was where they had grabbed the kid from yesterday. The bed covers were still halfway off the mattress. Lastly, he pushed open the bathroom door and checked in the shower stall. Not a single person to be found. There was no one home.

"Shit, that only leaves two places," he thought. Marcelo was checking on one of the locations, so that meant Ferdie would have to check the other.

He stepped from the home and closed the front door behind him, though he knew it wouldn't latch. He used a tissue from his pocket to clean any prints from the knob. Then he turned and headed away from the house. A neighbor across the way watched Ferdie's exit from where the man stood in front of his garage. Ferdie started across the yard aiming directly toward the neighbor.

"What the fuck you want?"

The man cowered a bit, but then tried to regain some composure.

"Look buddy I'm just minding my own business," he said, trying to conceal his fear.

That was what Ferdie wanted to hear. It made him smile a little, "Damn right you are," he answered and then turned and made his way back to the BMW.

He opened the door, slid inside and started the car. He tried to picture the route to his next location. He had actually trailed Watts from the house to the place yesterday morning. Marianna's husband had gone to see a private detective guy named Stafford. Maybe Watts would still be with the dick, Ferdie thought.

Ferdie started the car and pulled away from the curb. About a block down the winding road a car came speeding by in the other direction. It caused Ferdie to swerve away a little; something that always pissed him off. He was about to give the guy the finger when, at the last minute, he noticed that the speeding car was a white Crown Victoria. There weren't any bells or whistles on it, no special antenna or even public plates, but the stiff behind the wheel looked familiar. In fact, he was sure he'd seen the man before.

Ferdie just hoped the cop hadn't seen him.


Jim Stafford was about ready to leave town. He unlocked the door to his office and trudged up the stairs. He felt a little better now, having showered, and changed out of the bloody, sweaty clothes that he had been wearing. The old clothes were now in a trash bag stuffed under the front seat of his car. He'd have to dispose of them somehow, but right now he needed to concentrate on tying up a couple of other loose ends.

Unfortunately, the stairwell up to his office was miserably hot, and Stafford began to perspire again. By the time he reached the top of the stairs he could feel the sweat running down his spine. He walked over and cranked on the window air conditioning unit.

Stafford went to the computer desk and sat down. There were a couple of files he needed to delete and one he wanted to retrieve some data from before erasing. He double clicked the mouse and "Stafford Investigations" popped up on the screen. That was going to be short lived, he thought. Today was the end of his investigation business.

Stafford worked the mouse a minute until he found the information he was looking for. The data of interest was the personal address and phone number of one Mr. Conor Howard. Stafford had worked a job for Howard about a year ago, and during the course of rendering services, it had come to light that the client had some expertise in offshore banking. Stafford had made a mental note of the fact, in case he might ever need to ferret off some ill-gotten gains one day.

Well, that day had come.

Stafford jotted the information down and then moved the mouse over to the delete button. There was now no longer any record of a connection between Conor Howard and the investigator, as best he could tell. Stafford moved to a couple of other files and deleted those also. Then there were a couple of odds and ends he wanted, but most importantly, he couldn't forget the strongbox in his bottom desk drawer. He wandered around the office a few more minutes before retrieving the box from the desk, and then he looked around. The office had its good memories, but truthfully, most of the memories weren't all that wonderful. The poverty he had experienced over the last few years had not been fun.

He turned and headed for the stairs. When he got to the front door he left it unlocked. There was always a chance somebody might come in and ransack the place.

That would be useful if he were so lucky as to have that actually happen.

Outside, Stafford placed the little safe in the trunk along with a couple of other items. The briefcase with the money inside sat over in one corner. His bags were in the trunk too, two suitcases full. He was trying to avoid putting anything in the rear seat for now. The interior was still filled with blood and the stench was becoming pretty strong. He'd need to either clean it up later, or maybe just ditch the whole car. His thirty-eight was on the floor of the rear seat too, he remembered, under some newspapers. The revolver was still covered in blood. Stafford wasn't sure if the gun was worth keeping, it was possible it might not even function any more. And he wouldn't be able to carry it on a plane anyway. But he decided to hang on to the weapon for now.

Stafford entered the car and started the engine, and then looked at his scribbling of Conor Howard's address. The man lived in Las Vegas. Out of state, that was good. Stafford liked Vegas, too; it was a good town. After Vegas, he'd probably ditch the car and take a flight to a different state. Then he'd drive across another state line and catch a flight out of the country.

But first he had to get some help from the man in Vegas. You couldn't declare $140,000 in cash on a flight abroad.

Fernando Alba had no difficulty in finding the office where he had tailed the Watts fellow to only the day before. It had a big sign out front that said "Stafford Investigations", but no dedicated parking lot. Ferdie had to park several spaces back down the street from the office front. He would have preferred to locate himself right in front of the door, but hey, he supposed they didn't know he was coming.

Now all he had to do was wait. The question was, whether he would get lucky or not. Was there really any way in hell that David Watts would once again come by the investigator's office? Probably not; but you never knew. Actually, Ferdie had a lot more confidence that Marcelo would track down Marianna over at the Espinoza place than he did in himself finding Watts here with the investigator. But like he always said, you never knew.

Ferdie had no way of even knowing if the office was occupied or not. At night you might see interior lights or something, but during the day? During the day you wouldn't know shit.

But somebody might be in there right now. Or somebody might come by. If he could just find any of those four people, Watts, Marianna, the dick or Espinoza, then maybe they would lead him to Watts or the money. Or, even better yet, Watts and the money. He owed Watts one for stiffing him at the bus stop. And that Marianna whore, he owed her big time. If he ever got his hands on that bitch again he'd make sure she never got a second chance to double cross Fernando Alba.

Ferdie left the car running because of the heat. After about a half an hour of waiting, he was becoming impatient. He had about decided on trying to enter the joint when a man exited through the lower level blacked out glass door. He was tall and wore a Hawaiian shirt and cargo shorts. He was also very Caucasian. Ferdie looked at the black door, it was hard to read, but it appeared to say the same as the large sign above it did, "Stafford Investigations."

No one else left the building after the investigator, who then climbed into a blue vehicle right out front.

"In my spot," Ferdie thought.

The blue car started and then moved into the street.

Ferdie turned the key and the BMW's motor roared to life. He pulled away from the curb and followed after the Dodge. He had to assume that the tall white guy would be the Stafford fellow. And, presumably, if he just followed the Stafford guy around a while the man would probably eventually lead him to Watts. Ferdie estimated that a kidnapping and a one hundred thousand dollar ransom warranted the man's client some attention from the investigator. Hell, if it didn't, Watts needed to fire the man and hire somebody who would actually do some work.

He just hoped the pursuit wouldn't take too long, however.

Ferdie looked at his gas gauge. He had a little over half a tank. As long as they stayed in the Los Angeles area he'd be OK.


Detective Stokes parked at the curb in front of Marianna Watts' home and went to the front door. Immediately the detective noticed something was amiss. The latch and knob of the door were askew, having apparently been impacted by some significant blunt force. The detective drew his weapon and pressed lightly against the door with his other hand; it swung open.

"Police! Anyone home?"

There was no answer.

Stokes stepped inside with his weapon still drawn in front of him. He saw nothing unusual, so he carefully moved further. He searched the house from end to end and found no one. The home showed no sign of looting or other evidence of a crime, except for a broken picture on the floor of the hallway. The only real indication that a crime might have been committed was the smashed mechanism to the front door. Stokes remembered that the Espinoza-Watts woman had said the kidnappers had taken her from in front of her home. But then she had given the wrong address and even the wrong name. Perhaps the crime had taken place here, at her real residence, and the kidnappers had broken in and taken the woman and her daughter. If that were the case, then the damaged doorknob would likely be evidence of that very occurrence.

Stokes holstered his firearm and stepped back into one of the bedrooms that appeared to have been in use as an office. The central feature of the room was an ornate mahogany desk, which the detective immediately approached. He made a cursory survey of the top before carefully opening a couple of the upper drawers and looking inside. All indications were that the desk belonged to David and Marianna Watts. All the correspondence and financial documents included their names; he certainly had the right residence. There were also check stubs from the LA Unified School district for both parties. They were obviously both employed by the same municipal department. The school district would be the next logical place for Stokes to investigate, especially for the husband.

The Detective tried to think of what else he might look for that would help him with the case. As he passed back into the kitchen Stokes noticed the framed photos on the baker's rack.

"So that's the Watts family," he thought to himself.

There was the Marianna woman's likeness and also that of her daughter Julia. There too, was a Caucasian fellow of middle age and slightly portly dimensions. That had to be the husband, David Watts. Stokes was looking forward to talking with that gentleman. His side of the events of yesterday would probably prove quite interesting.

With nothing more to see at the residence, Stokes exited the house and tried to shut the door so that it would stay closed behind him. He headed back for his unmarked cruiser, but before he got there the detective noticed a man across the street keeping an eye on him. He walked over to the individual and asked what he might know of his neighbor's whereabouts.

Stokes flipped out his badge.

"Hi there."

"Hi," said the man, squinting at the officer's identification as he approached.

"I'm investigating a possible occurrence at your neighbor's house over there," he said, nodding back in the direction from which he had just come.

"Yeah, well it's about time?"

"About time?"

"Yeah, you just missed one guy."

Just missed someone? "What do you mean?" Stokes asked.

"There was just a guy here snooping around over in the Watts' house, just like you were. He drove off just before you got here."

"It wasn't someone who lives there then?"

"Oh, no. This was some scary looking guy with tattoos. He was in the house for a few minutes and then left. But I didn't see him take anything."

"Did you call the police?"

The man got a funny look on his face and shook his head. "No. Maybe if that was the only thing, then maybe. But this morning the Watts lady and some Mexican guy…" the man paused and looked at Stokes, obviously considering whether he might be "Mexican". "Uh, you know, a darker skinned guy."

Stokes nodded his head, "Yeah, I understand. Go on."

"Well they went in the house, too. This morning. And then came out a little later. But they didn't take anything out either."

"What time was that?"

"I don't know? Maybe around ten o'clock or so," the man replied.

"And you didn't know the Mexican man?"

"Right, never seen him. But he gave me a dirty look before they drove off. The lady didn't even say anything to me. I mean I don't know her well, but you'd think she'd say something."

"What kind of car was it?"

"I don't know; green. Probably like a Japanese car, maybe a Honda, or Toyota."

Stokes had his note pad out now and was writing the information down.

"And what about this last guy? Did you know him? Was he Mexican, too?"

The man drew in his breath and shook his head a little. "Hell no, I didn't know him. He was a scary looking guy, a little tall with a whole lot of tattoos. I think he might have been Mexican. He had dark hair and kind of dark skin. Kind of like yours, maybe a little darker."

"And what kind of tattoos did he have? Anything recognizable?"

"Well I couldn't make out any certain one, he just had a whole bunch." The man now ran his hand up and down one of his arms. "He had his whole arms covered, both of them."

Suddenly the description of the individual seemed familiar. "You mean he had full sleeves?"

The neighbor looked at the detective like he was crazy. "No, no, he had short sleeves; so you could see his arms."

"OK, I understand." Stokes thought about explaining "sleeves" to the man but then thought better of it. "And what about his face, his neck, any tattoos there?"

The man thought for just a moment, "No, just the arms."

Now the description sounded really familiar. "Kind of long hair?"

"Yep."

Stokes had about all the information he needed. He asked the man for his name and phone number and jotted that down with the other items on his pad.

"OK, thanks. I might be calling you."

"Hey is everything OK? With the Watts' I mean? Like I said, I don't know the wife very well, but I've known David a couple of years; seems like a nice guy."

"So far we're just investigating," the detective replied. "I think everything's probably fine. I'll talk to the husband at work."

"Oh, he's working now?"

This surprised Stokes a little. "He doesn't work?"

"Well, off and on. But I thought he was laid off for a while."

Stokes wasn't sure how to answer that, so he lied in order to end the conversation. "Yeah, well I think he's been brought back in," he said as he walked over to the cruiser.

"Thanks for your help."

"Yeah, well I hope you catch them."

Stokes didn't know who "them" would be exactly, unless the man meant he should arrest the people who had visited the house for looking "Mexican" or something.

Stokes started the car and looked in his mirror before pulling into the road. He reached for the a/c and flipped it on. It was still pretty hot.

So Marianna had visited the house that very morning with an unidentified man, Stokes thought to himself. But they hadn't taken anything. What the hell could that possibly mean? The woman had only been released late last night. And hadn't identified herself as Watts, but as Espinoza. Francisco Espinoza lived at the address she had given as her residence. Maybe Espinoza had been the man accompanying the Watts woman this morning? Maybe not, but it seemed the most likely possibility. But why had they come to her home? And why hadn't she ID'd as Watts? She also hadn't wanted him to call her husband and let him know she was OK; she'd specifically asked him not to. So what did that mean? Did it mean that Marianna Watts didn't want her husband to know she was free? What would that get her? Could it possibly be because she wanted her husband to go through with the ransom demand? Ah, now that would be a motive; money was always high on the list of possibilities when you were looking for a motive. But how would Marianna benefit from the ransom being paid? Was she in on it? Stokes didn't think so. The woman had really seemed upset about her ordeal. And it had looked quite apparent to him that she had been legitimately held against her will. So how did it all add up? It didn't make any sense. But at least he now had a new lead.

Stokes hadn't realized it at the time; he hadn't really gotten a good look at the man's face the morning before. But the description just offered of the "scary Mexican" man at the Watts' residence was strikingly similar to that of the tattooed man Stokes had seen dropping the women off at the duplex the morning before. The guy had then left the scene with another man in the same car the whole group had arrived in. He hadn't really gotten a good look at either man. But, now that he thought about it, the description just given by Watts' neighbor and the picture in Stoke's mind of the person from the prior morning all added up to the same man; one man, in fact – Fernando Alba.


Marcelo edged his way into the Boyle Heights alley and stopped his car. He wasn't exactly sure what time it was, but it didn't really matter, there wasn't any need to hurry. He had just tried to call the boss with his cell phone, but found that the battery had died. That wasn't a problem, he'd just call Ferdie later; Ferdie was going to be really happy with him.

Marcelo bent forward and stuck his arm under the front seat. He reached around a moment and then pulled out what he was searching for, a little metal box. His kit.

The address to which he'd pulled up lay to his right. The property was a non-descript stucco bungalow. He was to the rear of it though, where the detached garage opened out into the back alley. It was better not to park on the street out front, because the guy who lived in the bungalow dealt product, and lots of traffic in and out of the place would tip off the cops; Marcelo didn't want that. He especially didn't want that because the guy was actually one of his dealers, and not the kind of dealer Marcelo would go to buy from, either. The man was the kind of dealer you sold to, a street dealer, and he was part of the Tachos' network; he was one of Ferdie's dealers.

Marcelo stepped out of his vehicle, carrying his little metal box and headed for the door. The security door in the rear fence had a large combination lock. He knew the combination by heart. He took advantage of the location frequently.

Though the man inside the house bought from Ferdie and Marcelo, Marcelo and his boss didn't actually keep drugs in their possession, at least not in street quantities, that was the dealer's job. So when Marcelo needed a fix, if he didn't have a personal stash on hand, he just came here and got some, and, of course, he got it for free. The man inside had everything you could want; uppers, downers, pot, coke, heroin, meth, you name it. But Marcelo stuck to the heroin, it was the best; it did him right. He couldn't understand the hombres who went for the uppers, especially the meth. He'd seen that shit mess people up and drag 'em down in no time. Sometimes even some of the muscle guys went in for the tweeking; it helped 'em get stoked when they needed to make a hit or something. But not Marcelo, he'd seen too many tweekers fuck shit up. They'd get so high they wouldn't even know what the fuck they were doing. No, if you needed the meth to do a man's job, then you weren't really a man in the first place. Heroin was the thing; it just kept you mellow.

And Marcelo was going to get very mellow.

Ferdie would be very appreciative when he found that his main man had secured the $100,000 from that punta Paco. He'd probably even fork up a big reward for Marcelo, like maybe five or ten G's, maybe more. It was a good day. And Marcelo had handled his affairs with aplomb; he was an excellent muscle man.

Having negotiated the security fence, Marcelo stepped up to the rear door and knocked on it. He had a smile on his face.

Today he'd go for a double load.


Ferdie tried to get Marcelo on the phone, but his call went directly to voice mail. Either the man was on his phone or he hadn't turned it on. Or then again, there was the possibility that Marcelo's battery had died; the cheap, disposable phones that they used didn't hold a charge very long. Ferdie always lamented that in order for his calls to be untraceable he had to use such a piece of crap phone. He also owned one of those nice ones, with internet and all, but it seemed like he hardly ever got to use that one.

They had been heading west on the I-10, until
Stafford, with Ferdie tailing him, had turned off at the
Pomona exit. Ferdie's fuel reserve was running pretty low
and he didn't know how much longer he'd be able to keep
the pursuit up, even if he wanted to. They were going to
be heading into the boonies soon. Where the hell was the
guy going anyway? Watts wouldn't be somewhere out
here, would he? Ferdie was pissed he couldn't contact
Marcelo, it sure would have been nice to know if his man
had found Marianna, or at least Paco the taco, maybe then
he wouldn't have to continue following the idiot detective
guy all over creation.

They came to a traffic light and Ferdie got caught
behind another vehicle that wouldn't run through on the
yellow. Stafford made it through the light, but not him.

"Shit."

That was the problem with trying to follow someone
through the city streets. You stay too close and they make
you as a tail, too far back and you get separated in the
traffic. It had been easy out on the highway, hell, you
could stay a quarter of a mile back there, but here, in the
traffic, it was a pain in the ass. But just as Ferdie was
ruing his luck, he saw that he would get a break.
Stafford's Charger slowed about a block ahead of the
light and turned off into a gas station.

"Hell yeah," that was what he needed. Ferdie could
catch up and even pull in and get some gas, too. That was
perfect. Ferdie might even walk right up to the man and
converse a little, maybe. The cracker wouldn't recognize
him; he had no reason to.

The light changed and Ferdie drove ahead before
pulling the BMW into the same gas station. He was about
to choose the pump right next to Stafford, but at the last

minute decided it would be better not to give the investigator such a close look, not just yet. He might need to approach the man later when Stafford contacted Watts, if he contacted Watts that was.

Ferdie stopped at another set of pumps. He got out and stuck a platinum card in one of the machines, then punched in his zip code. He went for the premium grade. He glanced around a little. The station was pretty new, clean. Ferdie scanned the sky for any sign of a cloud, but there was none. It was even hotter, too.

"Fuckin' Pomona."

Why were they in Pomona? Ferdie had his guesses. But a new possibility had recently begun fomenting for Ferdie, which could answer some of his questions. Maybe the reason Watts hadn't shown up for the ransom drop was because the man had gotten a clue and had now gone on the run. Either he alone, or in conjunction with Marianna, hell, even possibly with the investigator, had the money and was fleeing the area. Fleeing before Ferdie could find them. That certainly would explain Watts' disappearance and the fact that Ferdie still didn't have his money.

Ferdie glanced over at the Stafford fellow. He was still filling his tank at the pump, he looked a little nervous though. It would have been fun to rap a little with the guy. Oh well, maybe he could toy with him later. For now he'd just get gas.

Then follow the pendejo to wherever the hell it was he was going.

Detective Stokes sat in his cruiser considering the description of the perp at the Watts house when his cell phone rang.

He picked it up and pushed the "talk" button.

"Yeah, Stokes."

"Stokes, it's me."

The detective hated when people did that, like everybody was your best friend. At least this time he recognized Evans' voice.

"Evans?"

"Yeah. Hey, we got the warrant."

"That was fast."

"Yeah, well I convinced the judge there was a probability of flight, maybe ongoing criminal conduct, you know. I'm heading over there right now. Thibeut's rounding up a team, too. You going to be able to make it?"

Stokes thought a moment. "Yeah, yeah, I want to be there. Where is it again?"

"Forty-third Street, just north of Vernon. We're going to coordinate with Newton Division on it. "

Evans was referring to the other Central Bureau Division in charge of the southern downtown area. "Yeah, I'll head right over. What's the address?"

Evans gave him the particulars and then said he had to go.

Just as Stokes put the phone down his radio crackled with a man down alert. This one was in Griffith Park, near the observatory. It was stacking up to be a bloody day. Stokes had already heard reports of shootings in East LA and one in Watts. Now even the parks were getting into the act. And who knew what might come of the Vernon Avenue situation? When they had tried to get these guys before, at the duplex, they ended up with two stiffs on their hands. Stokes just hoped this time one of the stiffs wouldn't be a cop.

Julia Watts looked out the rear door of the strange house she was in. There was a whole bunch of flashing lights outside. She wanted to go out and see what was going on, but she wasn't sure if she should.

Her Uncle Paco had told her to wait for him until he came back. But that was before; before that other man had come and talked to her Uncle and scared him away. Then the man had made really loud banging noises with his gun. That seemed like a long time ago though. Julia wished her Uncle would come back, but since the other man had come and gone Julia had not seen her Uncle Paco again. She was scared and wanted her Mommy. Julia's Uncle was supposed to take her to her mother, but now that he had run away, Julia didn't know how she was ever going to get to see her. Maybe her mother would come get her soon. But what if her mother didn't know how to get to Julia? Maybe her father would find her. But Julia didn't think her Daddy would know where Uncle Paco's house was, either. Maybe no one would find her.

She could be all alone, forever.

But then there were the lights. Julia knew she wasn't supposed to go outside. But the lights were pretty and the men walking around were dressed special, and they looked like they were nice.

Besides it was scary being in the house all alone.

Detective Stokes pulled onto the street to where Evans had directed. He immediately saw a couple of black and whites, along with several other official vehicles. Down the road, apparently on the other side of the subject residence, he could also see a tactical unit vehicle. It was one of those large command center vehicles, and a SWAT team was exiting from it for the near side of the street.

As Stokes edged to the curb a paddy wagon pulled in behind him. At the other end of the street a squad car blocked the road and another black and white was, even now, backing past Stokes' cruiser to block the entrance on this end. It was a big operation. Evans wasn't going to be in charge this time. Neither would Stokes, of course. Since it was an inter-divisional operation there would be an inter-departmental command, even over Thibeut's head, probably someone from Central Bureau.

Stokes exited his vehicle and walked along the near side of the street, so as to remain out of view of the subject residence. Though he figured that, by now, the police presence surely must have been spotted by whoever was inside the target building. If it hadn't, then the guys inside were brain dead or half asleep.

The possibility of who might be inside ran through Stokes' imagination. Surely, this time, the young women they were looking to help would be in there. And the bad guys; how many of them would there be? Was it going to be the same cast of characters that they usually caught trafficking women? Not that you could always predict with certainty who the traffickers might be. Often enough these things were south of the border operations, but it wasn't unknown to find eastern European or even Russian mob types moving women in and out of the country. Poor kids from the Balkans or the Ural steppes seeking a new life in America were just as lost upon reaching the States as young Mexican women were, maybe even more so. There were plenty of lost kids, of all types, to go around.

So, from a criminal standpoint, whatever nationality, or ethnicity, the perps inside happened to be, wasn't really of any consequence. Just so long as they were caught and taken off the street, that was all that mattered.

But, from a personal standpoint, there was one intriguing possibility for Stokes, of one particular criminal that might be inside. A possibility he actually held out hope for. There was a chance that a certain old nemesis of his might be within the surrounded house. The man seemed to somehow be involved in all this mess. Stokes had had run-ins with the guy several times before when Stokes was still in the Narcotics Division. But the department had never been able to get anything to stick. And now, apparently, the crook was somehow involved in the current kidnapping scheme. But had Stokes identified the correct man? The criminal could have changed his appearance in the years since Stokes had last seen him. After all, there were quite a few people running around with full sleeve arm tattoos, but when you added in the long hair, tall, muscular build and absence of facial tattoos, that narrowed the field. And a man looking like that had dropped the Watts woman and her daughter off at the duplex, Stokes had seen him, though at the time it hadn't registered. And then another man of that description, possibly the same man, had visited the Watts' home, too. Both men fit the description of the drug dealer that had eluded him once before, Fernando "Ferdie" Alba.

The problem was, there didn't seem to be any direct tie-in between the kidnapping at the one duplex and the trafficking occurring at the duplex right next door. Could they be unrelated? It was beginning to seem as if maybe they were dealing with two different events, two different crimes. So maybe even though Alba might be involved somehow, Stokes wasn't certain that Alba was going to be mixed up with the human trafficking. If he were, it would be the first time that Stokes knew of, the man had ventured into that particular criminal endeavor. Of course, kidnapping would be a new gig for Alba, too. So, either way, it really didn't add up. Then maybe Stokes was wrong. Maybe the guy with the sleeve tattoos wasn't Alba; but the evidence was starting to point that way.

The detective looked at his watch; it read 4:57PM. Less than twenty-four hours since the shootings at the duplex and they had already tracked and encircled the suspects at their next location. That was pretty good.

"Now if that Alba character would just show up here," thought Stokes. Then it would really be good.

Jim Stafford was a little tired, but he was less than an hour out of Vegas and things were starting to look up. He'd made the trip without any hitches so far and he would soon be passing out of the state of California for Nevada. Crossing a state line was an added level of paperwork that authorities would have to surmount should they just happen to be in pursuit. Stafford just needed to keep changing locations faster than the LAPD could do the footwork to follow. Once he, and his money, were far enough away, the tracking would become all but impossible. He could disappear to the Caribbean or somewhere similar for a while, maybe even change his identity and return to the states after things cooled down, there were a lot of possibilities.

But the first thing he needed to take care of when he got to Las Vegas was to ditch his car somehow. Stafford had thought about it; there just wasn't any easy way to clean the blood from the upholstery, at least not to a level so as to be inconspicuous. The car had to go. Then he needed to track down Howard and get some of the money into an untraceable offshore account. After that, he would get out of Vegas, maybe head for Denver and catch a plane to the East Coast. Then he could think about heading out of the country.

Stafford smiled; hell, he even had a passport already, which he kept in the little strong box.

Things were working out. Now if he could just get the image of Harold Reed's face out of his head.

It was now obvious to Ferdie where the investigator guy was headed. He was quickly closing in on Las Vegas; they were, in fact, almost to the Nevada state line. Ferdie didn't think the guy had spotted him yet; he was tailing the man at a pretty good distance, so that wasn't a problem. However, Ferdie was getting hungry, it was nearing dinnertime and he hated when work interfered with his eating arrangements. Fortunately, they would be in Vegas shortly and he could dine there. But he would need to finish up with Stafford and Watts before he could go ahead and satiate his appetite. He'd need to take care of business as soon as possible upon reaching the desert town.

Ferdie was mulling this over, when a sudden puff of smoke from well up ahead caught his eye. The sight came accompanied by a low muffled bang. Over the top of the car in front of him Ferdie saw a big rig in the center lane swing to the right about a quarter mile away. Stafford's blue Charger just happened to be in the other lane as the truck swung in, and the car had to swerve off the road a little to avoid the semi. The tractor-trailer immediately began to slow and pulled off the highway onto the shoulder. Stafford's Charger, however, and another car that pulled a similar maneuver, continued on down the road, albeit at a somewhat reduced pace.

"Fuck that would have been funny," Ferdie said aloud. If the guy would have t-boned the truck it might have taken the man's head right off.

Ferdie passed the semi on the side of road and followed on after Stafford, though he had to reduce his speed a little so as not to run up on the Dodge. Funny thing was, Ferdie seemed to keep gaining on the car no matter how much he slowed his pace. After about a mile of this he was barely doing forty when the blue car up ahead pulled to the side of the road and came to a stop on the shoulder. Ferdie didn't know what to do, except to pull over himself and see what happened. So he eased his own car onto the shoulder of the highway.

Ahead, the door of the Charger opened and Stafford got out. He walked around the hood and looked down at the front passenger side tire. Ferdie hadn't come to a complete stop yet and he decided to continue on, to edge the BMW forward a little. The investigator bent down for a moment and then stood back up. He went back to the

driver's side and stuck his head in and popped the trunk.
As he walked to the rear of the car the man was now
facing in Ferdie's direction and he frowned upon seeing
the dark sedan coming has way. Ferdie sped up a little and
closed the final tenth of a mile and stopped the car.

"Hey I saw what happened!" he yelled, sticking his
head out the window.

Stafford put his palm up in the air as if to signal "no
thanks", but that wasn't the answer to his greeting that
Ferdie was looking for, so he ignored it. Ferdie stepped
from the car and approached.

"I saw what happened, you OK?"

"Yeah, I'm fine. Thanks. I don't need any help,"
Stafford replied, trying to dismiss the overly helpful man.

But Ferdie pressed on, "What seems to be the
problem?"

"Oh, nothing. It's just the front tire. But I've got a
spare, it's no problem."

Ferdie was right up to the trunk now. He glanced into
it; there were a couple of suitcases, a spare tire, a little
metal box and a large briefcase.

"On your way to vacation and you get a break down.
That sucks man. You going to do some gambling?"

Now Stafford began to look angry. "Look buddy I
don't need any help, hear? I'll be fine."

Ferdie just stood there.

Stafford lost it. "Look asshole, if you don't get out of
here I'm going to have to do something that I might
regret! You understand?"

Ferdie considered that a moment. The man was a
little bigger than himself, he might not win a fight with
the guy, and what's more, he had foolishly left his pistol
in the BMW. But Ferdie wasn't one to back down; he was

fairly strong for his size, and younger than the man in front of him, so he invented something.

Without warning Ferdie's right fist swung at the bigger man's jaw and connected. The man, knocked off balance, fell back into the trunk of the car. Ferdie grabbed the trunk lid and swung it violently downward. It impacted Stafford somewhere on the top of the head. The second swing landed just below the knees where the private eye's legs still stuck out from the rear of the car.

Stafford bellowed and Ferdie quickly repeated the procedure. The investigator was trying to pull his weight back up over the trunk lip but Ferdie fought to keep him from gaining such an advantage. There wasn't much for the man to grasp a hold of, and after slamming the trunk lid on Stafford for a fifth time, Ferdie grabbed the man's legs and lifted them up and over the rear lip. This time when he closed the trunk, it swung all the way down and latched.

"Shit."

Ferdie glanced around quickly to see if anyone had witnessed what had transpired. But no one had pulled over. If someone had seen, they hadn't stopped. And that was all that really mattered.

Suddenly, the trunk lid popped open and the Stafford man rose up from the interior. Ferdie was at first caught off guard, but he quickly recovered and grabbed the lid, slamming it down once again on the man. It hit Stafford squarely on top of the head this time and Ferdie pushed down hard on the lid. The man had an arm out now, however. Stafford grabbed for the rear bumper area as Ferdie continued to thwack him on the head. Ferdie also balled up his fist again and punched the man's wrist as hard as he could. The hand let go of its grasp and Ferdie shoved the arm back inside while simultaneously pushing the trunk closed. It latched again.

Ferdie realized, however, that it would only take a moment for Stafford to find the emergency trunk release again.

"What a crappy invention," thought Ferdie. It certainly wasn't helpful for people in his line of work.

He had a dilemma. How was he going to keep Stafford in the trunk? If he had a gun he could just shoot through the lid and shut the guy up. But the gun was in his car behind him and Stafford would probably pop out before Ferdie would be able to retrieve it from that far away anyhow.

Ferdie tried a different approach.

"Look asshole, don't unlock that thing again or I'll kill you," he yelled at the man in the car.

There was a fumbling sound from inside the trunk and then the lid started to rise again. Ferdie hit it with all his weight and it closed once more.

"God Damn it! I've got a gun. So help me, if you fucking pop your head out of there again I'm gonna blow it off!"

This time there was no commotion from inside. Ferdie waited a second or two to be sure and then made for the BMW. He opened the door and slid into the driver's seat before reaching over and opening the glove box. He retrieved his 9mm pistol from under the registration and exited the car, leaving the door open so Stafford wouldn't hear it shut.

As he returned to the front vehicle Ferdie saw that the trunk lid had remained closed. That pretty well sealed the man's fate. Now Ferdie was armed, he had the upper hand.

But what about Watts? He hadn't planned on assaulting the guy on the side of the highway, but the man's flat tire had forced the situation. And now it was doubtful whether Stafford would carelessly lead him to the Watts fellow. That just wouldn't happen, he decided. So Ferdie needed to get some answers as to where the money was. Hell, maybe Stafford had it with him.

"So, where's Watts?" he yelled, trying to overcome not only the trunk lid, but also the traffic passing by.

"Who?" came the muffled reply.

"Don't fuck with me. David Watts! He hired you!"

"I don't know who you're talking about."

Ferdie suddenly realized he wasn't being cautious enough and he stepped back from the vehicle. It dawned on him that there was a possibility that the investigator might keep a firearm in his trunk. If so, he could maybe locate Ferdie's voice and pop a shot off through the lid at him. He decided to take a quick look inside the passenger compartment and see if there might be a bag of money up there, besides that would place him out of any possible line of fire while he thought for a moment.

Ferdie stuck the handgun under his shirt and moved beside the vehicle. He was astonished by what he saw inside. The interior of the car was a bloody mess. He opened the driver's door and leaned in. The top of the driver's front seat had blood spatter all over it and the rear seat and floor area were absolutely covered by the dark red coloring. Some of it even appeared to still be wet.

"What the fuck?"

Ferdie looked around the interior, but there wasn't much of note within the passenger area, just a few papers on the rear floor, sopping up the blood. What the hell had happened in there? Ferdie thought a moment, but then answered his own question; somebody had gotten the shit blown out of them is what had happened. But who? Actually, that was an easy question, too; the "who" would obviously be David Watts. Stafford had killed the man and taken the money. That was the most likely scenario. So where was the money? Stafford would have it with him, especially if he was running, and it certainly appeared as if the man was doing just that. Then Ferdie remembered his short look at the contents of the car's trunk. There had been a briefcase in there, a sort of large briefcase, large enough to hold $120,000; that was where the money would be.

Ferdie climbed out of the car and headed for the rear of the vehicle. He still wasn't sure if the man inside the trunk had a weapon or not, but in a moment it wouldn't matter.

"You got the money in there with you?" he shouted.

There was a pause before the confined man answered.

"Who the fuck are you?"

Ferdie laughed to himself, he pictured the helpless man in the trunk. The guy hadn't even asked "What money?" Stupid punta.

The money would be there.

Ferdie estimated the car's gas tank was most likely going to be right under where Stafford was lying. He didn't want to puncture it if he could help it. In the movies when somebody shot an automobile gas tank the car always blew up, real big too. But in real life, Ferdie knew from experience, that didn't really happen, at least not usually anyway.

But, there was no reason to take an unnecessary risk, so Ferdie opted for a different angle on the job in front of him. He pulled the pistol from under his shirt. He didn't have the key to the trunk so he would have to get Stafford to open it for him. The man probably wanted out anyway, he would oblige.

"OK, listen. I'm going to let you out of there. But I need you to do just exactly as I tell you, OK?"

"Yeah, yeah. OK," the investigator answered from inside.

"Good. Now unlatch the trunk and open it. But just a little, I want you to come out real, real slow. Got it?"

"Yeah."

"OK. Do it."

Ferdie heard the same sort of fumbling sound as before, and then there came a quiet click. The trunk lid lifted ever so slightly and Ferdie moved forward and placed his left hand on top of it. When the lid had opened about six inches Fernando stuck the business end of the 9mm into the opening and fired. A sudden force impacted the trunk lid upward, but it was only momentary, and Ferdie had no problem keeping the lid from flying up. Then he fired three more times. He tried to aim for the upper torso, but it was all just guesswork. After a brief pause Ferdie carefully lifted the lid up and looked inside. The Stafford man was lying there, squashed around the spare tire and suitcases; he was looking at Ferdie but seemed to be barely alive. There were large patches of blood on his upper body and it looked like a chunk had been taken out of one of his cheeks, too. The Tachos boss put the gun to within about a foot of the man's forehead and pulled the trigger a final time.

The briefcase was in the back corner of the trunk and Ferdie carefully reached over Stafford's dead body to retrieve it. He closed the trunk and wiped the top of the lid with his shirttail. Ferdie then moved around to the driver's door handle and removed any possible prints there, too. As he headed back to his own vehicle he was pleased to see that no one had pulled over to offer assistance as yet. He climbed in the BMW and set the case in the passenger seat. There were a couple of small spots of blood on the top of the case and Ferdie grabbed a tissue from one of those little travel packs that he kept in the car. He carefully wiped the spots off and then cracked the door open and disposed of the evidence onto the freeway. Then he turned his attention back to the case.

There was a pop latch on the front of the briefcase and Ferdie flipped it over with his thumb. The case sprung open. He lifted the lid further, revealing the contents.

And just like that, Ferdie had solved his problem. The case was filled with sleeved stacks of one hundred dollar bills.

He closed the container and started the car's engine. Before pulling out on to the interstate, he placed the pistol back inside the glove compartment and then quickly looked around for any sign that some one might have observed what had just occurred. But it was clear that there just wasn't anyone who could possibly have paid any attention. They were in the middle of the desert and the vehicles on the highway were flying by at over seventy-five miles an hour. Nobody had seen anything.

Ferdie waited for a break in the traffic and then pulled out around the blue Charger and on to the highway. He pushed hard on the accelerator; it was late and he was in a hurry.

There was a meal waiting for him in Vegas.

By 5:30PM they were ready to go.

Stokes and Evans looked on from across the street as the armored tactical team took up positions to enter the target residence, just north of Vernon Avenue. Mendez and Wystrom were also there, about a half block west of Stokes' position. They were all there, not only in support of the LAPD Newton Division, but also in hopes of nailing the leaders of the prostitution operation that had caused the death of their fellow officer, Lourdes Garcia. Of course, they were also concerned with saving a group of young women from a terrible life on the streets, but that would be icing on the cake compared to catching those responsible for Garcia's death.

The detectives watched as six heavily armored SWAT officers approached the front door of the residence. About a dozen others of the team moved in, tightening their perimeter ring around the building. One of the officers at the front door carried a large metal battering ram. As the team at the front sidled up to the door an explosion echoed from the rear of the structure. Stokes could see a group of SWAT officers out back and realized they had probably deployed a flash-bang grenade to distract the occupants of the house toward the rear of the home. Upon hearing the grenade from the other side of the house the officer with the battering ram stepped in front of the home's entryway along with another officer, and the two wielded the battering ram in unison against the front door. It only took one swing and the portico immediately caved inward. The two officers with the ram stepped back and two other SWAT members rushed in through the opening. This was accompanied by shouts of "Police! Put your hands up!"

At first there was no reply or sound of any type, but then screaming could be heard from inside the building, followed by popping noises. The first shots sounded like pistol fire, then the unmistakable chirping of the SWAT's AR-15 automatic rifles echoed through the afternoon heat, followed by more screaming from within. Had the shouting been of a deeper timbre, like what might have resulted from the perps being hit, then Stokes wouldn't have minded. But the screams were high pitched, and unfortunately, they were almost undoubtedly coming from the women being held inside.

"Damn! Are they shooting the girls?" Stokes yelled, knowing no one could possibly have an answer to his question.

Stokes and Evans had now edged out from their position of relative safety behind a parked vehicle and had begun to move across the street.

"I don't know, but they better secure that building in a hurry or there won't be anyone left alive in there for us to save," replied Evans.

Around them the other detectives and uniformed officers had automatically moved forward also, heedless of their personal safety, given what seemed to be transpiring inside the building in front of them. Stokes looked upward to the second story windows to see if he could make out what might be happening inside that part of the house. Motion could definitely be seen in one of the rooms. Stokes turned and looked back at the roofline of the homes behind where they had just stood across the street. Sure enough, on top of one of the houses two snipers were poised, their rifles aimed at the second story windows of the target property.

"Maybe the girls are upstairs! The snipers don't seem to be firing at the second story."

Just as Stokes got this statement out, a second floor window opened and a head of long dark hair pushed its way out and onto the steeply sloped porch roof. Quickly enough, a body appeared behind the head, and the complete form of a teenage girl exited the window. The young woman's hands were out in front of her, but they didn't hold, and she began to slide forward down the metal sheathing. Stokes broke into a run and headed into the front yard of the house. Unfortunately, he arrived just a moment late. The young woman hit the end of the roofline and her arms buckled before she pitched over the edge face first. She then flipped over feet outward, with her face toward the sky. Stokes just managed to get a slight touch of the girl's ankle before she landed flat on her back on the ground. Fortunately her momentum had carried her just past the home's concrete footwork and she landed in the yard. The young woman's arm, however, caught behind her when she landed and the cracking noise could be heard even above the continuing gunfire from inside the house.

Stokes had just started to reach down to lift the girl and carry her to safety when he saw that another head of long dark hair had made its way out of the window and onto the porch roof.

"Turn around! Don't come out head first!" he yelled.

"You catch that one, I've got the one on the ground!" It was Evans, he too had seen what was happening and had only been steps behind his fellow detective.

Evans reached down and swiftly lifted the young woman from the grass. The girl's arm flopped beside her, but she made no sound of protest as Evans threw her over his shoulder and carried her off.

Stokes only saw this out of the corner of his eye however, as he was now focused on the next girl who was careening down the roof toward him. This time he was in position and when the young woman slid directly off the roof without flipping he caught her on his shoulder, the two of them falling backward onto the ground.

Upstairs, the screaming continued and more shots rang out from inside, as the glass from one of the other upper windows shattered and slid down the porch covering.

The young woman who had just landed on Stokes jumped up and a uniformed officer grabbed her by the arm, quickly leading her away.

"De pie primera! De pie primera!"

Stokes rose to his feet and found Mendez next to him yelling toward the girls still exiting the upper window.

Two more were working their way downward, the first, a shorthaired girl, simply flopped over the edge and into Mendez's arms. Stokes was about to reach for the second child, but another uniformed officer beat him to it. Another girl quickly appeared out the window, and this time the youngster came down feet first and was able to better control her descent. When she came to the edge she pushed off and landed right in Stokes' arms.

Four more young women exited in like manner, all caught by an increasingly large group of officers. All totaled, nine girls took their chances escaping via the porch roof. All appeared to be pre to early teens, and all appeared very relieved to be out of the house. When no more women came to the window, Stokes and the other officers retreated back across the street.

The shooting soon ended however, even before the group reached the cover of the parked vehicles. Suddenly everything became quiet. The screaming had ceased with the exit of the young women from the second story window. Stokes hoped that the screams had simply been the result of fear on the girls' part, and not as a result of actual wounds received. But who knew what sort of casualty mess might be inside. It would probably be a while before the actual results of the melee became known.

One of the SWAT officers appeared at the front door and motioned for two more of the team to enter the building. Shortly after that, the ambulance crews, ready just down the block, were called into the residence.

Stokes could feel the adrenaline still pumping through his body. He tried to calm himself a little. The worst of the action seemed to be over and he needed to bring himself back down.

Just to their east, Stokes saw that Detective Mendez was still with the group of young girls, speaking with them in Spanish, trying to calm them. There were also several female officers attending similarly to the group. One of the SWAT team checked on the young women and Stokes saw that Mendez got a word with him.

The detective was probably still concerned about what might have occurred inside the home.

"I'm going to check with Mendez, see if he might have heard about what happened inside." Evans still stood with him on the sidewalk across the street. Evans looked a little shaken from the excitement, but he had responded well, they all had. "Good job, by the way."

Evans smiled, "Yeah, you too." Then he let out a slight laugh, " I'm just glad it was you that caught that big kid."

Evans was kidding with him; the girl that had knocked Stokes over couldn't have weighed more than ninety pounds. It was actually the velocity with which the child had hit him that knocked him over, not the girl's weight.

"Good thing it was me she hit and not you buddy," he replied as he left from the curb.

Detective Stokes made his way over to where Mendez stood, just down the street. The girls were being bundled into a paddy wagon for safe keeping, except for the one young woman with the broken arm, who was getting an ambulance ride directly to the hospital.

"So what's pie primavera mean?"

Mendez turned and saw that it was Stokes addressing him, and then he laughed.

"De pie primera? It means feet first, like you were yelling at them."

"Oh, OK," replied Stokes. "Yeah, that's what I was trying to yell to them. They were flying out of there fast enough to break their necks."

"Yeah, well you need to improve your Spanish man, aren't you like half Mexican yourself."

"One quarter."

"Well you should learn it better," Mendez replied. "But, hey I can't fault you on springing into the action there, that was pretty brave, even if your kid catching skills could use a little work. I mean you missed the first one completely and then the other one knocks you over."

Stokes was going to have a hard time living the kid catching thing down. But at least it was all in good humor and for a good cause at that.

"So I saw you talking to the SWAT guy. Did he give you the head's up on what happened inside?"

Stokes assumed the news couldn't have been too bad; Mendez seemed to be in a pretty light mood. "Did all the girls get out?"

"Yeah, your kid catching skills actually saved the day. That was all of them, the only injury was that first girl's fall."

"What about our guys?"

Mendez went on to explain that none of the officers had received any serious injuries. Inside, they had encountered four armed men. One of the perps had been killed and two of the others were wounded, the last guy surrendered in one of the upstairs bedrooms.

"Do you know Ferdinand Alba? Goes by Ferdie on the street."

Mendez shook his head, "No. Why?"

"Ah, it may be nothing."

Stokes looked at the blank reaction of the other detective and realized he had to finish the thought.

"He's a drug dealer I ran into back in Narcotics. It's just that I thought he may have been one of the men that had been involved in Garcia's shooting at the duplexes."

Mendez's eyebrows raised at the mention of a connection to officer Garcia's death.

"He's hard to miss. Good-looking guy, kind of clean cut except for some long hair, well spoken. But then he's got these full sleeve tattoos, which are out of character. No other tats though, just the sleeves."

"Doesn't sound familiar. You think he might be in the house?"

"I don't know. There's a possibility."

Stoke's cell phone rang in his pocket. He didn't really want to remove his attention from the situation at hand, but he looked to see who was calling. The number was from the Hollenbeck Homicide Department, so he decided to take it.

"Hang on," he said to Mendez.

"That's OK, I got to go. I'll catch up with you back at the station," the other detective replied.

Stokes put his hand up to signal goodbye as he answered the phone.

"Stokes."

"Uh, hey Stokes. This is Detective Padron. I interviewed you about the Garcia shooting."

Detective Padron had debriefed Stokes regarding the deaths at the duplexes only earlier that morning.

"Yeah. Padron." Stokes didn't really want to talk to the man at the moment. "I'm over here at the 43rd Street bust, all hell's broken out over here. Can I call you back in a little while?"

"No, can't do that Stokes. I'll be off duty in fifteen minutes."

"Well, what can I help you with? Can you make it quick?" Stokes thought he had answered pretty much any question the detective could have needed.

"Yeah, just trying to do you a favor man," Padron answered.

"OK. What's that?"

"Didn't you say you were looking for some Espinoza woman, the one who had been kidnapped and held at the Garcia shootout location?"

"Yeah. You found her?" That would certainly be good news, but with Padron being in homicide, an ID from him could easily mean that a body had been found instead of a live person.

"No, not her. But I've got a stiff report from the County Sheriff of an Espinoza, a Francisco Espinoza, over in East LA. Looks like a hit. Just thought you might be interested."

Stokes had somewhat put the Espinoza name on the back burner in favor of the Watts name. Besides, there could be any number of Espinozas in the greater Los Angeles area. But he had an idea on how he might qualify the lead.

"What's the stiff's address?" he asked.

Padron's answer to the address question definitely qualified it for him.



David Watts stared at the ceiling of the Intensive Care Unit at Los Angeles Doctor's Hospital. It was pale green and filled with fluorescent lights. David tried to raise his head to take in his other surroundings but simply couldn't. He'd already found that he couldn't speak, not one word. Only moments before, an ER technician had informed the doctor that the patient on the gurney had suffered a heart attack, which had then precipitated a massive stroke. David had tried to communicate with either of the individuals, but no sound had escaped from his mouth, neither was he able to lift his hand to gather their attention. He was in a sorry state.

The initial pain of the heart attack had been overwhelming, but now he just felt numb. David wasn't sure if that was from some medication he had been given or was simply the result of the stroke debilitating his nervous system. It didn't matter; for him, it seemed the rightfully painless manner in which one would begin to slide from this life into the next.

That was OK. The only thing that hampered his thoughts was the chaos of the situation he would be leaving behind. What would happen to Marianna and Julia? Would his brother-in-law and the investigator be able to make the ransom delivery? Why had Stafford wanted the empty briefcase? Would the fact that they were $20,000 short of the ransom amount doom the girls to death? And where had the money in the bank account gone? Was his wife an accomplice in the kidnapping the whole time? Somebody would surely take care of the situation. Wouldn't they?

"Just relax now. Everything will be all right." The voice floated in from the firmament.

And quickly, his troubles did seem to ease away. All would be fine. The situation on earth would take care of its self. Loving warmth came over him.

David Watts would have no more worries.

As Detective Stokes made his way east on Whittier he realized he was in a very positive mood. With the rescue of the young girls from the prostitution ring, something good had finally happened. Actually at this point it was still an alleged prostitution ring, but none-the-less the girls were assuredly happy to be out of the clutches of whatever had been transpiring in that house. It had been a good end to the day. The day before had been just the opposite, full of mishaps. First Detective Garcia's death, then the failure to secure any prostitution rescue at the duplex and then finally the Watts woman's strange attempt to disguise her identity. It had seemed as if even the small success of rescuing the woman and child had all been for naught. But the rescue of the young women at the Vernon location, if not completely making up for the terrible events of yesterday, at least made Stokes feel that there still existed some righteousness in the world, that the efforts of he and his fellow officers were making some difference.

The I-210 overpass came into view and Stokes began to look for the turn-off for the Espinoza residence. The fire hydrant that had been open earlier was now shut off and not a trace of evidence was left of the pool of water that had earlier sat in the street. The wind and heat had sucked every bit of moisture back into the atmosphere.

As Stokes turned left onto the subject street he immediately caught sight of the LA Sheriff's Department cars ahead of him. Two were parked out front of the Espinoza residence. The detective found a spot along the curb just past the patrol cars. Across the way Stokes noticed a couple of the youths he had seen earlier in the day. The kid who had done most of the talking earlier was not among them, however. When the detective exited his vehicle a couple of the kids turned to one another, obviously recognizing the officer from his earlier trip to the residence.

Stokes made his way back around the row houses as had done before. At the edge of the alleyway, where it met the rear parking lot, a body was being tagged and placed in a bag by the Coroner's Department.

"Whoa! Wait a minute," Stokes shouted, as he jogged back toward the activity.

The two men in the coroner's outfits paused and looked up at him, while a plain clothed detective stepped forward.

"Detective Stokes, LAPD Vice," Stokes said to identify himself. "I just want to get a look at the stiff for an ID."

"No problem detective. Happy to oblige," the plain clothed officer replied.

The body was already in the bag, but it had not been zipped up yet. One of the technicians pulled the bag wide for Stokes to get a good look. He glanced up at the LAPD detective and addressed him.

"Anybody you know?"

Stokes looked at the cadaver's face; it was completely unfamiliar.

"How'd he die?"

"Three bullet wounds to the back. Probably bled to death within a matter of a minute," responded the sheriff's detective. "Looks like a hit, maybe gang related. He still had his wallet in his pocket. Cash, ID; it's all there."

So the Espinoza character, who lived at the residence that the Watts woman had given him, was dead. Murdered in fact. Could Marianna Watt's have done it, Stokes wondered?

"Did you check inside the residence?"

"Not yet. We're just getting ready to go in there."

Suddenly Stokes remembered about the little girl. If Marianna had been the one who killed the Espinoza fellow, then the girl would be gone. But if she wasn't …

"Hey, do you mind if I accompany you inside? I have a missing persons on a woman who gave this address and also her little girl. I have reason to believe either of them might actually be inside."

"Sure, be my guest." The sheriff's man held his arm out toward the rear of the row house residence. "Found the key to the house in his pocket. Frank's about to try the rear door now." The plain clothed officer turned in that direction and yelled. "Hey Frank!"

A tall uniformed officer looked toward them.

"This LAPD wants a look inside with you!"

The officer hunched his shoulders up, "OK. Whatever."

"You done here detective?" asked one of the coroner's technicians.

"Oh, sorry. Yeah, go ahead … I'm done."

The man who had asked the question nodded to the other technician at the foot of the corpse. The man then threaded the zipper together before pulling it upward and enclosing the body of Francisco Espinoza.

Stokes made his way over to the rear of the residence. As he passed a green Honda parked out back he noticed a set of car keys dangling from the passenger side lock. Beside the car a suitcase and a duffel bag also sat open.

"Is this the dead guy's vehicle?" he asked the tall officer; the one the other detective had called "Frank".

"Yeah. Those are just car keys. Don't touch 'em. We found a separate house key on the body."

Frank stepped up to the rear doorway. "You ready to go?"

"Yeah, sure," answered Stokes.

The officer pounded on the door with his fist. "Anybody home!" He paused a moment and repeated the procedure, this time adding, "Police!"

Then the officer tried the door handle. He turned the knob and the door opened; it wasn't even locked. The officer gave a nod of his head for Stokes to follow him in, and then opened the door.

The rear doorway opened into the kitchen. The room was a little messy, but nothing seemed out of the ordinary. At least no burner was on like there had been when they entered the duplex the previous day. The two officers moved to the front room and found it empty. A stairway ran upstairs out of the front living room.

Stokes looked around the room to see if there might be anywhere a child might hide, but he didn't spot any likely locations.

"Marianna! Julia! It's Detective Stokes!"

The uniformed officer looked at him with surprise, but both men stood silently while they listened for any reply.

"You expecting someone here?" the tall officer finally asked.

"I'm looking for a woman and her child. I know the little girl was here earlier."

The sheriff's deputy raised his eyebrows indicating his surprise at the detective's knowledge of the situation. "I hope you'll fill us all in when we're through here," he added.

"I will. But we need to see if the girl's here first. If her mother is the one that did in the stiff, then my guess is the little girl will be long gone."

"Fair enough."

Stokes went ahead and took the initiative and made his way up the stairs. At the top of the stair three doors opened up. One was to a bathroom and the other two led into separate bedrooms. He paused and listened before proceeding. At first there was just silence. But then he heard something. It was very faint, but it sounded like a muffled sniffling noise. The sound came from the bedroom on his left. He moved into the room and approached the closet. He listened another moment and then knelt down before slowly opening the closet door.

There, behind a couple of shirts hanging from the rack, sat Julia Watts. She had been quietly crying. But upon her discovery by the detective she could no longer hold back. The child let loose with full lung capacity and the tears immediately began to fall.

"Well there you are," Stokes said, relieved at finally catching up with the elusive little girl.

From the hallway heavy footfalls sounded moving up the stairway. "Hey!"

Officer Frank appeared at the bedroom doorway. Julia looked up at the second man now standing behind the person crouched in front of her. Stokes couldn't believe that the child had the ability to cry any harder, but somehow the little girl managed it.

"Ah, its OK honey. Don't cry," Stokes told the child. "Don't you remember me from yesterday?" The girl's tears lessened just a bit. "I remember you. Your name's Julia isn't it?" Stokes made an exaggerated nod of his head. "I think it is."

Julia now looked up at the detective as if assessing whether his demonstration of kindness were worthy of her relenting from her anguish.

"That the kid you were hoping for?" Frank asked from behind.

"It certainly is," Stokes replied to the deputy, before re-addressing the girl. "You remember you and your mommy came and visited me at my office."

The child seemed to relent some, but then relapsed at the thought of her mother. "I want my mommy," she said, crying anew as she drew out the word "mommy".

"It's OK sweetie. We're going to find your mommy for you. Now come on out of there."

Julia hesitated a moment, but then let the detective take her in his hands. Stokes stood and turned with the child in his arms. "You have any female officers down there?"

Frank thought for a moment. Stokes now had time to read the deputy's badge up close; it said "Johnson".

"I don't think so. Just the coroner might have a lady with their group, but not us."

"All right, well I'll walk Julia downstairs and we'll see what we can do for her. See if we can find her mommy."

"So you think her mother isn't the shooter then, if the kid's here?"

Stokes started down the steps. "No she wouldn't have left her. I don't think anyway."

Julia's face was still wet, but the crying seemed to have temporarily dissipated with the ride in the detective's arms. "Yeah, we're going to find your mommy for you," Stokes told her, hoping to keep the tears at bay.

As the detective made his way through the kitchen and exited the rear door he met the plain clothed sheriff's detective heading in.

"So what you got there?" the man reacted.

"This is the young lady that I told you about before," Stokes answered, then directed his next comments for the child also. "I was going to find her and her mother. I found her, and now we're going to find her mommy."

The other detective was obviously sensitive to the child's situation. "Sounds good. All little girls need their mommies."

Stokes wasn't really versed in child interrogation, but he thought he'd give it a brief try anyway. There was some information that he needed that the child might easily provide. "So Julia, did your mother say where she was going?"

The child didn't react so Stokes prompted her, "Huh? Did she say?"

The little girl shook her head.

"Did she say when she was going to be back?"

"Uncle Paco was taking me on a trip to see her."

The sudden blurt of information surprised the detectives.

"Uncle Paco?" the sheriff's detective asked.

Who was that thought Stokes? Uncle Paco? The dead guy who apparently lived there was a Francisco, not a Paco.

"You mean Francisco Espinoza? You call him Paco? Uncle Paco?" It was the sheriff's detective again asking the question.

To Stokes' surprise the little girl nodded her head.

"You mean Francisco Espinoza is your Uncle Paco?"

The child nodded once again. Stokes wished he had a picture of the guy to show the child to confirm they were talking about the same man. He briefly considered showing her the corpse, before realizing that idea would be way off.

"So this is your Uncle Paco's house, right?" the other detective asked.

Julia nodded again.

That added information and the puzzle started to make a little sense, Stokes thought. It looked like the Watts woman had used a sibling's address instead of her own to confuse the police. Then Marianna had either fled to the residence or, at least, left her child in her brother's care at the home.

Of course now the sibling, "Uncle Paco", was dead and they had no clue as to Marianna's whereabouts. She had apparently left, and not taken her child. But then Julia had said that Paco was taking her on a trip to see her mother. Maybe that was the truth, the packed suitcases sure indicated as much. It was just going to take a couple of days to sort the whole thing out.

The trouble was, in the mean time, they'd have to do something with the little girl. The child's Uncle was dead and her mother and father were nowhere to be found.

"Can you guys take her for now?" Stokes asked, obviously referring to the child in his arms.

The plain clothed detective smiled, "Are you kidding, I'm not taking her. Besides, she looks right at home with you."

Stokes bent his neck and looked into the little girl's face.

"Anyway, isn't she part of the case you're working on?" the detective continued.

Stokes considered that. In truth, Julia Watts was probably more closely linked to the LAPD case than to the shooting here. Though she could prove instrumental in solving either of the mysteries.

"Yeah I guess," he finally agreed.

"You take her. We can get a female detective and somebody from child services to come over and talk to her later."

"All right. I'll take her back to headquarters with me and get somebody from juvenile to handle her for now." Stokes looked into Julia's face again, "And then we can find your mommy for you."

"Thanks," replied the sheriff's detective. "I still have a team coming out to go over the interior of the house and search the vehicle. If we come up with anything I'll let you know."

Stokes and the other detective exchanged business cards.

There was nothing left for Stokes to do but to return to Hollenbeck with the girl. On the way back to the cruiser, the child continued to look sullen, but the crying remained at bay and she seemed at least a little more comforted than before. Having no children of his own, Stokes wasn't completely confident of handling a young child of Julia Watts' age, but the girl seemed to take to him just a little.

On the way back to headquarters he sat her in the front seat next to him. He knew that wasn't correct procedure, but without a child safety seat, Stokes wasn't sure whether strapping the young girl in was the safest thing to do anyway. He remembered from his time on street patrol that it was dangerous to strap little children into standard seat belts. Besides when he attempted to put Julia in the back seat she balked and started to cry again.

So he placed her beside him and held on to her the best he could. She even held on to him.

It was a nice feeling.

# Tuesday, September 6th

Detective Stokes entered the last of the data into the computer form on the screen in front of him. He then clicked on the "print" function and downloaded the report to the main printer at the far end of the room.

The underage prostitution ring case was finally wrapped up.

Actually, they had solved the prostitution case in a pretty rapid manner; it had only taken around two weeks from the time of the initiation of surveillance, to the final report.

In the end, it had become obvious that the Watts kidnapping and the underage prostitution operation were two separate cases. Stokes had just happened to get lucky spying the Watts women being ushered into the duplex across from the department's stakeout. Their kidnapping had nothing to do with what was going on just across the driveway. So when the shooter launched his attack from the other building, it wasn't in defense of his criminal buddies next door, it was more likely due to some paranoia that the cops might be moving in on the prostitution operation. The guy somehow thought he was defending himself. Normally a person wouldn't go to such irrational extremes as the shooter had, but then most people weren't normally high on methamphetamines, either, as toxicology had confirmed the man to be.

So the prostitution thing had wrapped up pretty tidy. Two of the perps were dead and three other men were in jail for attempted murder, kidnapping and solicitation of a minor. The young women, as it turned out, had all been illegally transported into the country from Central America. Being as they were not legal residents, the girls had been turned over to the U.S. Citizenship and Immigration Services bureau, the agency formerly known, as the INS. Stokes wasn't really sure what would happen to the young women after that. Most likely they would be deported back to their countries of origin. Unfortunately, that probably meant back to a life that wasn't all that much better than a life on the streets here.

Or maybe not. The detective realized he didn't really know. Maybe some of the kids had led happy normal lives at their former homes and had been taken against their will; it was just impossible to know. But Stokes had lost some of the euphoria that had swept over him after saving the young women. There just were no perfect endings.

So the prostitution case had ended up with no loose ends. Too bad Stokes couldn't say the same for the Watts/Espinoza case. There were plenty of loose ends there.

In the time since the discovery of the kidnapping, four case related individuals had shown up dead, each of the individuals' bodies having been perforated by at least one bullet wound. Another individual, perhaps the only key left available to unlocking the puzzle, had been located several days after the shootings. That individual was David Watts, who happened to be alive, but that fact hadn't made the fellow any more useful. The man was currently in a coma at Los Angeles Doctor's Hospital just West of downtown. The patient's prognosis was hit or miss; he could wake up tomorrow and fill in all the holes in the case, or he could remain in the coma indefinitely, the doctors just couldn't say.

The first body to have been discovered was that of Francisco "Paco" Espinoza, in the parking lot of his row house complex in East LA. His death appeared to be a professional hit. Afterward, it had become assumed that the motive for the man's murder was that of robbery, robbery of $110,000 in cash.

The second body found was that of Marianna Watts. She was discovered later that same evening, outside the location where Stokes had found the woman's daughter, Julia, hiding in the closet in the Espinoza residence. The woman had been shot once in the head and dumped into the trunk of Francisco Espinoza's Honda Accord. The forensics team had discovered her body when they went over the car, which was parked out back of the East LA residence. It was determined that the Watts woman had died earlier that same day, just as the Espinoza man had. Also discovered in the car, under the front seat, was a chrome thirty-eight revolver. Ballistics matched the bullet found in the trunk of the car with the weapon found under the front seat. Powder marks on Francisco Espinoza's right hand indicated that he had fired a similar weapon, probably the same day as his death. Print marks on the revolver also matched the Espinoza man, and so Francisco Espinoza was now considered the most likely suspect in the Watts woman's death. Once again, the department was under the assumption that the motive had to have been robbery, robbery of the same $110,000 that had subsequently been taken from Espinoza's possession.

The $110,000 in cash, which was not found in evidence on either of the victims, was assumed to have been the motive for both killings, because of what the police had found to have occurred earlier in the day. According to bank records from the SoCal Trust Bank, Marianna Watts had withdrawn a total of $110,000 in cash from three different branch locations that morning. A security camera at one of the locations had caught Marianna Watts on tape as she exited the passenger side of a green Honda Accord. The Crime Lab had been able to enhance the raw video footage enough to get an ID on the car's California license plates. The plates matched those issued to Francisco Espinoza. It was apparent that Espinoza had accompanied the Watts woman on her cash collection journey around town. It was also apparent that Francisco Espinoza had wanted the money for himself; and wanted it badly enough to kill Marianna Watts for it. And then, apparently, someone else had come along with the same high regard for such a large sum of money and had killed Espinoza himself, for the same loot.

What hadn't been answered yet was where the Watts woman had gotten such a large amount of cash in the first place. A second question, and possibly more important, was who had ended up benefiting from all that money?

This seemingly singular set of circumstances, all occurred around East LA and seemingly revolved around Marianna Watts and her acquisition of some newfound wealth.

A whole different set of circumstances seemed to revolve around the Watts woman's husband, David.

David Watts had been found out front of the Echo Park branch of the SoCal Trust Bank on the same day as the shooting of his wife in East LA. The man was found suffering from a heart attack and was basically incoherent. Eyewitnesses to the scene had said that a tall white man had accompanied Watts out of the bank, but that the other individual had not helped the heart attack victim when the man had collapsed. Rather, the tall man had apparently forcibly taken a briefcase from the stricken Watts and then sped off in a late model blue sedan. The bank officials inside had explained to police that David Watts had attempted to withdraw the very same money which his wife had already withdrawn only hours earlier. They of course, had told the man that there was no money to be had in the account. Watts then exited the bank, where he had the heart attack, before the tall white man deprived him of the apparently empty briefcase he was carrying. Watts had been uncommunicative from the very beginning and, obviously, been unable to provide any information.

Related to these same events surrounding David Watts that day, a man was found shot to death, execution style, in a parking lot in Griffith Park. This body had actually been the second of the Watts/Espinoza victims discovered that day, having been reported shortly after police were notified of the Espinoza shooting. In this case the victim was an estranged relation to the Watts man, the victim's sister having been formerly married to Watts, making the man Watts' ex-brother-in-law. From all accounts, including that of the ex-wife, Susan Reed, the deceased man, one Harold Reed, had been out of communication with David Watts for years. As a matter of fact, the deceased's whole family had been. The Reeds lived in New York, and since the finalization of the divorce, the family had pretty much shunned David Watts as an outsider. Susan even told the police she was pretty sure her brother Harold had a strong dislike for her ex-husband David, possibly even bordering on outright hatred. That begged the question, what had Harold Reed been doing in Los Angeles and how was he connected to the Watts case?

It hadn't actually been hard to connect Reed to Watts. Being that his relation as an ex-brother-in-law was a stretch in family relations, the man's relationship hadn't popped up right away, but it wasn't long before the police realized there was a connection. What had been hard; was connecting the Reed victim to the ongoing Watts/Espinoza investigation. At first there had been no obvious link to the case. But further investigation had divulged an ironic similarity between Reed's finances and the financing situation surrounding the Marianna Watts withdrawals. The day before his death Harold Reed had wire transferred $120,000 to a bank, which he utilized only on rare occasion, that just happened to have two branches in the downtown Los Angeles area. The day of his death, the same day as the deaths of Francisco Espinoza and Marianna Watts, Reed withdrew $100,000 in cash from the two Los Angeles Bank branches where he had wire transferred the money the day earlier. Apparently Reed had booked an early morning flight and flown directly out from New York to Los Angeles that very morning. Interviews with the bank management unearthed the discrepancy between Reed's wire transfer amount of $120,000 and his subsequent withdrawal of the slightly lesser amount of $100,000. Apparently the bank had not had sufficient time to gather together the full amount in cash, which was over the typical amount kept at any one branch location. Sixty thousand dollars had been withdrawn at one location, but the second branch was only able to provide forty thousand dollars in cash, while retaining an adequate reserve for day-to-day business. So then the police had understood what Harold Reed had been doing in LA, but they still didn't know why he was doing it, or what had happened that had caused him to end up in a parking lot in Griffith Park with two holes in his head. That information was put together about a week later.

Review of the security camera tapes of David Watts' heart attack in front of the SoCal Trust Bank uncovered evidence of two accomplices to the Watts fellow's mission that day. One accomplice was the tall white guy described by witnesses at the scene. As Watts had exited the bank Watts had appeared to swoon, whereupon the tall man moved toward him as if to help. But instead the man had torn the briefcase Watts was carrying from the stricken man's hands and taken it with him back into a blue Dodge Charger parked at the curb. The man then hurriedly backed the car away from the curb and took off out of sight. That was the seemingly relevant action on the security videotape. However, there was one other bit of information as to another occupant in the blue Charger. Mid-way through the tape an older, well dressed, man stepped out of the rear seat of the vehicle and seemingly spoke out to the tall man as he stood on the sidewalk. The man was easily identifiable as Harold Reed.

So then things had started to make a little more sense, at least in Stokes' mind anyway. The day of the murders, the morning had started off with an alleged kidnapping of Marianna Watts and her daughter Julia. The kidnappers had apparently demanded some amount around $120,000 in ransom from the head of the household, David Watts. Watts had then called, and phone records corroborated this, his brother-in-law in New York, Harold Reed, whom he knew had the financial resources to be able to come up with such a large ransom amount. Certainly, from looking at the financial records, the Watts family themselves would not have had such resources. But that was where the storyline seemed to fall apart. If the Watts family was as impoverished as they seemed to be, how was it that they had a joint bank account with $110,000 in it? A check of bank records actually showed that the account had only recently been above $120,000 but that $10,000 dollars had been withdrawn just a couple of weeks ago. The entire $120,000 figure was also due to only six large deposits, each of exactly $20,000. So that was one question. The next question was why would the criminals kidnap someone from such a seemingly non-well-to-do family. And then why would they demand $120,000? If, in fact, that was the ransom demand. It was certainly not a scenario you would expect. And especially not from Fernando Alba. That was if Alba had been the man Stokes had seen at the duplex with Marianna Watts that first morning. But Stokes was still convinced that it had been. It was just odd, because Alba's thing was drug dealing, not kidnapping. But there was a scenario that could include all these various characters, their preferred criminal activity, and the various money amounts.

There would have been no way Alba would have asked for such a large sum of money from the Watts family unless he knew they had it. And the only reason he would know they had it, was the same reason that they were in possession of such a large amount of money to begin with; because David, or Marianna, Watts had stolen the money from Alba in the first place. It made perfect sense. Suddenly a hundred grand shows up in the Watts bank account out of nowhere, and then, just as suddenly, Fernando Alba comes along looking for that same amount. That had to be the reason. He had only stooped to the kidnapping in order to retrieve the funds that had been stolen from him. And how had the money been stolen? Most likely during the transaction of his normal business in the drug trade. Maybe Marianna Watts had even worked for Alba, that wasn't beyond consideration.

Still it was odd that David Watts had called in his brother-in-law and, in addition, had tried to retrieve the cash from his own bank account. Why would he do both? The man had been late to the money at his own bank, Marianna having cleaned out the account before he could get there. Maybe he hadn't known about the money? Maybe Marianna had hidden it from Watts and the man only found out about it somehow at the last minute. That would explain the Watts woman's insistence that her last name was Espinoza. Maybe she didn't want her husband to know she had been freed from the kidnappers until she could get to the bank. Then she could high tail it out of town with the cash and leave her husband holding the bag. That was cold, thought Stokes.

Then there was the subject of how the department had solved the mystery of Harold Reed's demise. The department had gleaned the license plate number from the bank video of the blue Dodge Charger that Reed and the other tall fellow had left in. The car had ended up being registered to a Jim Stafford, who was a licensed private investigator in the State of California. A statewide alert was put out for the car and it wasn't twenty-four hours

before they got hit on the vehicle. The department got a
response from the San Bernardino County Sheriff's office
that a car matching their description and plate number had
been found along interstate 15 near the Nevada state line,
just the day before. In the trunk was the body of the
vehicle's owner, Jim Stafford, who had been shot to
death. There was also a handgun in the car and a lot of
blood in the interior of the vehicle. As it turned out the
blood inside the vehicle hadn't come from the dead
investigator, it had come from another previous occupant
of the car, Harold Reed.

In piecing that information together, the situation
appeared amazingly similar to the storyline of the dead
Watts woman and Espinoza man. Harold Reed had
withdrawn a lot of money, just like Marianna Watts had,
those were known facts. After the Reed withdrawals,
David Watts, who was the apparent intended recipient of
the money, had had a heart attack. Inexplicably, Watts
was then left in front of the bank to fend for himself. The
driver of the car that drove off, Jim Stafford, had been the
one who had abandoned Watts on the sidewalk and was,
therefore, seemingly not very interested in getting the
money to the intended recipient. It was possible the
investigator was just going on to the ransom drop, but that
would mean Stafford had been showing compassion for
the one Watts party's plight, while he left the other one on
the sidewalk to die. That was highly unlikely. So, what
was more likely was that the Stafford man had decided
he'd rather have the money for himself. So, just like
Francisco Espinoza had done with Marianna Watts,
Stafford had driven his own cash cow to a deserted
location, put a bullet in the cow's brain and then taken off
with the money. And then, again, as with the Espinoza

fellow, the Stafford man had met his own demise when someone else decided they needed the money a bit more than the fellow who had just stolen it.

Now came the real $200,000 question; who was it that had killed Espinoza and Stafford and taken the money? The obvious answer, for Stokes anyway, was Fernando Alba, or whoever it was that had committed the kidnapping in the first place. The only problem with that solution, however, was that one person could not have committed both slayings, the timing of the murders, and the distance between the locations, precluded a single individual from being responsible. There was just no way to travel that far, that fast. But, of course, it was possible that there could always have been more than one killer. Maybe only one of the murders was attributable to the kidnappers. Maybe the other individual had just fallen victim to some random criminal, or possibly to an as yet unknown player within the same criminal web. Or, finally, somebody like Alba could have had help with the murders, contracting either one or even both of the hits out. There could be two killers, but only one mastermind. Two hundred thousand dollars would give someone those types of resources.

So far the department hadn't come up with any leads on the perpetrators of these final murders. The killings of the brother-in-law and of the Watts woman were sloppy and the murderers had been easily identified. Of course, the bodies of the murderers had been offered up for the police at the various crime scenes, so that did make the job a little easier. But the killer or killers of Stafford and Espinoza had been a little more clever; they would be harder to track down. Nobody had seen anything at either of those murder locations, even though both shootings had occurred in a public place and in broad daylight, one happening along a busy interstate and the other in an open parking lot.

The one along the highway was going to be an especially tough nut to crack. Stokes had even driven out with one of the homicide detectives to see if he could add anything to the investigation. But the car had been clean as far as the probable killer was concerned. All the prints in the car had come from the three stooges from the bank withdrawals, Stafford, Reed or Watts. The blood inside the car had all been from Reed, and the rest had been from Stafford, where he had been found inside the trunk.

The shooting of the Espinoza man was proving not much less difficult, either. But Stokes held out hope that the killer there might yet get apprehended. Though no one had come forward as a witness, Stokes was sure someone had seen something of the murder there. All those young people that had approached him when he went to the Espinoza residence earlier on the day of the murder, those kids were the type that kept an eye on the happenings in their "hood". One of those kids just might come forward and provide some testimony; at least it was a possibility.

Another possible line of investigation was that forensics had pulled a partial print from the Espinoza crime scene. The print was developed from an area that was highly unlikely to have been contacted by anyone other than the deceased, too. Yet the print had already been determined to not be that of Francisco Espinoza. Apparently, someone else, hopefully the killer, had decided they needed access to the interior of Espinoza's green Honda. Whoever it was had needed to turn the key in the passenger door lock and had inadvertently left a partial print on the hard plastic housing of the base of the key.

So that was good news. Especially if forensics could develop enough of the thumb, or finger, print to be able to run it through the database. But, of course, even then, if the killer weren't in the database, then no matter how good the print, no match would come up.

That thought made Stokes smile. Fernando Alba was definitely in the database.

Fernando Alba looked through the real estate portion of the Los Angeles Times as he sat on the couch in his rented Boyle Heights home. He was considering a move up. And why not, his star was on the rise. The only trouble was, in order to buy a property without any proof of legitimate income; you really needed to pay cash. And that was the sticking point. It wasn't that Feride didn't have plenty of cash, he did, it was just that using all of it to buy the type of home he wanted would leave him without sufficient funds to make the large-scale drug purchases that he had become involved with of late. And he didn't want to revert to the old penny-ante scores that he used to deal in. The big jobs were much more lucrative.

Ferdie added it up. He had something like $550,000 in cash immediately available to him. That was a big jump up from what it had been only a few weeks back. Not only had his two men returned from Suarez with a successful purchase, which they had then turned for a good $80,000 profit, but he had also come into an unexpected sum of money from the escapade with the Watts woman.

That one was really funny. Not only had he gotten most of the money back that the woman had stolen from him, but he also received a gift of an additional one hundred grand from the woman's husband. Ferdie was pretty sure he knew how that had occurred. Apparently the woman's husband had been unaware that Marianna had stolen the money from Ferdie in the first place, so the man had gone out and found the ransom amount from another source. That money had ended up in the hands of the private investigator that Ferdie had off'd on the side of the road. There still hadn't been any sign of the husband, David Watts, and Ferdie was still assuming that the investigator had killed the man for the money.

In addition to that cash, Marcelo had located the money Marianna had stolen, in the possession of her ex-husband Paco Espinoza. Marcelo had then eliminated Espinoza and doubled their loot. At first, Ferdie had been under the assumption that Marianna was still running around loose somewhere, but then, only a couple of days ago, Ferdie heard word that the woman's body had turned up in Espinoza's trunk. Apparently Paco had blown his ex-wife's brains out. That was funny, too. Money made people do strange things.

"Ferd?"

The call came down the stairs from the master bedroom.

"Yeah, mi amor!"

"I'm going to take a shower. I got to be over at my mother's soon."

"Yeah, fine," Ferdie replied.

Gloria's mother was still kind of protective of her nineteen-year-old daughter. And she should be, thought Ferdie. What with pendejos like himself running around loose in the world, it wasn't safe. Gloria was one of about three or four girlfriends Ferdie could count on when needed. They all pretty much knew about each other, too. It didn't matter; he even encouraged them to socialize together. Sometimes they even entertained him together, it just came with the territory.

Ferdie was an important man; he was respected in the community. Soon he'd be more than just the local Tachos boss, too. With half a million in cash he was now looking at moving into the big time. Maybe another score or two and he'd even have a little extra cash for some play toys.

For now, it didn't hurt looking in the paper at the million dollar homes.

The phone on Detective Stokes' desk rang. He thought about not answering it. It was getting late in the afternoon and the detective was intending on making it an early day, he hadn't had one of those in a while. But duty got the best of him and he picked up the receiver, hopefully to dismiss whomever it was until tomorrow.

"Stokes, make it quick."

"Ah … Detective Stokes, this is Marion Barnes with Child Services."

Marion Barnes was familiar to him, she had been the woman who had come by to get little Julia Watts from his office, on that day two weeks ago. But it was odd that the woman would be calling the detective, there really was no official line of communication between himself and Child Protective Services.

"Oh yeah, Ms. Barnes. How do you do?"

"Hi Detective. I'm just fine, thank you. Say, do you think you have a minute that we could talk? I just wanted to fill you in on a couple of things going on with Julia Watts. You remember her I'm sure?"

How could he forget the kid, the little girl was adorable. She'd even seemed to take a liking to him, he thought. He was still a little confused about the nature of the call, however, but he tried to be polite.

"Yeah, of course. What can I do for you?"

"First, just let me tell you that Julia seems to be getting along OK, but we haven't placed her in foster care just yet. As you may know, when a child is left homeless by the death or disability of the child's parents, it's the job of our office to locate the closest living relative and to attempt to place the child with that relative, if at all suitable."

"Sure, I understand that," stated Stokes. "Is there some problem with that in this case?"

"Well, let me explain a little further," Ms. Barnes said before pausing briefly. "You see, in this case both of the child's parents are now deceased. As it turns out Francisco Espinoza was the father of the little girl, Julia. He and Marianna Hernandez, whom you know as Watts, were married in Mexico about seven years ago and had one child together, that being the little girl in question. She was born a little over four years ago to the couple, who then separated. Interestingly enough, Julia was actually born in this country and therefore is a legal citizen of the United States."

Wow, thought Stokes, trying to take all that in. So "Uncle Paco" was actually "Daddy Paco". And that meant Marianna Watts had been killed by her ex-husband. It also meant that Julia's real mother and father were now both dead.

"OK, but what about relatives. There must be someone. And what about David Watts? Doesn't his marriage to Julia's mother count for anything?"

"Oh most certainly it does. But as you know David Watts is currently incapacitated and may be for the foreseeable future. So, at this point we can't really consider Mr. Watts as a credible living arrangement for Julia."

That made sense. "But what about other relatives?" Stokes asked.

"Well, frankly there aren't many options there either. We did locate a great Aunt in Saltillo Mexico, but she is handicapped and frankly not in a financial position to offer a stable home at this point. Besides, with the child being a U.S. Citizen, the office here comes under a lot of pressure to try to find a caring home here in the states rather than in some other country."

Ok, that also made sense, thought Stokes. "But what does that have to do with me?"

"Well Detective, that brings me to my point. As I recall when I came by your office to pick Julia up you made a remark to me as I left. I'm hoping you were serious in your statement and not just trying to play the good guy."

Play the good guy, what did the woman mean by that? Stokes tried to remember what statement he might have made. "I'm not sure that I follow you."

"As I remember when I started to leave your office with Julia she began to cry and wanted to go back with you. You remember that?"

Stokes did remember that. The two had bonded a little. "Yeah, I remember."

"It seemed that the child had taken a liking to you. And then as I told Julia we were going to find her a nice home, you piped up and said something about how if the agency couldn't find the child a loving place to stay, that you and your wife were always available."

Now Stokes remembered, he had said that. But was the woman now suggesting that she was going to take him up on the offer? He hadn't really been serious at the time, not because he didn't care about the little girl, but because he just thought there would be no way that they would allow him to jump to the front of the foster care line like that. Weren't there already families set up to take children in?

"I'm sorry, Ms. ... Barnes," he almost forgot the woman's name, "Are you saying that you are considering placing the child with me?"

"Well Detective, you did express interest. And I checked a little, you and your wife seem to have a stable home life, and no children of your own."

"But aren't there other foster families?"

"Not as many as you'd think. There's actually a bit of a shortage right now. And as you must be aware, the child seemed to have taken a liking to you."

"Yeah, I know. Frankly I took a liking to her, too. But I got to tell you, when I spoke up I wasn't expecting a call to suggest that the child might actually be placed with us."

"Have you discussed the situation with your wife?"

"No. Well, I mean … I discussed Julia, but nothing further." Stokes recalled how Debra had reacted when Stokes had related the child's attachment to him. She'd actually mentioned at the time how fortunate they would both be if they were ever blessed to have a child themselves.

"So Detective, you're saying you're not interested?"

No, that was not what he meant to be saying. "No, that's not it. I'm just a little stunned by this turn of events is all." It was hard to believe. "You're not kidding me are you?" he asked the Child Services worker.

There was a bit of a giggle on the other end of the phone. "No officer, I'm not kidding with you. It's no prank. I think you have a legitimate at shot having the child placed with you. If you want her that is; I mean it's a commitment, a serious commitment."

Stokes thought a moment. "And how long would it be for? Would it just be temporary, or could it be a permanent arrangement?"

"Well, that all depends. If Mr. Watts regains consciousness and is able to function well enough to provide a normal life, then he would have a claim toward parental rights to the child. Depending on how that went, a court could decide either way on whether to keep the child with you or to return her to the man she had considered her father up to this point."

"And if Watts doesn't recover?"

"I would think if that were the situation, then there would be every reason to believe that you would keep the child permanently."

This was all too much, but he asked anyway. "You mean we could adopt her?"

"Yes. After a reasonable period of time the court would consider an adoption proceeding if you so desired."

Stokes couldn't believe it. Couples waited years, even decades to adopt children, and here a beautiful child had possibly just fallen into their laps.

"Are you saying you're interested then?"

Stokes tried not to overreact, "Um … Ms. Barnes, I think it would be safe to say that we would be very interested."

"That's what I was hoping detective. I think you and your wife would make an excellent match for Julia."

Wow, thought Stokes, it was really hard to believe that the woman was even suggesting any of this.

"Detective, let me leave you my number and you can talk with your wife a little further. In the meantime I have to go now. Do you have a pen?"

Stokes wrote down the phone number and then asked the Barnes woman to confirm it for him again. Then he hung up.

In his wildest dreams Stokes had never considered that there would be any possibility that the little Watts girl might somehow end up in his care. And now the likelihood was just astounding. He couldn't wait to get home and surprise Debra with the news. He knew she would be overjoyed. And the thought of Debra mothering their little girl, Julia, was just overwhelming.

He decided he really couldn't wait till he got home.

Stokes lifted the receiver and called Debra's cell number. It rang about three times before she answered.

"Honey?" he interrupted before she could say anything.

"Oh, yeah, hey Bren."

"Debra, you are not going to believe what I have to tell you."

"Oh, no Bren," his wife sounded discouraged on the other end of the line, "you're not working late again are you? I thought you had said you were coming home early."

"No honey, I'm coming home right now. We'll go out to dinner. I've got some incredible news."

Debra's voice picked up a little with that. "Oh yeah, what? Tell me."

"Like I said, you're never going to believe this."